The Sun and Stars

Thank you
for supporting
Friends!
Old

~Elizabeth Adam

The Sun and Stars

by

Elizabeth Adair

BearCat
PRESS

San Francisco

Library of Congress Control Number: 2012930267

Casebound: 978-1-937356-16-3
Trade paper: 978-1-937356-17-0
Kindle: 978-1-937356-18-7
EPUB: 978-1-937356-19-4

Publisher's Cataloging-in-Publication Data

Adair, Elizabeth.
The sun and stars / Elizabeth Adair.
p. cm.
ISBN: 978-1-937356-16-3
1. Henry VIII, King of England, 1491-1547—Fiction. 2. Great Britain—History—Tudors, 1485-1603—Fiction. 3. Historical mystery novels. 4. Murder—Fiction. I. Title.
PS3601.D349 S86 2012
813—dc22
         2012930267

Published by BearCat Press: www.BearCatPress.com/

Cover art by Gayle Feyrer, after Arthur Rackham
Book design by the Frogtown Bookmaker
BearCat Press logo by Golden Sage Creative
Washington Alternates font
Copyright © 1999 by D. Steffmann. All rights reserved
Heraldic Devices font ⚔
Copyright © 2011 by Intellecta Design
Trinigan font
Copyright © 2002 by Fontgrube. All rights reserved.

Floats the Dark Shadow excerpt
Copyright © 2012 by Yves Fey. All rights reserved

To Mary,
my mother
whose stories
made the people
of the Tudor court
seem very near.

Chapter One

ing Henry lifted his hand. All eyes fixed on it, and all breaths halted. He signaled. With a glitter of armor and thunder of hooves, the two knights charged. Lance struck shield and splintered with a loud crack, the fragments sailing into the air. With a rending crash the defender hit the ground, but his esquire dashed to help him up and at once he drew his sword. His opponent dismounted, swept out his blade and attacked.

Metal clanged and the defender staggered, but his blow struck home, veering them both around. His second stroke went wide for the sun in his eyes. Seeing this, the challenger shifted again, giving up his unfair advantage and winning the crowd's cheers for his chivalry. But he spared his opponent no other quarter. Gauging himself the stronger, he elected to take the next blow full-on. Then his stroke crashed down, felling the defender. Lying on the ground, Sir Edward Nevill raised his visor to signal himself beaten.

King Henry VIII applauded both his boon companions as the Duke of Suffolk helped his opponent up. Nevill smiled at his defeat with good grace. His red hair and large face looked remarkably like his kinsman the King's.

"You won the first wager." Isabel Holland turned to her cousin.

Sir Hugh Lovell grinned. "I told you."

"Well then, Sir Oracle," she challenged, "predict the next." She exchanged a glance with their friends, Jane Giffard and Thomas Wyatt. Hugh was opinionated, and teasing him good sport, but his advice might be worth a wager. He would be making a brave show today himself, but for the wrist he had injured during practice.

"Not so straightforward from now on," her cousin answered. "Last night's rain soaked into that gravel. The horses' hooves are starting to expose patches of mud."

"And they'll be sliding like skittles." Isabel made light, but misgiving seeped into her exhilaration. She surveyed the tiltyard. The shadows of the gay pennants fluttered over dark streaks where the gravel was damp. A breast-high wooden barrier divided the ground to protect the jousters and their mounts from collisions and flying hooves, but even in play, combat could be fatal.

Hugh flexed his sprained wrist slowly, disgusted at his luck. It was strong, sturdy of bone and sinew, the hairs on it as fair as those on his head. He was vigorous and strapping, with a short nose and blue eyes. Isabel did not resemble her cousin. She was slender and of middling height. Her face would do, but it had neither the white and rose complexion nor the spiritual otherworldliness men admired most. She prided herself on her wide-set grey eyes and the contagious lilt of her laughter, but she would have given half her land for splendid red hair. Hers was light brown, a tawny gleam its only hint of her Tudor blood. She took after her mother, by all accounts. She would never know for herself. Twenty-one years ago a young lady-in-waiting had surrendered her virtue to handsome young Prince Henry and gotten for it a babe but no husband, and death in childbed.

Isabel looked across the crowd of courtiers to where her father sat beneath a velvet canopy. His massive vigor gleamed larger than life. His doublet of cloth of gold was trimmed with garnets and set off by silken hose of a delicate yellow. On his head shone the Sun and Stars, the crown he had captured in France. Whiter than the sun its huge diamond blazed, surrounded by constellations of smaller rubies, sapphires and amethysts. Yet, brilliant as his jewels shone, his golden-red hair rivaled them. His face was large, his features small, regular, and at the moment lit by a smile as expansive as the fair day that had freed him from a long imprisonment indoors. A wet May had thwarted his will, and King Henry took ill any thwarting, even by the heavens.

Yet he was not merely a hunter and athlete. He relished an argument in Latin as much as a competition with the bow, and when Isabel turned old enough, a tutor from Plymouth came to stay at the manor in the rolling uplands of Devon where her grandparents raised her. She'd had a stringent education for a girl of the country gentry, and when old enough was summoned to court to wait on the Queen.

Isabel glanced at Queen Katherine sitting by the King. Her proud Spanish decorum concealed a troubled mind. Isabel's existence was not the only proof of King Henry's interest in other ladies. Besides her brother, Henry Fitzroy, it was rumored that at least one of the children of Sir William Cary's wife, Mary Boleyn, was fathered by the King. Affection for her husband's bastards could not be expected, yet Isabel could attest to the Queen's graciousness. She would be watching today's tournament among the Queen's maids of honor, if not for the King's broad hint that she should take time off. It was not Isabel who need fear her royal father's displeasure, he'd intimated. In all their years of marriage, the Queen had borne only one surviving child, Princess Mary. The throne lacked a legitimate male heir, and gossip raged that King Henry was secretly at work to annul his marriage.

Yet, a secret tattled about by all the court could hardly be secret from Queen Katherine. That was the meaning of her father's hint. Trouble was brewing, and Isabel should take care not to be caught on the wrong side. The loyalty she owed the Queen being duty only, Isabel had vacated the palace with a clear conscience. With the rains of April muddying the Devon hills and turning the Torridge to churning brown floods, the remote countryside held few of the attractions it would in high summer. Isabel had moved in on her Aunt Margery, Hugh's mother, in London.

"I see you gawping at the Queen's ladies-in-waiting," Jane teased Wyatt, whose glance had followed Isabel's.

Wyatt smoothed his short brown beard with a restless finger. "That I am not," he answered indignantly.

"Thomas is a poet," Isabel added, "and so, incapable of gawping . . . though it might be wise to gawp a little less at Mistress Anne."

Wyatt pointedly refused to answer. But Jane sniffed. "Anne Boleyn? She's skinny as a switch and has hair like crows' feathers. What King Henry sees in her is beyond me. Now as for the gentlemen in the royal party, there's one I'd hoped to see. What a disappointment the French ambassador's secretary is in bed with the rheums. Have you noticed him, Isabel?"

"The round one, like a little capon?" Isabel could not resist baiting her. Every handsome new gentleman at court turned Jane's head. Isabel just hoped her friend's parents wouldn't marry her to some man with the brows of a monkey or the teeth of a horse.

"What do you take me for? No, the slim, dark eyed one, of course. Monsieur Des Roches."

"With the point to his beard, like Mephistopheles."

"Does no man find favor with you?"

Isabel frowned. "I'm no condemned soul—yet. I'll put off thoughts of marriage until I'm commanded." She turned to her cousin. "Well, Hugh? What have you wagered on Tom Seymour?"

"Seymour?" Hugh smiled. "Nothing. Lord Colford will best him."

"Never!" Isabel answered, stung. "He'd better not, I've bet two marks on it," she added quickly. That evening in the garden last October must not be guessed. Tom Seymour's compelling eyes, the scent of him like leather and smoke, and the heat of his lips on hers could send them both into exile and disgrace if gossip caught wind of it. Though his family were West Country gentry like her mother's, she knew right well her father would never countenance such a match. Tom was a younger son with few expectations but what he could make for himself, and though he'd demonstrated soldierly bravery, Isabel had to admit he'd showed few signs of prudence. Since then, she'd avoided him. At least she'd see him again now, if only from afar.

"What, Hugh?" Wyatt asked. "Since when is it your habit to back your enemies?"

"Colford was no gentleman in France," Hugh acceded, "but he's shrewd, and more seasoned than Seymour. I back winners."

Braying rent the air, a horrific, discordant sound, yet it slyly managed to bring to mind the trumpets of a royal fanfare. Through the near archway ambled a bizarre figure. Mounted on an ass, he wore an overturned wooden bucket for his helmet and for his breastplate, a crockery platter. His steed was equally splendid, its caparison a bedspread and the mount itself no less than a unicorn, as proved by the carrot tied to its poll. As knight and steed passed below the stands where Isabel and her friends sat, the ass planted its hooves, threw back its head and protested stridently. The rider flourished aloft his lance, a scraggled broom, but the ass sat, delivering the warrior rump down in the gravel. Untroubled by this misfortune of war, the valiant doffed his bucket and leapt into a cartwheel, patched buskins and shining gauntlets spinning.

"Will!" Isabel called amid the laughter and catcalls of the crowd. "Noble Sir William, Champion of the Joust!"

Picking out the sound of her voice, Will Somers faced her and bowed solemnly. Nothing abashed, Isabel rose and returned a blithe curtsy, to the cheers of courtiers and commoners. Like the jester, she was a favorite at court. King's jester and King's pet bastard, many took one no more seriously than the other. Since childhood she had sensed her place was privileged, but inconsequential. In the end, her father would marry her off as a reward for some man's loyalty, or an inducement where loyalty was uncertain. Never officially recognized by her father, she did not have any particular legal status. Like Will, she could only prosper by pleasing. Because of this, they had always shared an unspoken alliance.

Will cupped a hand to his ear, hearing some elfin challenge inaudible to the coarser senses of the crowd. Retrieving his lance, he brandished it fiercely and leapt astride his unicorn, but the saddle slid until he hung upside down. The onlookers roared with laughter as clinging to the ass in this indelicate embrace he trotted from the yard, roaring with all the fury of a thwarted Mars.

"That takes skill," Hugh said, grinning. "I've always said Master Somers would have made a champion if a lowborn man weren't forbidden to bear a knight's arms."

"Methinks he finds ways to even that score," Isabel returned, applauding as Will disappeared through the archway with an upside-down parody of knightly hauteur.

"Look." Hugh hushed his voice. "Here's an entrance not unlike that exit."

Outside the low wall, servants wearing Cardinal Wolsey's badge were cleaving a passage through the common folk. The path they forced was unnecessarily wide, and displaced people who had stood all day to get their vantage point. Some shouted and shoved back but subsided to resentful quiet as the gentlemen of the Cardinal's household marched into sight as grandly as if in the train of the Pope himself. The Cardinal's secretaries followed, then two attendants, one bearing the velvet purse containing the Great Seal of England, the other carrying a pillow upon which sat the Cardinal's scarlet hat. Finally, in full red robed regalia, came Cardinal Wolsey himself. He paced with measured tread by reason of his vast dignity, and no doubt also by reason of his vast bulk. His expression was of supercilious disregard, and as he passed through the common people he held to his nostrils a pomander of orange peel stuffed with spices, to save him from smelling their sweat.

"Detained by matters far more important than the King's pleasure, no doubt," Jane whispered. Her cautiously lowered voice was wise. The Cardinal had many spies. "I hear the Duke of Norfolk himself had to ask three times before Wolsey granted him an audience."

"What, only three?" Wyatt quietly bantered. "I call that gracious, in a priest who's richer than the King. Even the Pope begs his table scraps."

"A most studied lack of study," Isabel agreed, as the Cardinal mounted into the stands, sparing not a glance for his ecclesiastical peer, the Archbishop of Canterbury. He reached the chair that awaited him, canopied by a scarlet baldachin nearly as elaborate as the King and Queen's. Not until he was settled did his gentlemen permit themselves to sit.

"They say his cardinal hat is specially made in Paris," added Jane.

"English dye isn't scarlet enough for him," Hugh rejoined, and challenged Isabel, "Cap that, coz."

"Nay, a cap that red's too hot to touch," Isabel answered. "And it caps a hellfire of ambition. Yet, he has one good friend." She would not, and need not, speak clearer. Her father depended all too utterly upon the Cardinal's administrative genius.

The trumpets cried forth, and Isabel fixed her eyes on the near archway, the crowd shrinking to tiny, droning insects and the entrance for the defenders' team looming like a portal of heaven or hell. At last, Tom Seymour rode into the lists, proud in his armor, his almond eyes determined beneath his raised visor. Yet his gaze remained unswervingly ahead. If he knew where she sat, he gave no sign of it. Though it was she who'd warned him to avoid her, his aloofness plunged her into misery even as the sight of him made her soar into joy. Over the gleam of his armor his surcoat was blazoned with the Seymour arms. The plumes in his charger's crest blew gay and brave in the breeze, but he wore no lady's favor. He turned his head slightly, and for a fleeting instant his eyes met hers. Radiance poured into her. Isabel smiled, then made herself look away.

Through the far entrance rode Lord Adam Colford. His surcoat and his mount's caparison fluttered crimson, but whose favor was the silver gauze wafting from his helmet Isabel neither knew nor cared. She had never known Colford to speak to, nor liked the cold arrogance of his bearing. Even had he not been her cousin's enemy, he struck her as a hard man, his noble breeding unwarmed by any human feeling.

The combatants trotted the length of the tiltyard while the

heralds announced their names and titles. Reaching the center, they pivoted smartly to salute the King and Queen, then gave the customary salute to each other. "There's a hawker, go fetch me an orange," Jane directed her serving woman, who went to obey, blocking the view. Isabel swallowed sharp words. When the way cleared, the two knights were poised, lances at the ready.

At the signal they charged. Wielding lances in one hand, shields in the other, they guided their mounts by the grip of their thighs, depending only on balance to stay in the saddle. Gravel flew from pummeling hooves, reminding Isabel of the dangerous footing. If a horse in full armor fell on its rider, death was near certain. As Tom closed with his opponent he raised his lance and couched it. Steel clashed. Isabel rocked forward as daylight showed between Tom and his mount. With a grinding crash he was down. Colford turned in the saddle. Even in the heavy armor the movement managed to convey a discourteously predatory satisfaction. Anxiously Isabel watched Tom's esquire help him to his feet. Swaying, but upright beneath the weight of his armor, Tom Seymour drew his sword for foot combat.

Lord Colford dismounted. Undazed and possessed of dense, compact sinews to Tom's tall slenderness, he had the advantage on foot, and Tom was not bound to go on with it. But Tom raised his sword. Chivalry demanded Colford should allow him to gain a point to salve his pride before striking in full force. Tom might use that chance to grasp victory.

Colford paused, making sure Tom was steady on his feet, then approached. But he did not make even a polite pretense of attack. As if bored with the whole matter, he glanced up at an approaching bank of clouds as if the weather for the evening's entertainment were his only concern. Tom paused, uncertain what to make of it. A strike on an unguarded opponent would win him no glory, and he was not the man to take such an ignoble advantage.

Or was Colford trying to make him do exactly that? Isabel knew of no quarrel between them, but the aristocrats of the old guard were always trying to show up ambitious gentry like the Seymours. Or perhaps, Lord Colford's disdain extended to everyone but himself. Suddenly, his sword flicked. Tom parried, but Colford had not struck; it was only a feint. Isabel heard a few scornful sounds at Tom's hot headedness, and clenched her teeth. Tom dared him with a sharp feint of his own, but Colford did not bother responding. Though his face was hidden by his visor, Isabel knew Thomas Seymour must be breathing fires of wrath. Yet he stayed himself when Colford's sword flicked again. But this time Colford moved with it. Tom parried, but encountered only air and staggered. Seizing on his imbalance, Colford felled him with a single perfunctory stroke. Tom's esquire assisted him to the far exit to cheers and snickers.

Wrath scathing within her, Isabel looked to her father. He was a stickler for chivalry. He would surely show his disfavor at such a churlish victory. But no, he was chuckling as if he thought it clever. Lord Colford raised his visor, receiving his praise. He had won favor with the King. He cared not how, or at whose expense.

"The villain played his trick like a master." Hugh pulled off a few sections of Jane's orange and devoured them.

"A master of what? Scorpions? But what do you care, your wager's won—and nothing proved but how easy it is to appeal to base instincts. The win was dishonorable."

"Adam, Lord Colford," Wyatt intoned. "You are challenged to a duel by Lady Isabel, Upholder of Honor, Good Manners and All That's Fair. Choose your weapons."

"Tongues!" Hugh answered. "My wager's on you, coz."

"Begging your pardon, sir," a child's voice distracted them. A freckle-faced boy of about ten stood in the walkway. "Are you Sir Hugh Lovell?"

Hugh turned, still smiling. "I am."

"Then I've a message for you, sir."

"Have you?" Hugh took the folded paper he was offered and handed the boy a farthing.

After the knavery in the tiltyard, Isabel would rather have swallowed poison than commit any dishonor, but she felt mightily annoyed when Hugh angled the note away from her. His blond brows lowered, then sprang up. "You'll grant me your leave, ladies? I won't be long." Clutching the paper, he bounded along the walkway and down the stairs.

"There's gallant protection for you." Jane sucked on the last section of her orange.

At last Isabel spotted Tom Seymour entering the far side of the stands, where his brother Edward and other Seymour connections were. Anxiously she assessed the damage. His fair skin was whiter than usual, making his dark grey eyes startling under the russet of his hair. His face was controlled, but not drawn. He smiled as his brother clapped his back, but that was like him, whatever he felt. He sat tenderly, but not as if in severe pain. He had taken no grave hurt—at least, no bodily hurt. She ached for his pride.

"No wonder they're taking so long to start the next joust. His Majesty's gone."

While the Queen chatted with one of her Spanish ladies he had wandered off, making a wager or two with his friends, Isabel supposed, as was his wont. Her attention went back to Tom. He drank from a flask his brother handed him but did not glance her way. No doubt hers was the last gaze he wanted to meet just now. "May Lord Colford be afflicted with a plague of Egyptians!" She was somewhat mollified when Jane burst into merry laughter at her sleight of tongue.

At last King Henry reappeared, his gold doublet and white hose conspicuous as he moved through the crowd, his guards exhausted with the effort of keeping up with him. Resuming his seat, he exchanged a few words with the Queen.

"Something's wrong."

"What?" Jane asked. "His Majesty seems pleased with the games, now they'll go on."

"Marvelous pleased. But . . . his hose."

"His what? Have you been too long in the sun?"

"No longer than it takes a chestnut to ripen." Isabel's curiosity pricked. Before, his hose were pale yellow. She would wager anything on it. Now, they were white as a swan's plumage. But why retire to change hose? She frowned, piqued by this challenge to common sense. "Mark me, mischief's afoot."

Queen Katherine's manner betrayed nothing, but Isabel watched as the King put forth a hand to receive his huge, jewel-encrusted cup from a page. The gesture was curiously placid, lacking the nervous energy she knew so well. "My father's up to his old japes. That's Edward Nevill!"

"No, never," Jane answered with certainty, then frowned. "Well, maybe his shoulders aren't so broad. But his face—no, it's not His Majesty's! Though they look so much alike that at this distance anyone could be fooled. You recognized him by his *hose?*"

"They were a different color before, so I looked sharper."

"Your astuteness is close to miraculous." Wyatt seemed uncertain what he thought of such an accomplishment in a lady.

"No miracle, much toil under a very determined tutor. I can also calculate the area of a circle, remember the feast day of every saint, and translate Julius Caesar's writings—for all the good it does anyone. I'll never make a lawyer or priest, and my lord father will marry me to a dullard if it suits his purposes." She glanced at the counterfeit king, noting now that his crown was also different, which stood to reason. Though King Henry allowed his kinsman to impersonate him for a rollick, wear his doublet, even drink from his golden goblet, a royal crown was sacred. Nevill's must be an imitation, left over from some masking entertainment.

The trumpets blew. Isabel and her friends exchanged knowing glances as the jousters entered the lists; for the defenders Sir Nicholas Carew in his fanciful helmet like a gargoyle's snout, his lady's favor flying from the crest, and for the challengers a knight with a closed visor, his armor a mysterious black. "Look at them." Wyatt indicated the squinting, craning courtiers.

"Next they will scratch their heads in puzzlement," Isabel said, and was rewarded when Sir Piers Knevet, sitting near the Seymours, chose that moment to do so. "I imagine it's more than the fun of the jape," she added thoughtfully. "The Privy Council carps against my lord father for risking himself at the tilt. I suspect he had a mind to escape their clack—at least, beforehand."

"Afterward, he'll say they're too late."

"And so they will be," Isabel answered, smiling. She watched her father ride the length of the stands while speculation swelled to excitement. To see the King joust was rare these days, but he'd once been a champion. So had Carew, who'd embellished his own reputation with feats like riding across the tiltyard hefting a whole tree trunk for a lance. This should be a match, indeed.

About to salute the Queen and his counterfeit self, the Black Knight paused. His gauntlets went to his helm as if he only now noticed its bareness. Spurring to the stands, he bowed in the saddle to the nearest lady. She played along with his fancy, pretending to be taken aback at the alarming stranger, but nimbly unhooked the gold chain from her waist and tossed it.

Catching it deftly, the Black Knight fastened it about his massive shoulders, saluted her with raised gauntlet, and rode back, to applause.

"I'm not the only one who has something in common with Will Somers," Isabel remarked, feeling a touch of ironic affection.

The counterfeit king signaled, and the knights burst forward. Henry couched his lance, but his mount's hindquarters floundered sideways. For a breathless moment horse and rider slithered on the muddy patch, then the horse went down. Isabel leapt to her feet, her temples pounding. Her father had been thrown clear, but he lay unmoving. His esquire reached him and unfastened his helmet. Isabel glimpsed blood before the competitors and esquires surrounded him, hiding him from view.

Their silence was ominous. Her breath broken into painful shards, she whispered prayers, she scarcely knew what. Amid her fear she heard Wyatt's quiet words. "If he's taken from us, who will rule?"

Beyond her anxiety for her father, a nightmare landscape opened out. Princess Mary was only a child, and many felt Queen Katherine too apt to bend to the Emperor in Spain, who might swallow little England to feed his own ends. If they had their supporters, so did her half-brother Richmond, among those who would not stomach the rule of a woman.

It would mean factions, bloodshed, the people now surrounding her killing one another, as their parents' generation did in the Wars of the Roses. *Please God, grant it may not be—*

A cheer went up. Black armor glistened in the sun as King Henry stood, leaning on Nicholas Carew's shoulder. They had bound a cloth about his forehead. For a moment he stood still, then with an impatient movement waved them away and sent an esquire after his horse. When the man brought it, he mounted. Isabel shouted in gladness, joining the general roar as her royal father galloped the length of the yard, proving he was uninjured.

But when he dismounted near the archway, he was swaying. Sir Thomas More descended the steps to his aid, and Colford's brother, Sir Giles Colford, and the spectators were treated to the rare spectacle of Cardinal Wolsey himself puffing as he hurried down.

"Away, I've taken no hurt," King Henry ordered, but Isabel could see the accident had shaken him. "You worry like clucking old women! A tumble or two is all part of the game." Despite his bluster, the King steadied himself with his hand on More's arm. "I scared you that time, eh Wolsey? And my good Giles?"

His councilors answered too quietly to hear from where Isabel sat, exchanging glances of relief as they expressed as much of their anxiety as they dared. Henry laughed.

From beyond the archway cries arose. A palace guard burst through and fell on his knee before the King. "Murder! Treason!" he gasped. "Your Majesty, the Sun and Stars! Two guards lie slaughtered, and your crown is stolen!"

Chapter Two

od's Teeth!" King Henry roared. "Stolen! And both our guards murdered? How?"

"Cut down by sword work, Your Majesty. There's been fighting in the arming tents, by the look of it."

"Where's our guard commander?"

An officer stood forth, his face very white, and the king conferred with him in quieter tones. Isabel could not make out their words, but the faces of King, Cardinal and councilors turned grimmer with each word. Cardinal Wolsey questioned the competitors in turn, nailing each with his eye, and Sir Thomas More, beside him, listened intently. Lord Colford stepped forward and demanded that Sir Brian Harrow, who stood half armed for the joust, repeat the whole matter for his sole benefit. When Harrow had finished, Colford turned without reply to where his brother, Sir Giles, conferred gravely with the King. Colford spoke, and Henry's answer thundered with anger. "By Saint George, he'll not escape! Allow no one to leave these grounds until we have both him and the crown."

"By the sound, they know who stole it," Jane said.

"An odd robbery." Isabel frowned. "The thief won't get much use out of that sort of headgear. Selling it'll be nigh impossible, and it won't keep his ears warm."

Cardinal Wolsey spoke to a herald. The man trotted to the center of the tiltyard and filled his lungs. "His Majesty calls forth Sir Hugh Lovell!"

"Hugh?" Jane exclaimed. "What do they want with Hugh?"

"Hush." Isabel leaned over Hugh's empty place toward the gathering below, straining to make out what they said, but the alarmed speculation in the stands drowned it out. "Have you any notion where he went?"

"None," Wyatt answered soberly. "If he doesn't show himself it'll look ill."

Yet Hugh did not come forward. After further directions from the Cardinal, the herald announced with ominous gravity, "The right royal Henry, King of England, commands any who see Sir Hugh Lovell to apprehend him or make his whereabouts known to the guards. At all costs, prevent him leaving these grounds!"

"What kind of mistake—?" Jane began.

Isabel saw motion by the spectators' entrance. Beyond the low wall surrounding the tiltyard, two uniformed men dragged Hugh along. He resisted the ruffianly treatment, but another soldier joined them. Hugh demanded something, and two of them answered at once. They pushed him, now shocked and unresisting, through the spectators' entrance to where the King awaited with livid countenance. Before Hugh could bow, the guards shoved him to his knees.

Lord Colford's lips twitched with disdain, and he spoke to Cardinal Wolsey, who nodded agreement. Isabel burned at seeing Hugh thus humiliated.

"Sir Hugh Lovell," Henry spoke low, but portentously carrying, "where is our crown, the Sun and Stars?"

"I don't know, Your Grace," Hugh protested.

"You were not a competitor today. What were you doing in the arming tents?"

"I got a message, Your Majesty. Sir Robin Tremayne asked to meet me near them. He failed to arrive, so I went seeking him."

"Oh?" King Henry asked. "And what matter was of such great import that you must pursue it regardless of the tilt?" Regardless of *his* turn at the tilt, Isabel knew her father meant. He found it convenient to forget he had been competing incognito.

Hugh paused as if considering what to answer. At last he said miserably but clearly, "I beseech Your Majesty's pardon, but the matter may not be disclosed with honor. I give my word my business was harmless, and had naught to do with any theft."

"Murder, and the theft of a royal crown, which is treason," the King stated grimly. "Whatever word you've given to hold your tongue, we release you from it. Upon your allegiance, we command your answer."

Hugh looked full up at him, his face candid, but determined. "Upon my honor, I may not."

"Cold stone walls may cool your fervor. Take him to the Tower. Away!"

As he was hauled off, Hugh threw a desperate look at his friends. Bewilderment, determination and fear reshaped his features in swift succession, but the guards shoved him on.

Half-seen figures seethed with mysterious purpose, looming and receding on the tapestry as the candlelight flickered. Isabel turned away from them, pacing the room.

Despite the open window she felt stifled.

Her aunt sat in her high-backed chair of dark oak, her embroidery untouched in her lap. "Sir Thomas More has always spoken well of Hugh," she said, "and there's no better lawyer in England."

"So says the King."

"Yes," her aunt answered, "there's that. His Majesty may have set More to work already, against Hugh."

"Calling Father hasty would be calling a conflagration tepid, but More's the opposite," Isabel answered hopefully. "If he's been appointed to discover Hugh's guilt, he'll see the weakness of the case—whatever the case is. Surely More wouldn't convict a man he knew to be innocent." She paced to the tapestry again and turned. "After all, that wouldn't recover the crown."

Lady Lovell did not answer immediately. She looked over her embroidery, not seeing it. In the uncertain light the squared bones of her cheek and jaw, so like her son Hugh's, seemed stark as they never had before. At last she said, "More is the King's man and can't let himself be seen to fail. Nor can the King. They need the thief and many will prefer to say they have him."

They won't, Isabel wanted to answer, but she knew better. She realized the all-consuming importance of saving face at court, and how ambitious rivalry pushed otherwise decent people to betrayals. She did not believe they would knowingly send an innocent man to the block, but they might let themselves be convinced of what was to their advantage—if someone near the King was unscrupulous enough to do the convincing.

"A pox on Hugh's obstinacy," she burst out. "He shouldn't be in the Tower, he should be in the stable with the asses! Why won't he say his business in the tents?"

"If it's a matter of honor, he won't be forsworn." Her aunt's voice was firm.

So both Hugh and Isabel had learned from the cradle. Even death was preferable to the loss of honor or breaking of troth. Hugh Lovell was nothing if not honorable.

"What do they think Hugh wants with the Sun and Stars?" Isabel quickened her pacing, the better to speed her thoughts. "Gold can be melted and jewels sold separately, of course, but that crown's real value is in its history. For that alone, its theft amounts to treason. The risk makes no sense."

"Not to us," her aunt Margery agreed. "That's why we need Sir Thomas More and his knowledge of state matters. Will you close the window? The evening grows chill."

They had sent the servants from the room. Much as Isabel wanted the air, she latched the window. Through its mullioned panes the moon shone, and on the lawn running down to the Thames its crystalline clarity was a counterfeit of calm simplicity.

"Matthias must have reached More's house with my message by now," Lady Lovell added. "His reply will come soon."

Perhaps she was right that little could be discovered by two women without official authority. Yet Isabel could not help guessing where More's inquiries might lead. Even if stealing the crown for gain made no sense, its loss had importance. Fifteen years ago, in 1513, young and untried, King Henry had crossed the Channel to make war. Not since the old days had a monarch pressed the English claim to the French throne, but the young King had ambitions to renew the glories of Henry the Fifth. His proudest victory was the Battle of the Spurs, named for the ignominious French use of those accouterments in the face of the English charge. He took the towers of Tournai with their treasures, the greatest of which was a small but finely wrought crown set with a single magnificent diamond surrounded by a constellation of gems. Though he returned home without conquering France, carrying off that symbol of French kingship was a symbolic victory, and a sore blow to old Louis XII, whose successor, Francis I, had continued to demand that Henry return the crown. To no avail. On the last such demand, Henry had laughed. "Let Francis come pluck it from my head, if he dares!"

What if King Francis had done exactly that? Or at least, had paid another to pluck it for him.

"Last year, when Hugh served with the embassy to France, he made powerful friends at the French court," she said. "That, and being in the wrong place at the wrong time, might account for the suspicion against him."

"Air castles," her aunt said. "We need help from someone on the Privy Council."

"Right desperately!" Isabel agreed, but could no more stop worrying about her cousin than give up breathing. What of Robin Tremayne, who had sent Hugh the message to meet him in the arming tents? As far as Isabel knew, he was Hugh's trustworthy friend. He had never been to France, nor made friends of the Frenchmen at the English court. He inclined rather to the faction that favored Spanish interests. Of the French sympathizers, the most important had been in sight during the King's ill-fated joust, either in the stands or among the competitors watching from the archway. There were the French Ambassador and his staff, of course. Cardinal Wolsey was rumored to have secretly parleyed with the French even while the King planned war against them. The Duke of Norfolk had French friends, and in youth had even accompanied King Francis on forays of mischief in the Paris streets. The fact that the Ambassador, Cardinal and Duke had been in plain sight in the stands during the theft meant little, since these men would hardly have played the burglar themselves. But neither could some gang of ruffians. Close watch was kept on the arming tents during a tournament. No one would be admitted but the competitors, or those known to them.

Another with French friends was Lord Adam Colford. He had served on the embassy to Paris beside Hugh. It was there he and her cousin had their falling out. Lord Colford had been on the tiltyard immediately after the theft, perhaps too soon after to have taken part, but it was he who had spoken to the King just before he summoned Hugh. If he'd not been involved, he'd been very quick to point blame.

"Aunt Margery, what exactly is the quarrel between Hugh and Lord Colford?"

"Colford betrayed a confidence, something unwise Hugh said about the Cardinal. It cost Hugh a court appointment—" Lady Lovell ceased speaking as Hugh's page entered holding a note. She took the paper, waved him away, and eagerly broke open the seal. The first words seemed to cheer her. Then her breath left her in a low sound.

Tensing, Isabel waited.

Lady Lovell crumpled the note. Without speaking, she walked back to her chair. "Sir Thomas More writes that the King has not engaged him against Hugh." She uncrumpled the paper. " . . . *but by reason of divers considerations, not the least being Sir Hugh's refusal of the King's command to speak, I misdoubt that defending him would be in the interest of our sovereign and nation.*" She looked up. "The King's man. Matters must be bleak, or he would never write thus." The tears she had held back since Hugh's arrest spilled down her face.

Isabel hurried to her, and for a long time held her, feeling her impotence to give any real comfort. "Saint Francis, patron of dumb animals, deliver my silent fool of a cousin," she vented her exasperation.

"Don't cry, all shall be put right." Her aunt patted her back.

Isabel had not been aware of her own tears. Though the candlelight was blurred, she felt not grief but anger. "All I have, and whatever influence I command, are at your disposal. If I can do aught to see him cleared, I will."

"Wealth or rank will avail us little in this."

Isabel's royal father had granted her manors in Devon and Cornwall. She had thought herself well off, but they were worth less than ashes if she could not use them to help those she loved. In a burning tumult she silently cursed More's rebuff, and all those who'd goggled at Hugh's humiliation. And Colford's unknown words to the King and Cardinal.

"There is something you can do. You stand a better chance of gaining a way into the Tower than I. Comfort him as best you can, and tell him I will find him a good advocate."

Isabel said nothing. She had little faith in whatever obscure lawyer could be hired to pursue Hugh's interests, once More's refusal made the King's mood clear. If Hugh must obstinately keep his secret, she could still discover what forces were ranged against him. Then at least he could fight for his life.

Chapter Three

sabel had never heard a key turn a prison lock before and hoped she never would again. Iron scraping iron made a grim, implacable sound, naked of every illusion that covered the truth of mortality. Especially, the illusory security of power and privilege. Ambition was a near neighbor to overstepping, and even those who did not meddle could become the targets of others' plots. There was not a man or woman of the court who did not imagine that dismal sound in their nightmares.

The Warden of the Tower opened the door and stood back for her to enter. Hugh sat in a meagerly furnished stone room, his legs stretched out before a stool too short for him, his elbow on a table that had once belonged in a rich chamber, but was now old and scarred. When he saw it was her, he stood quickly. "Aha, coz!" He grinned valiantly. "Now I see this is all your doing. Never again will I make a wager against your liking!"

"Let it be a lesson to you," she reproved. His doublet was rumpled, his eyes heavy with sleeplessness, but to her relief she saw no sign of ill treatment. The Warden shut the door with a thud that made them both start, but by tacit agreement they ignored the grind of the key in the lock. "I brought things from your mother, linens, blankets and changes of clothes. And from me, books. They'll bring them presently. The Warden insisted on searching them, no doubt for concealed daggers, garrotes and heavy artillery."

Hugh laughed, but it had a hollow sound within the stone walls. "All the magnificence of my palace is at your disposal." With a flourish he invited her to sit at the battered table.

Isabel perched on one stool and he sat upon the other, wrapping his long legs around it. "How is Mother taking it?"

"She's bearing up. I'm to tell you she is procuring an advocate, and that if you must remain silent, she trusts your judgment. Have you been questioned?"

"Once. The investigator is Cardinal Wolsey's man, Master Cromwell."

A chill inched up Isabel's backbone. If there was unpleasant work to be done for the King, Wolsey's lawyer, Thomas Cromwell, was eager for it. His shrewd, porcine face was to be seen wherever secrets lurked. His small, penetrating eyes quested for tidbits others wished to hide, and his pale fingers found their way into every pie.

"He's not pleased with me," Hugh admitted.

"Because you refuse to tell your business with Robin Tremayne?"

"He has no interest in that. He says Robin denies sending any message, and several witnesses corroborate that Robin never sent a note, nor left the stands. In fact, good Master Cromwell has gone so far as to accuse me of directing a note to myself to fool all of you."

"A very labyrinth of deviousness you must be."

"Some folk judge all others by themselves. Cromwell's

questions have many themes, but they all run in the same key. He wants to know the names of my cohorts, and where we've hidden the Sun and Stars."

"Since you can sing no such tune, your duets must lack somewhat in harmony."

"I fear there'll be discord soon."

Though his tone remained light, Isabel tensed. "What do you mean, Hugh?"

"Thinking me merely stubborn, he has touched me gently with certain iron implements, and left me to reflect on how those touches would feel with the metal red hot. If I don't reveal the crown within five days, Master Cromwell promises I shall feel heat on the sixth."

"Then you must be proved guiltless within five days?"

Hugh's jaw tensed visibly. "Cromwell's not making that easy. As I see it, two facts argue my innocence. He scoffs at both."

"The message. If your friend never sent it, someone else wanted you near the tents during the theft," Isabel replied. "What other fact have I missed?"

"One you don't know. When I reached the tents and found no Robin, I passed the time with some of the competitors. Among them, the King's plan to joust was an open secret. We saw His Majesty and Nevill go into a tent, and two royal guards on duty outside.

"When His Majesty went out armed, the guards remained at the tent, but everyone else rushed out to watch. I grew tired of waiting for Robin and went to find him. All was empty and quiet but for the voices of the grooms as I passed the stable.

"But as I left the competitors' courtyard, I passed a man entering. He looked like a servant, about thirty, brown hair, middle height, strong. A hat some master might have cast off was pulled aslant over one ear. Then the breeze parted his hair, and I saw he had no ears. Only holes surrounded by long-healed scars, as if he'd had his ears cut off for some felony. Odd that anyone at court would employ a man whose past misdeeds were so visible, I thought. But some men do mend their ways, and honest men get mutilated in war. I thought no more of it at the time."

Isabel squinted and tucked her chin. "A convicted felon arriving just in time for the crime. A likely story."

Hugh tried to smile. "Your Cromwell is all too like him."

The effort it took him shamed her. "Forgive me, coz. I have a gnat's nature."

"I'd never change you."

With her fingernail she traced a scar in the wood of the table top. "Your business with Robin. Counterfeit or not, the message sent you dashing like a cat that hears the milk dish set out. It meant something to you. If you told them what, could that save you?"

"I think not. They'd still say I sent myself the message."

"All the same, it might appease Father's anger if you were open with him."

"Maybe. But even if he would hear me privately, it's not a thing I can tell him. Of all people, I certainly can't tell Cromwell." He leaned forward, elbows on the table, looking her in the eye. He seemed to make a decision. "Someone in the family should know why I'm keeping silent. Besides, I need a favor. But you must promise not to reveal it to anyone."

"Not even to save you from torture?"

"Not even for that. Your word?"

She took a breath, but could see no help for it. "My word."

Leaning across the table, he spoke very quietly. "It's simple enough. I love Cecily Raight, and she loves me. Whenever we can, we meet."

"Lady Raight of Brumhall?" In her alarm she had to force

her voice back to a whisper. "Her husband's no man to run afoul of."

"Lord Simon Raight is a brute," Hugh answered bitterly. "Cecily here at court and their son in the country are both in his power. That's why he must never know."

"And her brother Robin carries messages between you?"

"Aside from you, only he knows."

"And possibly, another. Whoever sent the false message."

"That fear kept me awake last night. Yet, the longer I thought of that, the less likely it seemed. The hand was the same sort as Robin's, but the wording was not just vague. It was odd. So businesslike I thought Cecily was angry with me. Now, I believe whoever wrote it supposed Robin and I had business dealings."

"I hope so for Lady Cecily's sake. Yet," Isabel busily traced the scar in the wood, scarcely aware of its roughness, "perhaps even if the sender knows, she's safe. The flimsier your excuse for being at the tents, the better for the real thief. –Ouch!" She picked out a splinter and sucked her finger. "You really must find better lodgings, coz."

He smiled. "As soon as I can. Blank stone walls aren't to my liking, I've decided. Before that, though, will you do me a favor? Speak with Cecily. Assure her of my silence." He looked down, a little embarrassed. "And my love."

"Done."

He smiled again. "My thanks, coz." But the smile faltered. Quickly he rose, turned away and paced to the grated window. "Whoever trapped me did it neatly. They're clever. What few signs I can offer of my innocence sound so farfetched it's no wonder Cromwell's brushing them aside. If the King of France is behind it, what chance the crown will ever be recovered?"

"So you're thinking in that direction, too?"

"I don't like it, but I am." He turned to face her. "If all else fails, will you plead my innocence to His Majesty? I know it could anger him. I'd never ask, except the idea of the scalding iron—" He forced himself to silence, ashamed of his fear.

His silent anguish was even harder to bear than his giving way. "If it means begging, I'll beg with all my heart," she answered. "But I won't leave it at that. Your best safety lies in discovering the real thief. To find him, I'll spare nothing."

Hugh nodded, spent.

"Try to sleep. Think of anything else that might convince them they mistake the sparrow for the hawk." She put all her heart into making her smile reassuring. "And when your thoughts chase each other too relentlessly, I brought you the *Hundred Merry Tales.*"

Hugh gave a short, startled laugh. "What, that new book of jokes everyone's talking about?"

"Yes. Perchance you can teach some to Master Cromwell."

At the very idea, his laughter ran clear, the dam of his fears breached. She rapped on the door for a guard to let her out, glad to have brought him at least a little hope.

As she stepped into the murky corridor, the guard gave her such a nervous look she wondered what was wrong with the fellow. Then, beneath the guttering torch in its sconce, a squat shape moved.

"Good day, Lady Isabel." Thomas Cromwell came forward, his small, pale eyes sharp under his thin brows.

"And to you, Master Cromwell." She schooled her alarm to the semblance of disdain. "Though what joy you find passing it in a dark corridor is beyond me."

"I'm on my way to question the prisoner, of course," he replied, his unconvincing excuse a ranker affront than his eavesdropping. "Your family feeling is most praiseworthy, my lady, but I advise you to leave off meddling. This is an official matter."

So he had heard her promise. Isabel was thankful Hugh had whispered his secret about Cecily. He was right, it was not safe in the hands of such a lurker as Cromwell. She felt dirtied having to go in fear of such a creature.

His thin lips twisted upward at her outrage, but the smile did not reach his pale eyes. "My lady, this is a serious investigation, the province of men. Attend to your amusements, and leave it to those with legal knowledge."

Isabel's anger burgeoned with every condescending word. "Well enough—if you men with legal knowledge will investigate it seriously," she retorted. "I demand an accounting. What of the man with no ears? Have you found him yet?"

"No such man serves any of yesterday's competitors, nor is in Greenwich Palace. Nor's likely to be." His expression had not changed, but his voice dripped gouts of sarcasm on Hugh's story. "I'll make myself plain, my lady. Knighthood will not protect a man guilty of treason. Not even a cousin who's a king's daughter can shelter a traitor from justice."

Or, from Cromwell's greed for advancement. For that, she had no doubt he would torture without a qualm. And if it failed to yield the crown, would he save face by fabricating evidence, then silencing his victim with execution? To save his own position, he might.

"What hope has an innocent man, leaving the investigation to such experts as you?" Isabel flung into his face. "You've already decided your course and have all but hung his head on London Bridge!"

Cromwell's gaze flicked up and down, his examination devoid of sensuality, yet that only increased its obscenity. So he must have looked when he touched the cold iron to Hugh's skin. His colorless eyes darted back to her face, and she saw a decision in them. "A wondrous interest you show in the matter, my lady. I marvel at it, truly. You're right, our investigations aren't over. Since Sir Hugh didn't have the crown when he was taken, someone else must. That someone must have a very strong interest in our investigation."

Her mouth went dry. His threat was clear. If she made matters awkward for him, he would not hesitate to implicate her. King's bastard or not, he judged her within his power to bring down. Or, within his master's. Whatever Cromwell's purposes, behind them lay Cardinal Wolsey's. Her heart thudded against her very gorge, but she would die before showing him her fear.

God's nightgown! she thought, but held her tongue. Not ten Wolseys, not the Devil himself, would threaten her off the truth. Whether or not it untidied their neat solution, she would see justice done for Hugh. Turning her back on Cromwell, she stalked away without a glance back.

Chapter Four

y noon, it had begun to rain. Isabel found her aunt sitting in her study, household accounts before her on the desk, but she was staring out the window. She told her how Hugh did, and about the encounter with Cromwell. "If I do nothing, he'll leave me alone. Yet I can't stand by and let Hugh be tortured. I wish I knew whether Cromwell really believes him guilty or only wants a scapegoat."

Lady Margery frowned absently as Eleanor of Aquitaine, Isabel's white cat, picked a dainty way across the floor and jumped onto the desk. Isabel hastened to lift her off before she upset any of her aunt's papers. She sat, settling the cat in her lap. Eleanor purred, but jumped to the floor beside her feet. She was a loving cat, but wanted her own way. Of Turkish ancestry, she was angular, with long, silky fur and opalescent eyes. Her aunt merely tolerated the cat, who rarely bothered to catch vermin, but Isabel would not leave Eleanor in the care of the Queen's other ladies, who might forget to feed her. She was too fond of her.

Much, Isabel thought, as her father was fond of her—as a pet to be indulged, but only half-regarded. When he thought of her at all. Perhaps he would hear her plea for Hugh, but if the case presented to him seemed to prove Hugh a traitor, no amount of begging would save her cousin's life. As a member of the mere gentry, Hugh would not be granted the aristocratic dignity of beheading. It would be the hangman's noose. Since he could not tell them where to recover the crown, would they draw and quarter him too?

Isabel shut her eyes, refusing to think of it.

"What?" her aunt asked sharply.

"Nothing." She bent over to scratch behind Eleanor's ears. So the whole court saw her, a mere royal pet. Though at her age most women had married, borne children and buried some, her father still saw her as a girl. Partly, she suspected, he did not want to think himself old enough to have a grown daughter, and maybe for that reason the courtiers followed suit. Or, most of them. Not Tom Seymour, who was the same age and sick of being treated like a child by his solemn stick of a brother, Edward. Since Tom's kiss, Isabel had done nothing to try to impress her maturity on her father. She dreaded being married off to anyone else. Only last month as he spoke with Queen Katherine his eye had lit on her among the Queen's ladies and he'd asked her whether she would like a husband. She denied it with a pert pun, just off-color enough to make him roar with laughter and drop the matter for the time being. She herself had encouraged them to think of her as only a giddy maiden. How could she expect the competitors at the tournament who might have seen something important, or solemn men of the law, to take her seriously?

Yet, that might be an advantage. *Attend to your amusements*, Cromwell had said. Dancing, silk sleeves for her gowns, and tender fancies of courtly love, men imagined these filled a maiden's mind. Let them. Since even a wizened, sober widow with a proven head for business would never gain access to the official records or the authority to investigate, let the frivolity expected of a spoilt young maiden be her disguise, and her weapon. Two men already lay dead because someone wanted the Sun and Stars. To find out why, she might indeed have to enter a realm where weapons were necessary.

Hearing footsteps, she glanced over her shoulder. Ursula, her waiting woman, came in, carrying a tray with two plates. Lady Margery eyed the bread and wine and motioned her toward Isabel, who shook her head.

Ursula's long, thin face took on a severe expression. "You ate no dinner yesterday and scarce breakfasted this morning, my ladies." Pushing the papers aside, she clacked the tray down on the desk. "Starving yourselves won't help Sir Hugh."

Isabel's stomach growled. Ursula was right. She needed strength. Besides, it was time to begin. Scooting her chair close to the desk she pulled off a hunk of bread. Surprised at how good it smelt, she wolfed it down.

"Well," Ursula declared, startled. "That's a change of heart."

"Only of stomach. Aunt, may I ask Ursula to sit with us? Come, good Ursula, share the loaf before Eleanor carries it off to Aquitaine." Taking the wine, she poured a cup and nodded toward the one empty chair.

"I don't need it," the waiting woman protested, taking the cup. "Now, my lady," she asked shrewdly, "what help do you want?" Ursula Gibbs was a Londoner born and bred, a widow with many friends and a wise head on her shoulders.

"We have five days to prove Hugh innocent," Isabel said.

"Or that mucky blacksmith's son heats up his little tongs?" Ursula's knife sliced the bread as if it were Cromwell's hide.

Isabel was surprised, but not much. At court, Ursula was

worth a dozen paid spies. "Did you also hear that he tried to scare me off?"

"Master Cromwell?" Ursula's brows rose nearly to her linen coif. "How, my lady?"

"He was very touchy about interference. Why should I show so much interest, he insinuated. As if I had the Sun and Stars hidden in my linen chest!"

Her aunt glanced up sharply. "I don't care for the sound of that."

"He went on the attack to save face. I'd caught him eavesdropping." Isabel mused, nibbling a crust. "We've assumed Hugh's arrest was a similar diversion, an attempt to make it appear His Majesty's men have matters under control. But what if he's a scapegoat for someone?"

"You mean, *Cromwell* might be the thief?" Ursula asked.

"Or his master, Cardinal Wolsey. Think of it. Who would want the Sun and Stars?"

"King Henry's crown is too dangerous to have in England," the waiting woman said, "but I suppose a buyer might be found in some foreign country."

"Who might trade the thief to the King along with the crown, for an even richer gain?" Lady Margery asked. "Too risky."

"That's my point," Isabel agreed. "Who but a king is far enough away, and powerful enough, to risk our King's wrath? Yet kings have baubles of their own and need not pinch one another's. Unless more is at stake than a trinket. That's why His Majesty is so fond of the Sun and Stars. Each time he wears it he rubs salt into the wound of the French king's pride."

"King Francis?" Ursula reached for the wine. "But the thief will have the devil's own time trying to smuggle it out of England. Search points will be on every road, and inspectors at every port."

"A tight watch can't be kept forever," her aunt said. The thief need only tarry a month or two."

"Is that why they gave Hugh five days?" Isabel wondered. "If they do believe him guilty, they may hope to spur his cohorts into an attempt before he reveals them."

"But since poor Sir Hugh can reveal nothing, the real thief need only sit tight," Ursula answered. "And laugh."

"Unless Cromwell is involved. Then he's in a bind. He dare not silence Hugh so quickly it reveals his own guilt, yet the longer he waits, the more danger to him. What of the rumor that the Cardinal was negotiating with the French behind the King's back, even while we were allied to Charles of Spain?"

"What, the Cardinal in a secret deal with King Francis? A traitor to England?" Lady Margery stared at Isabel, shocked.

"Foreign politics are marsh mud to me," Ursula declared. "All I know is that Queen Katherine is the Emperor Charles' aunt. If the King casts her off and puts the Boleyn on the throne, Spain may declare war. Then, we'll need French backing."

"And the price is the Sun and Stars?" Lady Margery commented bitterly. "Robbery is a base tactic for a King."

"Not too base for a lecher like King Francis." Ursula finished her wine. "They say his notion of fun is to ride with his cronies in the streets of Paris, lobbing eggs, garbage and rocks at his subjects—when he's not abed with three women at once, that is."

"Ursula!" Lady Margery chided. "Remember, your lady is a maiden!"

"Who hears worse talk from young wastrels like that scribbler Thomas Wyatt and the wild Seymour boy, I'll be bound." Ursula sourly cocked her head in the direction of Greenwich Palace. "Where are they, now Sir Hugh's under a cloud?"

Isabel stood watching the rain slant into the garden. Where *was* Tom Seymour, she thought. Where was his slightest message of goodwill or faith in Hugh? She turned away from the window. "I won't jump at straws. The Cardinal's not the only one who might be in the French King's pay. The French ambassadors are, of course. What about the Duke of Norfolk? He used to be King Francis' accomplice on those garbage-lobbing expeditions, by all accounts." She did not say so aloud, but even Anne Boleyn and her sister once served as ladies-in-waiting in France. Anne hated the Cardinal. Might she try to frame him?

"So you count out those with no love for the French?" Lady Margery asked dubiously.

Isabel scooped up Eleanor of Aquitaine, who mewed loudly. "I accuse no one, and I count out no one. The Spanish sympathizers are Queen Katherine, the Spanish ambassador, the Queen's ladies-in-waiting—the elder ones who came with her from Spain. Though Lord Adam Colford favors France, his brother, Sir Giles Colford, has worked to hold together our Imperial alliance." She rubbed the cat's silky ears. "But what would the Emperor Charles want with the Sun and Stars? And what of those whose sympathies are hidden? Norris, Carew and Harrow were all competitors, for instance, and the thief had access to the arming tents. –I'll not leave Sir Thomas More off my list, either."

"You're angry with him for not representing Hugh, but More's a man of principles."

"And so he refuses to help an innocent man because he's in disfavor? Besides, More's as moiled in politics as Wolsey."

"All the more reason not to make enemies of such men," her aunt warned.

"I don't give two plums for Cromwell's threats," Isabel answered defiantly. "What of the boy who delivered the false message to Hugh? Find him, and we have his master."

"Start asking, and it's the quickest way to alert the master," Ursula retorted.

Isabel ignored that caution, too. "And the man with no ears. If Cromwell's not lying and our earless friend is really not in service at court, he's a scoundrel hired for the theft—but Hugh saw just one man enter, and only a fool would send a single swordsman against two trained royal guards. There must have been at least one other swordsman. Hugh heard grooms in the stables, but grooms aren't trained fighters. At least one competitor must have known the King was to compete, and stayed behind when all rushed to watch."

Isabel paused as a memory that had eluded her surfaced. Though she had seen Tom Seymour enter the stands after the joust, she'd not seen his opponent. "Aunt! Lord Colford was with the King when Hugh was dragged in, but not before. When he rushed up demanding to have the tale of the theft repeated, he came not from the stands, but the direction of the tents."

"The thief is a cold-blooded murderer," her aunt replied. "If it may be Colford, take care that he knows nothing of your suspicion."

Isabel assumed an expression she hoped was dutiful. "Rest assured, I saw Colford's methods in the tournament yesterday. Chivalry is not his most conspicuous trait. I promise I'll steer clear of both him and Cromwell. Anyway, first I promised an errand for Hugh."

"Good," Lady Margery answered. Ursula arose and took up the cups.

Isabel stroked the cat with deliberate nonchalance. "By the way, Ursula, do you know any servants in the Lord Colford's employ?"

Ursula looked over her shoulder at her. "I might."

Lord Simon Raight's grandparents had been Yorkists in the
Wars of the Roses. Like many on the losing side, their fortunes
had fallen, and incontinent wagering had whittled away yet
more of his lands. The Tremaynes, from an old Cornish family
but not titled, had thought a baron worth a substantial dowry,
but Lord Raight had frittered much of that, too. He could not
afford a house on the Strand. He was one of those who, while
he could not bear the expenses of the court and had no duties
there, yet persisted in attempting to get a foothold. Escorted
through the damp, odorous streets of London by Hugh's young
page Matthias and two sturdy Lovell servants, Isabel rode to
Raight's house.

She had played with Lady Cecily long ago in Devon, while
her male cousins ran wild with Cecily's brother Robin, but
lately she had seen little of her former friend. Lord Simon
Raight did not make good company. He was an overbearing
man. Though with little of substance to say, he spoke loudly,
stifling others' conversations. Before Cecily was grown, the
Tremaynes had removed to the Netherlands where they had
shipping interests. There they gave Cecily in marriage to Lord
Simon. So far from London, they'd heard no talk about the
first Lady Raight. Maltreated and neglected by her husband,
she took comfort from another, until the lover met a gruesome
death in a hunting accident. Murder was never proven, but
many suspected Lord Simon. The lady did not outlive her lover
by long. According to Lord Raight, she died of an illness, but
some named that illness starvation.

The house was half-timbered, gabled and neatly kept.
Nothing about it looked sinister. Yet Isabel's heart misgave her.
Without doubt, Hugh was cuckolding unwisely. In that, he ran

true to form. Caution was seldom his companion. The servant who took her horse was courteous enough to her page and men, and a woman curtsied and showed her to a sitting room. Tapestries relieved the plainness of whitewashed walls, and timbered rafters arched to a simple peak. The leaded glass of two small windows diffused the grey afternoon light. To Isabel's relief, Lady Raight was alone. Startled, she arose, but when she recognized Isabel she gave a soft, glad cry and came to embrace her. Cecily had always been slight and fine boned, with fair hair, grey-blue eyes and a remarkable delicacy of feature, charmingly marred by a faint scatter of freckles across her nose. Isabel could understand what her cousin saw in Cecily, but three years of marriage had thinned and sharpened her. By the look of her, she'd slept no more last night than Hugh had.

"How kind of you to come visiting in this drizzle," she said. "Are you chilled? I'll have wine mulled."

"I grew impatient, cooped indoors," Isabel answered, guessing the reason for her old friend's formal tone, "but it was a damp ride. I'd welcome a cup of warm wine, with thanks."

When the servant had gone, Cecily listened to her diminishing footsteps, then said quietly, "Anything we say, Agnes might report to my husband. He's not in the house now, so tell me, what's this coil at court? Is your cousin really under arrest?"

"Cecily, no need to pretend," Isabel said even more softly. "Hugh told me. I've seen him in the Tower."

"Have they—"

Isabel shook her head. "He's well. And safe, for a few days. He asked me to reassure you. Whatever happens, he'll remain silent about you." Sitting, she glanced at the door, but saw no one, and no shadow that had not been there before. "Did you send him any word at the tournament yesterday?"

"I wasn't there. Lord Simon's mother suffered a dizzy spell. I left with her and saw her safe to an acquaintance's lodgings. Why?"

"Because Hugh received a message asking to meet near the arming tents. It bore your brother's name, but the investigators told Hugh that Robin denies writing any such note."

"I know no reason he would."

Isabel disliked worrying her, but a possibility needed considering. "Might Lord Simon have forged it?"

Cecily's eyes widened slightly, but she shook her head. "Not he. I'm certain he knows nothing of Hugh and me."

"Can you be?"

"My husband is a dissembler, but not subtle in his cups. Last night he was drunk."

The restraint of those few sentences spoke worlds. Isabel's heart went out to her.

But Cecily looked into her eyes unwavering. "I can't come forward, Isabel. I can't. But tell me straight out. Will Hugh die because of that? If I told them he had every reason to expect the note was genuine and go where it asked, would it save him?"

Doubt tensed Isabel's shoulders. Cecily had more at stake than her own honor and safety. Her child was in Lord Raight's power. "Your husband would harm his own son?"

"He'd no longer believe his son his own."

Isabel considered. At last, she answered honestly, "Your coming forward would not be enough to clear Hugh. I fear nothing will, except proving who is the real culprit. But is there no way out for you?"

"Even if I could somehow escape with little Alan, he'd come after us. Sometimes I've longed to beg my family's help, but Alan is his son, and what am I but another of his possessions? No court in England would deny his right to us.

I've watched you with the Queen's other ladies-in-waiting, so happy, like a butterfly, and I've been glad you have for so long escaped being some man's slave. You have no notion what it is, Isabel, after my kind upbringing, to live with a man like Raight. I'd heard of cruel husbands, I knew of the Duke of Norfolk's treatment of his wife, but in Flanders Raight was all charm. I never suspected what he was. The one spot of warm sun I have is Hugh Lovell. The one chance for life as it used to be. Short of destroying my son, I would do anything for Hugh." She closed her eyes, but not in time to prevent tears slipping from under the lids.

"Matters look dark for Hugh," Isabel admitted. "Sir Thomas More has declined to help, and I misdoubt whatever bumbler Aunt Margery may be able to hire. But Hugh told me one or two things that may help if I can learn their meaning, and it may be I've noticed others. Stay strong, and keep yourself and your son safe. I know that's what Hugh wants above all else."

Cecily nodded and wiped the wet from her eyes. "Do any traces show?"

Isabel took out her handkerchief and gently dabbed away the last of the damp. "Not now." She tucked it back into the velvet pouch hanging at her waist. "When did you and the elder Lady Raight leave the joust, by the way?"

"She took ill during the tilt between Seymour and Lord Colford. They were still at it when I left."

"There's not much hope of this, but as you went out, did you see a man lacking his ears?"

"Lacking ears? Not that I noticed. But Lady Raight is difficult when she's ill."

Isabel gave her a small smile. "You could have passed ears lacking a man and been none the wiser?"

"Too close to the mark," Cecily answered, beguiled into smiling despite her fears. "I remember a shout went up from the stands. That was one of the jousters unhorsed, I thought, but I said nothing, for Lady Raight would have collided with the French ambassador's secretary in her distress, and he seemed no steadier."

"What, Monsieur Salet had too much to drink?"

"No, the younger one, Des Roches."

"But he was never in the stands. Word was, he was ill."

"So he was. A misery of rheums and coughing. He should have stayed abed."

"Maybe he should've," Isabel answered, scarce able to contain the whirl in her head. The man with no ears, and now a representative of the French king, both present during the crime, both unaccounted for. "Maybe he should've."

Chapter Five

ou'd best wear your gay green gown tomorrow," Ursula
remarked.

"Tomorrow?" Isabel asked absently, her mind beset
with memories of the fine display of French swordsmanship
Monsieur Des Roches had given the court on his arrival. Two
months ago, his predecessor, an old man without fighting skills,
had been recalled to France for reasons not clear. "Oh! The
entertainment tomorrow night."

"I know you scarce feel like dancing, but you must go,"
Ursula answered, her comb sweeping through Isabel's long
hair. "His Majesty would read your absence as an
announcement you think he's wrong. He wouldn't like it."

"Have no fear, I'll give him no cause to roar and stamp—
wrong though he is. I wouldn't miss this evening for all the
treasures of Persia. A gathering of all my quarry in one room! –
All but Master Earless, I suppose."

"I've made inquiries. Cromwell's telling the truth, no such
man serves anyone at the palace."

Isabel turned so quickly the comb was pulled from Ursula's
fingers. "So he had no honest business in the tents! What of
your other errand?"

"I found an excuse to pass the time of day with a cook in Lord Colford's employ." Ursula laid aside the comb. "A crafty one, if I may say so."

Isabel could not resist. "A crafty cook?"

"A crafty excuse," Ursula answered, miffed.

Isabel hid her smile and gave Ursula's cleverness the interest due it. "What was your ploy?"

"The only one that would turn aside suspicion, since I couldn't hide that I was after tittle-tattle. His Majesty will soon seek a betrothal for you, and I've heard Lord Colford's looking for a wife."

"Ursula! You didn't!"

"I never hinted you favored him, give me some credit."

"If word gets to him—"

"Even then, he'll hear only that your old attendant, knowing he's a widower, poked in her nose without the slightest encouragement from her mistress. Everybody knows old women are busybodies and not worth much bother," she added with tart irony. "Since the lord might hear of my curiosity whatever my excuse, better to throw him wide of the mark. So I aimed for what I judged his most vulnerable point. His pride."

"You're incorrigible. Well? Did you learn aught of interest?"

"His fortunes are solid. My informant saw nothing strange in my curiosity about that, considering. He has a taste for fine clothes and horses, but no more than a lord should. If he's changed sides to the King of France, he didn't sell himself for need."

"There are rich men who'll forswear themselves to increase their riches—or their power."

"Power might be a sore point with him," Ursula mused. "Though he has the barony, his younger brother Sir Giles has the greater esteem from the King."

"No wonder. Sir Giles may speak too freely for the liking

of some, but Father will gladly shout down a too-forward tongue. What he mislikes is secretive silence."

"And brooding. Lord Colford's cook said right out that a lady of sunny nature shouldn't marry him. When I asked why not, she spouted gullible nonsense, but telling. His servants say Lord Adam Colford's a sorcerer and can make the very darkness of a room blacker with his thoughts. When he's in a foul temper they swarm like shadows round him, though he tells no one what those thoughts may be."

"What of his brother? Might he be an easier path to deciphering his lordship's broodings?"

"I didn't think to follow that line, but I did ask what sort of family the Colfords are. Relations between the two brothers are amicable enough. When room was short during the royal visit to Ludlow last March, they shared quarters. But they've never been close. They weren't raised together. Lord Adam was sent to a monastery for his early education, while Sir Giles grew up at home."

"Odd!" Isabel pondered. "You'd expect the younger brother to be farmed out so. A first step toward a career in the Church. But an elder brother and heir? Why?"

"She didn't say."

"Did he quarrel with his father? Was there any attempt to disinherit him?"

"No, that couldn't have been kept from court gossip. Mayhap he was wicked beyond governing, even then."

"Mayhap." Isabel mistrusted her eagerness to find sinister doings in every scrap about Lord Colford. To suspect Hugh's enemy was all too tempting.

"Lord Adam's worst fault, according to his servants, is his gimlet eye that pierces all their doings. He trusts no one. To the jaundiced, all the world looks yellow. To dissuade you from marrying him, the cook added one other sign of her master's lack of feeling. After the old lord, his father, died, Lord Adam straightway occupied the best manor house, while Sir Giles and the widow removed elsewhere. Though Lord Adam has the lion's share, he doesn't pay a farthing toward her upkeep. It all comes from Sir Giles."

"Wondrous family feeling," Isabel agreed. "A man who'd turn a cold heart toward his mother could do the same to his king. You've done well. In return, I'll tell you my news. The source is one I trust, though I can't say whom. Not only is the lord not accounted for during the theft, a secretary high in the service of the French ambassador was seen among the tents."

Ursula nodded, unsurprised. "Two mere women can muster as much wit as a Sir Thomas More, after all."

"I never doubted it. Yet the first of our five days is nearly gone, and we're not much closer to catching the thief. We have no idea who the earless man is, we can scarce question Lord Colford or Des Roches, and what of Cromwell? We go in such fear of him that we dare question no one at all! How can we trap a traitor this way?"

"Perhaps we'd best not trap any traitors."

"What do you mean, not trap them?" Isabel whirled on her in exasperation.

Ursula stood her ground. "As you said, what if Master Cromwell knows who's guilty? What if it's someone Cardinal Wolsey has ordered him to protect? What if it's the Cardinal himself? If Cromwell fails in that protection, it'll mean his career, maybe his head."

"Or Hugh's," Isabel answered stubbornly.

"Do you think you can win that battle, against a serpent like Cromwell? What if a lesser measure would do?"

"Lesser?" Isabel paused, clenching her fists, but listening.

"The evidence no longer points all at Sir Hugh. Go over Cromwell's head. Take it directly to His Majesty. Surely he would delay Sir Hugh's torture, at least until the Frenchman's been questioned."

"Buying time isn't enough."

"Maybe the questioning will turn up something. I can't let you go plunging in. Don't forget, whoever the traitor is, he—or she—has staked all on this crime. He's even killed for it. If you learn too much, would he shrink at killing you? Sorry as I am for Sir Hugh, I won't let you get yourself murdered. Whatever it takes to stop that, I will."

Even sacrificing Hugh, she meant. Ursula was in earnest and would stop at nothing to keep her safe.

That was why, for Ursula's sake, Isabel lied. If her lord father believed Hugh guilty, it would take more to stay his wrath than disconnected tales of an earless felon, Colford's absence and the sighting of Des Roches by a source unrevealed. Besides, His Majesty would probably add a royal command to stay out of the business. Yet she could no more do that than cease walking and sprout leaves. Though Hugh was her first care, two men were dead. In the glitter of the stolen crown, most had forgotten them, but two women who yesterday awoke beside their husbands would never know their embrace again. Two families were uncertain of security after the royal purse, a poor exchange for a life, was spent. Something fierce in Isabel wanted to see justice done for them.

First, she needed to connect at least one other suspect with the earless man. Hugh had heard grooms in the stable, yet if she began questioning the grooms, they would guess her reason, and soon the whole palace would know of her attempt to discover the thief.

Unless she made silence to the grooms' advantage. The clink of coins was a rare music to such as they, and therefore, sweet.

So without ado, she dislodged a topaz from her best French hood. Once Ursula was safely embarked upon the errand to the jeweler's, Isabel was off to the stables.

The large, timbered building was dim within and warm with the scents of hay and horses. Two grooms dropped their dice and jumped up from their bales of hay, and a third stared from within a stall as he brushed a glossy chestnut's flank. For a lady to demand her horse on the spur of the moment was not unusual, but for her to come into the stable herself, unheard-of.

Yet, luck was with her. The stablemaster was nowhere to be seen. A request, together with a small consideration, yielded the head groom for the joust, a wiry, bow-legged man who jerked off his cap to reveal a head bald and pointed as a duck egg.

Aware that the sight of a lady in the stables would be memorable, Isabel motioned him outside, positioning them as if her own tethered horse held all her interest. Satisfied that no eyes would spy on them but the liquid brown ones of her mare, and no ears prick at their words but long, velvety ones, she began, "Your name, friend?"

"Harry Hackett, my lady." His study of her was as shrewd as it was covert. This man judged all things by what he might get from them, she guessed. That was not entirely bad for her purposes.

She gave him a guileless smile. "I came to thank you for your alert service to my lord father. Your grooms were the first to his aid."

Now they were on familiar ground, and ground he liked. A devoted daughter was a fine thing, and her gratitude better yet. "Young Ned Prior was the first," he answered modestly. "'E's laid up with a twisted ankle from running to catch 'is Majesty's 'orse, mindful of my orders despite the hubbub."

"My grateful thanks to him, and to you. Please share this with young Ned."

"Thank you, my lady! I ordered 'em all to stay alert."

"It must be hard," she mused with the unworldly wonder of one who had never had serious duties, "keeping so ready for His Majesty's needs, yet watching all the horses at the same time."

"Nay, the 'orses weren't neglected. I'm no scatterbrains to go running out while there was any competitors among the horses."

"Competitors?" Isabel frowned.

"No chance for chicanery in *my* stables," Harry hastened to assure her. "I didn't leave till Lord Colford did."

Isabel petted her mare, not looking into bald Harry's sharp eyes but listening intently to every nuance of his voice. "I thought Lord Colford had already competed. He won his joust, didn't he?"

"Aye, my lady, so I heard. But 's mount went gimp."

"Gimp? You mean, lame?"

"A pebble lodged in 's hoof."

"So he gave his charger into your good charge," she punned pleasantly.

"Saving your ladyship, not exactly," Harry contradicted. "Lord Adam's very partic'lar. 'E ordered Ned to fetch an 'oof pick and tended 's mount 'imself, till 's esquire come hotfoot with news of 'Is Majesty's spill. Then we ran for the tiltyard."

"What, all of you?" Isabel idly twiddled a lock of the mare's mane, her heart plummeting like lead through icy water. "Lord, esquire, grooms and sundry?"

"There wasn't no sundry." Harry's voice hardened. "Wasn't nobody back there that didn't have business there. I never allow nobody unofficial 'mongst the knights' chargers, and you can tell 'Is Majesty so. If a knight had a mind to try tricks with another's mount, 'e'd never manage that with me on the job."

"I see." Isabel fought for a semblance of nonchalance. "I'm sure you're most vigilant. But if I may ask a favor, pray don't tell His Majesty I was here worrying about him. Clucking hens, he calls those of us who fear for him. Here, this is for your trouble."

"Don't fret," bald Harry answered, closing his hand around the coins she put in it. "They fall all the time in practice, and 'Is Majesty's as strong as King Arthur and Lancelot rolled in one."

"My thanks." Isabel turned to escape before disappointment shattered her composure.

Bald Harry's sharp features wrinkled into solemnity. "Sorry to hear about Sir Hugh's trouble, my lady. Whatever else 'e be, he's always a kind soul to an 'orse."

Chapter Six

he great hall stood polished and aired, its marble floor awaiting dancing feet, its damask hangings heavy without the stir of laughter and discreet dalliance. The place seemed to ache with emptiness. So felt Isabel's heart, chill, echoing and empty. For a brief moment, she'd believed she had found the missing connection to free Hugh. Had Lord Colford, the earless felon and Des Roches all been among the tents during the theft, it might have been enough to take to the King. Instead, Colford's whereabouts were attested by a witness. Only now, admitting the depth of her disappointment, did Isabel realize how much she had hoped her cousin's enemy was the traitor. To see a man she so disliked in Hugh's place would be no hardship.

Of course, that did not clear Lord Colford of masterminding a theft carried out by others, but the same was true of every gentleman and lady at the joust. She was back where she had started, with almost nothing.

Isabel climbed the narrow stairs to the musicians' gallery overlooking the hall. Sometimes, with the Queen's other maids

of honor, she practiced her lute here, the echoes unearthly
sweet in the cavernous space below, like the half-heard voices
of angels.

Now, with the silence weighing on her, Cromwell advanced
in her thoughts. If Colford needed a scapegoat, he had a reason
for choosing Hugh. Not so Cromwell, who bore him no grudge.
Yet here Cromwell was, at the center of things yet somehow
oddly invisible, both referee and contender in some twisted
game of his own ambition. In four days he would put Hugh to
torture. Hugh would not break easily, but in agony he would
finally submit to any confession urged on him. Everyone did.
Then, they would hang him, and if Cromwell had secrets they
would be choked with him. Personal malice wasn't necessary.
That made reason enough for him to sacrifice Hugh. "No! No!
No!" she whispered to the emptiness below. Among the ornate
rafters, echoes rustled like moths' wings.

Bald Harry's words about Hugh still reverberated in her
mind. From such a hard man, they were unexpected.
Perchance, embittered toward people, the groom cared only
for his animals, and thought well only of those who did
likewise. Yet the ring of his voice had sounded an odd note.
She was convinced he'd meant his sympathy and did not know
why it should trouble her. She leaned her elbows on the
balustrade, gazing listlessly down into the hall.

"Youth must have some dalliance,
Of good or ill some pastance.
Company methinks then best
All thoughts and fancies to digest."

Leaning over the balustrade, Isabel searched the shadows.
The song was a composition of King Henry's, but the voice was
not his. She recognized the baritone, gravelly and yet oddly
pleasing to the ear. However, its owner remained invisible. This
fish would rise only to worthy bait. She took up the song.

"For idleness
Is chief mistress
Of vices all . . ."

"And so it is." Will Somers stepped from a shadow in his green doublet, three glittering balls in the crook of his arm. "Your voice is sweet, lady, but methinks it's a turtle's."

"A turtle's?" She tried for indignation, but her spirits were too low.

"Coooor, coooor," the jester imitated the plaintive mourning that filled the palace gardens of an evening. "When can a turtle fly?"

"When she's a turtle dove." Isabel rested her arms on the smooth, cool stone of the balustrade, and her chin forlornly atop them.

"When she has wings," Will corrected gently. "And it's plain she has none today. So how does she come to be roosting so high?"

She half wished he would leave her to her worries, but if she welcomed any company, it was his.

A spark shot up in the gloom, the balls leaping into the air to describe a faintly glistening circle there. It moved toward the stairs as if on its own. She heard his tread as he climbed, as light as if he were not juggling at all, though she knew he was. From nowhere sprang a spinning silver arc, startling her into motion, and she found a glittering ball in her hand. Will's puckish head grinned at her, rising from the darkness of the stairs. Despite his mugging, she felt his sympathy.

"It will be hard, dancing and acting full of cheer. Yet His Majesty will expect that."

Will sat on the floor, leaning his back against the balustrade. "Methinks it would be wise. His Majesty's not in good sorts. He dislikes anything that seems an ill omen, you know."

"The loss of a crown?"

"I tried to tell him it's but a French crown. Yet that only put him in a worse humor." Will shrugged.

"Because the French King has hoodwinked him, doubtless."

"There's a fierce rivalry between those two," Will agreed. "King Francis is as mighty an athlete as His Majesty, and a good deal more the lover. If he's dealt our King some deceit, on top of the Emperor Charles' veiled threats, should the King not cry 'nuncle' . . ." A single ball made a distracting circle in the air.

That was as plain as Will would say it. Even a professional fool's impunity only went so far. Charles, to whom Queen Katherine was aunt and therefore King Henry, uncle, must know all about the King's Great Matter, his not-so-secret search for grounds to annul his marriage. Besides King of Spain, Charles was ruler of the Netherlands. If he'd threatened a Dutch embargo on English wool, her father's mood might be dangerous indeed. Like most people who enjoyed their power over others, he went livid if any dared bully him.

"And Hugh pays the price of his bad humor?" When Will did not answer, Isabel pressed, "Surely you don't imagine anything in this world could turn Hugh Lovell into a murdering traitor?"

"Sir Hugh Lovell? A faithful color, I'd call that Hugh," Will admitted. "Yet if traitors looked like traitors, any fool could avoid them. Perchance that's where your cousin comes in. That is, stumbles in, to a trap laid by a knave who's a wiser man than he."

Isabel gave him a wan smile, relieved it had occurred to others besides Hugh's family. "Yes, but what knave?"

"If I knew that, I'd not be sitting here, I'd be off to tell the King. He's no fun." Cradling the balls in his arms like a babe, he stuck out his underlip at them. "Hal want him toy back!"

"A fool needn't be a traitor to be a knave," Isabel

reprimanded, shocked at his insolence. But that was the special privilege of a court jester, and besides, when thwarted, her father could indeed be like a gigantic, fearsome, spoilt child. "Speaking of knaves, I have an unlikely question. Do you know of a man with no ears?"

"Knave he may be, but no jackass. What, a certain, specific man? I'm not acquainted with him. And hope not to be, he sounds not quite polite company."

Despite his professional fool's babble, she trusted Will's discretion. "What of the Frenchman, Des Roches? Is he recovered from his illness?"

"Not that I know. But you're not given to sighing over the handsome Monsieur Des Rheums." He gave 'rheums' a parody of a French accent that made it sound like a sniffling nose, and Isabel could not help laughing. "Dat's bettair," he sniffled. "Dere eez method een your questions, no?"

"Yes, I do suspect the French."

"The French alone? Or with help?"

"With the help of an enemy of Hugh's, I thought. But that trail led nowhere, and I've wasted one of Hugh's five days to no avail."

"Now you're the one talking in riddles, but I guess who you mean. It was not until the sixth day that God created Adam, but fair Isabel means to create Adam a traitor? Unlikely, I think. Adam Colford's no Thomas Seymour, but I'd rather a chill crossing than a coxcomb."

Isabel kept her face schooled. "Those without titles and lands can't afford ill manners," she returned lightly.

"Not unless they revel in them, as I do." He winked at her. But then he frowned. "Do you know, this Adaming and Thomasing has put me in mind of something curious. It's probably of no use, but as ladies like to be given useless curiosities, I'll present you with this. Last summer, I overheard an Adam berating a Thomas."

"Colford? Berating who?"

"The Thomas he brought low was—who's the lowest Thomas you know?"

"Tom the kitchen apprentice?" Exasperation filled her. She had hoped for a revelation. Surely this could not be some further insult to Tom Seymour. She tried the lowest Thomas she knew. "Pocky Tom the rat-catcher?"

"Wrong. A Cromwell is yet lawyer than those."

"Lord Colford berated Thomas Cromwell? Why?"

"For spying among his private papers. Master Cromwell denied it, but to no abatement of His Lordship's wrath."

Will was right, his information was probably useless in the matter of the Sun and Stars. She already knew Lord Colford and Cardinal Wolsey—and so also, Wolsey's lawyer Cromwell—had worked together last spring on some matter of mercantile licensing. And she already knew Lord Colford was insufferable and Cromwell a slinker. "I can't fashion a conclusion from your gift," she answered, disappointed, "but I'll keep it for a nosegay."

"No, I suppose it's not the curiosity you really want." He looked mischievous. "But then, it's curiosity a lady can least afford."

"And what curiosity is that?"

"The curiosity of a young man who says he loves, but not what he loves."

"What, not who?"

"Aye, and that's a difference. All the difference between a first son and a second. Consider the advantage to such a one, should he net a king's natural daughter."

"This time you go too far," Isabel returned sharply. She felt her face redden.

"It's not common gossip," Will replied mildly. "A fool's bread and butter is in noticing everything."

"I'm not led on by curiosity, nor he by greed, and we've done no wrong!"

"Sit down, sweet lady. Listen to thy Nuncle Will."

"No."

"Then stand and listen. Young Tom Seymour is not a man to pin your fortunes to, and you know it."

Some traitorous voice within her whispered agreement. "I know no such thing," Isabel denied staunchly.

"Soon His Grace will find you a husband. He's spoken no names, but it won't be Seymour. He'll marry you to a man of substance, one of the Boleyn kin maybe, or the governor of a Welsh border castle, somebody who's served him well and has a good head on his shoulders. If you're lucky, he'll make you forget Tom."

"I don't forget easily," she retorted, insulted.

He nodded, sympathetic, but there was nothing he could do. Or she. Her father would decide when and whom she would marry, and she must obey. "At least, your plight's better than your poor half-sister's," he said at last. "Princess Mary will be bartered to some foreign prince for a treaty. But you will stay here, among those who love you. Being nearby, your father will see to it your husband does not treat you ill. He's fond of you, you know."

"When the whim takes him to notice me."

"I've known King Hal long and well. A ruler will tell a fool much that he won't tell his council. You remind him of your mother, his first love, when he was not a king, only a man. He wants you happy, so rest easy about that, at least. I doubt you'll be forced to take someone you loathe."

"What of you, Will?" Isabel asked mischievously. "If I can't have Tom, I think I'd like you."

"With all my heart, lady." He leaned over and kissed her cheek, then tossing the balls in a silver flash, scampered down the stairs like a youth half his age.

Chapter Seven

In the mist the houses and quays on the river were no more than vague grey shapes. Fog rose from the leaden-dark water in curling wisps that gathered and hung heavy, muffling the plash of the oars. It was a peculiarly disturbing sensation, as if the riverbanks were only roiling, drifting banks of cloud. Isabel sat in the stern with her cloak wrapped around her. Though Ursula, huddled beside her, occasionally maligned the chilly damp, Isabel remained silent. She would have given much, could she but bring Hugh cheering news.

Without warning the massive battlements of the Tower of London loomed like some phantasmagoric spectre of power and menace, all the more threatening because only half seen. The boatman hauled at the oars, bringing the small craft toward the wharf with its rows of cannon.

As they drew near, Isabel made out a dark, cloaked figure in the mist, followed by two attendants. Seeing the boat making for the stairs, the foremost figure halted, no doubt waiting to hire it when she vacated. From the top of the stairs he—for the hooded shape was a man by the size—stood motionless, looking down on her. As the cannon slid by and the stairs neared, she saw against the cloak a strong swordsman's hand, and in the shadow of the hood an angled cheek and a stern mouth, the upper lip a deeply carven bow. With a jolt she recognized Lord Adam Colford.

Her boat bumped the wharf, jarring her. If he noticed how she started, he gave no sign. Under the hood his dark eyes remained unreadable beneath the slight, cynical arch of his brows. "Good day, Lady Isabel." He offered his hand to assist her ashore.

A good day for fishes, eels and other cold-blooded things, she was tempted to say, but instead returned a brief, "And to you, my lord." His hand closed cold around hers. Whatever he was doing at the Tower, he said nothing of it. Steadying herself by his hand as she stepped from the wobbling boat, she covertly studied him. His eyes, a variegated swarm of brown and green, were intelligent but hard. The suggestion of a haughty curl lurked about his nostrils, and his mouth even in repose betrayed a habit of ironic, ruthless humor.

"On an errand of mercy, my lady, or business?"

Startled, she glanced up at him.

Like one tossing a stone into a pool, he paused to watch the effect of his words, the impenetrable green-shot darkness of his eyes intent on hers. Illogically, his scrutiny made *her* feel the criminal. "I'll have the boat return for you." He descended past her and seated himself where she had sat. "Greenwich Palace," he told the boatman as his men climbed in after him with a rattle of their scabbards. As the boat cast off, Colford studied her with undisguised speculation. Though he meant her to see it, his amusement was private, as if he assessed her, and made some inward mockery of what he saw. His lips twisted in a brief, chill smile. Within her cloak Isabel clenched her fists.

"God's blood!" she vented her rage too quietly for any but Ursula to hear, and brazened it out, giving him adamantine stare for adamantine stare, as immovable as he had gazed down on her, until he was no more than a shadowy wraith in the mist. "Come, Ursula." She wheeled and marched up the stairs.

"Colford was here!" she told Hugh as soon as the Warden's footsteps receded.

"I know," her cousin answered calmly. "He was visiting me."

Isabel gaped at him. "With what? Plagues?"

"Good wishes, and books to occupy my boredom. We talked for a long while, and between us we've finally laid bare the truth about our quarrel in France. I blathered in my cups one night, then felt foolish and asked him not to repeat an unflattering remark about His Majesty. Lord Adam gave his word, yet it got abroad, and I thought he'd betrayed me. I accused him, and he took deep offense. Too deep to let him plead his own honesty. If I hadn't mistaken his pride for a betrayer's disdain, we'd have learnt the truth two years ago. Between us, we've identified the real culprit, my clerk who lodged in the adjacent room."

"Doesn't his sudden change of heart strike you as odd?"

"He thought me guilty at first, he said, but on consideration, misdoubted his assumption, based as it was on old pride and enmity. Adam Colford isn't the sort to admit his faults easily, but he's bitterly aware of them, and the friends they've lost him." Hugh shook his head. "For all that he's free, I wouldn't be Colford for the world," he added as if the very idea boggled his wit.

"But Hugh, he visited you before he discovered the truth of your quarrel. This unaccountable change—"

"Serves no ulterior purpose I can see. If he were using me as a scapegoat, his aim's already accomplished. Convincing

Cromwell or Cardinal Wolsey of his false good faith might serve his advantage, but to convince me, here in the Tower, surely that's a waste of breath. No coz, I understand his change of heart. I've seen the same thing in men before battle. If I'm to die, Lord Adam has no wish to part as enemies. He doesn't want our quarrel on his conscience. Nor do I, come to that."

Hugh fell silent. The reconciliation had made his doom real to him for the first time, Isabel realized.

"How is Cecily?"

"She's safe. Life with Raight has taught her to be circumspect."

"I've been doing a deal of thinking, locked up here. I mean to help Cecily escape, as soon as I can manage a safe way for both her and her child. You gave her my message?"

"Yes, and in faith, I believe she's foolish enough to love you in return. Ill as you've chosen to meddle, you've chosen a lady of great mettle. —Cecily's courageous behind her quiet."

A faint smile, but tender, hovered on his lips. "She's that."

"You're unwell, coz."

"Trouble sleeping, no more."

"Are they feeding you? Anything edible, I mean."

"Meals from a good public house, for triple the price. They're decent enough fellows, in their way. They've let Mother visit, and the Warden and I have a chess match in progress."

"And Wolsey's men, and the King's?"

"It's always Master Cromwell."

"He's let no one else question you? Why?"

Hugh nodded, seeing her point. "I could wish a change of scene from his face." He turned to the window and added, "Or this."

Isabel joined him. Through the iron gratings she looked down on a wide, grassy courtyard. "The Tower Green."

"That spot," he pointed, "is where they build the scaffold."

"They will build none for you."

"I know. I'm no lord. For me, it will be the Tyburn Gallows."

"That isn't what I meant."

"As to why only Cromwell, you know the rumors," Hugh resumed, his voice lower. "When the King wanted war against France, Cardinal Wolsey secretly hindered him."

Isabel paced to the table and stools, but felt too restless to sit. "Yes, but Wolsey has many enemies. A man as vindictive as he, wouldn't he use this chance to discredit one of them, not you?"

"My tongue isn't always well-governed. —If it were, I'd never have quarreled with Adam Colford. I may have offended my lord Cardinal without knowing. He did call me an insolent pup once."

"And half the court something worse." She sighed. "Just when I hoped to close the trap, I find it empty. First I thought I'd discovered a regular cabal in the tents, your earless man, the French ambassador's secretary Des Roches, and Lord Colford. But during the theft Colford was seeing to his lame horse. Or so says the head groom." She frowned, misliking the memory of Bald Harry's watchfulness, though she was convinced it was his habit. "And he mentioned other witnesses."

"It's not Adam. I'm certain of that, coz."

"Oh, so it's 'Adam' now?"

"So, Des Roches and Master Earless are still unaccounted for?"

"Yes."

"Then they're the ones to suspect."

"Perhaps." Yet she did not think so. Not they alone. Since Hugh seemed not to have overheard Cromwell's threats, she did not mention them. She saw nothing in the prospect of Cromwell's guilt, or Cardinal Wolsey's, to bring him hope. Those possibilities could only bring despair.

"If Colford's not part of the plot, what did that scrutiny of his mean?" Isabel spoke low, so as not to be heard over the sound of the oars.

Ursula frowned at the river bank as it slid by, then shrugged. "Maybe he heard of my talk with his cook."

"And wished to express his disdain of wedding a bastard? Then, my good fortune knows no bounds." But the memory of his scorn provoked a flare of angry pride. "*He* can boast of no Tudor blood," she retorted. "Yet if he only wanted to scorn a maiden's ill-founded dreams, why such wariness?"

"If he sees you as a danger?"

Ursula's words confirmed her own thoughts. Though Lord Colford had made a show of contemptuous amusement, unconcern did not clothe itself so. "Only alarm need cloak itself in a taunt."

"His lordship's hiding something," Ursula agreed.

"The real purpose of his reconciliation with Hugh must have been to gain information from him. But what information?"

The boatman moored the craft at the wide steps of the palace wharf, and Isabel spun him a coin. Ignoring Ursula's whispered scolding at such indecorous boyishness, she helped the older woman from the boat. The landing was quiet. Crewmen went about their business on a few of the moored barges, and some tradesmen were abroad.

"It could be we're staring right past the obvious," Ursula

resumed quietly. "The plot may be all the French ambassador's."

Isabel considered it again, but King Henry would never have let a foreign emissary in on his plan to joust. Such pageantry made a more splendid report for their royal masters if it took them by surprise. Amongst kings, prestige was measured to a nicety by such things. "Nay, an English courtier's in it."

As they reached the top of the steps, Ursula muttered, "Don't turn, lamb, but there's an idler staring at the river."

"Momentous," Isabel teased. Soon, she reflected, they would be fearing the sounds of their own footfalls.

"Well, if it isn't momentous, at least it's odd, for I saw the same man being rowed past us in haste just after we left the Tower, as if he had some business far more pressing than gawping at the water."

"Such as arriving first so he'd not miss where we went?" Casually, Isabel held out her open palm and surveyed the threatening sky, glancing along the wharf under cover of the gesture.

The idler leaned on a post, a nondescript short cloak about his shoulders. She checked for ears, but a perfectly good one was visible on the side toward her. Whether his sleepy gaze at the grey currents hid any watchfulness she could not tell. "Let's walk. Argue with me about the weather."

Ursula did as she was bid, and as they passed beneath an archway into the maze of the palace buildings, Isabel used the shadow of the arch to look briefly behind. "Still with us. Who sent him, I wonder?"

"I didn't like the way the Lord Colford watched you at the Tower wharf. Like you were a sailor on the riggings, and he, a shark."

"Or, Cromwell may have all Hugh's visitors followed, in

case Hugh tells his supposed cohorts to make off with the crown."

"We have naught to fear from Cromwell's spy, if that's his orders. If he's Colford's, what do you reckon is the point?"

"Lord Colford," Isabel mused. "Whatever Hugh says, the name has too many o's. Methinks there's a hole in it somewhere."

They emerged from the roofed walkway into one of the central gardens surrounded by the private quarters of the resident courtiers and set with crisscrossing paths. A glance, as if at her waiting woman, confirmed the man still followed.

"And you say Sir Hugh thinks he visited to apologize?" Ursula added. "A likely story, of a jouster who knocked down the Seymour boy like a sack of potatoes."

"A sack of potatoes?" Isabel returned indignantly. "Then plant them, for it grows in your telling."

"All I meant is I don't believe his lordship's remorse. Mark my words."

Isabel stopped on the courtyard path. "I do mark one!" *Sorry to hear about Sir Hugh's trouble, my lady. Whatever else 'e be, he's always a kind soul to an 'orse.* "Remorse, indeed! That's it, that's what's been bothering me all along. Good Ursula, let's present our shadow with a dilemma."

Ursula looked suspiciously at her. "What do you mean to get up to now?"

"If we separate, he can't follow us both. Won't that irk him?"

"While you go do something dangerous."

"I want you to draw him off, but it's broad daylight, you'll be safe."

"I meant, dangerous to you," Ursula grumbled.

"I'm only off to the stables. I want a headlong gallop."

"By my troth, you're fibbing. You aren't going there at all."

"By my troth and Saint Anne's left small toe, I am!"

Ursula sighed, knowing there was more to it. "Where shall I lead our footpad, then?"

"Oh, wherever makes the merriest fun." Quickly she drew from her pocket a list of things Hugh wanted from his mother, folded it tighter and handed it to Ursula. "Here, this should prick his interest." Without a glance back she headed across the grounds and heard Ursula's steps crunching the gravel path in the other direction. At the far side, she at last chanced a look. To her delight, the man was turning out of sight after Ursula.

Isabel doubled back for the stables, and when she arrived, called for her mount. She was fond of her little Spanish mare, but no sooner was the beast brought in her handsome trappings than Isabel startled her with an angry tirade against Ned Prior as a slovenly mucker of stalls.

The accused came running at her summons, a boy of about twelve with gypsy-dark hair and skin. From his sullen look she had guessed right that it was indeed the youngest grooms who did the mucking. As Bald Harry had led her to expect, he was favoring his ankle. "My mare stinks like a pigsty!" Isabel scolded. "Don't you ever clean her stall?"

"Your ladyship." Ned took it with the stolid heroism of a wronged soul forbidden to talk back, but then spoilt it by adding, "Jack does that row, your ladyship. My row's clean as nuns' cells!"

Isabel liked him. She frowned severely. "And what's your experience of nuns' cells?"

The boy stuttered with embarrassment.

Isabel reprieved him. "You're only telling me you're a clean, honest stable hand?"

"So please your ladyship, I am." With dignity the boy pushed his horse-long forelock out of his eyes.

"You're limping, I see. You wouldn't be the man I bid Harry reward for his excellent service to His Majesty?"

Ned squared his shoulders. "The ankle don't 'urt so much."

"Yes, you strike me as being above a little pain." Isabel took the reins and stepped onto the mounting block. "Still, it's been a busy week. And a gainful one, between my gratitude and Lord Colford's."

Ned froze. "Lord Colford! I've 'ad nothing from him."

"No?" Isabel stepped down, so close to him she could smell horse sweat and liniment. "Come, I know how it is. All the knights lay heavy wagers. A broken strap can lose a joust, and no real harm done. At least, not usually. Now, the King's spill the other day—"

"Jesu help me, your ladyship, it weren't nothing like that! If Lord Colford 'ad ordered *that*, I'd never for any money—" He stopped, hearing his mistake. "I mean—Oh no, 'Arry will—" His face crumpled.

"Beat you?" Isabel asked quietly.

Ned nodded, struggling fiercely to suppress the weakness of his tears. Clearly, a beating from Bald Harry was more brutal than a sprained ankle. "'E'll 'ave me 'ide for letting it out. Please, your ladyship, I'll do anything you want if you won't go tellin' 'im. I swear 'is lordship never went nowhere near the King's 'orse, nor any 'orse but 'is own!"

Isabel handed him her handkerchief. "Then, why did Lord Colford bribe you?"

"Bribe!" He looked at the embroidery on the handkerchief as if afraid his nose would send it to perdition, or else it, his nose. "It weren't no bribe, honest. 'E only gave us a—consider-ation, 'Arry called it."

"For saying he was in the stables when he wasn't."

"No, ladyship, 'e were there, right enough. That foreigner came an' spoke with 'im. Called the foreigner by some bug name, 'is lordship did. Ant? No." He thought a moment. "Roach."

"Roach?" Isabel repeated in soaring excitement. "Des Roches?"

"That's it, ladyship. His lordship paid us to let this Roach fellow in and not tell nobody. But 'Arry did keep a watch that the foreigner didn't meddle with the 'orses, and even if 'Is Majesty's mount 'adn't already gone out by then, we'd never, never 'ave let—"

"I believe you," Isabel answered gently, taking the handkerchief from him and wiping his nose. "Since it had nothing to do with His Majesty's accident, I see no reason to question Harry."

Ned looked at her doubtfully, used to the ill faith of the great toward the small.

"If I must get Harry in trouble over this, I promise he'll never learn from me where my information came from. Unlike Lord Colford, I give you no bribe, only my word."

Ned nodded, unconvinced.

"By the way, could you hear aught he or Des Roches said?"

"Not a word, ladyship. They huddled very close and secret."

"I see. My thanks for your help." Isabel stepped onto the block and leapt onto the saddle.

"Since you know, I'll tell you what else." Ned rushed to get the last of it off his chest. "Whatever the Lord said, 'is mount wasn't lame. I'd stake a week's pay that 'orse was a-walking smooth as oil. If you ask me, it was all a sham for 'is lordship to meet in secret with the foreigner." He paused. "Does your ladyship think—that is—could it 'ave something to do with . . . ?"

"The Sun and Stars?" Isabel's fingers went so numb she could scarce feel the reins. The boy was a talker. If he believed there was, then no fear of Harry would keep him from spreading wild chatter. She widened her eyes. "Do you think so? The gentlemen were under your guard. Is it your opinion they might be thieves?"

The boy frowned, then brightened with relief. "I wasn't part o' no crime, after all! Who'd play footpad in a place 'e knew was about to go bedlam?" He strove for manly authority. "Way I see it, ladyship, to find the top thief, better look for those as *wasn't* in the stables, see?"

"I begin to." Despite making her feel like a sea-going craft, young Ned Prior had a reasoning head on his shoulders. Isabel frowned as she gathered the reins. "I won't betray your generosity." At the merest pressure her mare sprang into an eager canter. As she left the palace gates, she turned away from London. Green folds of land stretched ahead as far as she could see. Her Spanish mare drove her hindquarters powerfully until trouble fell behind for a while, and their gallop was a pure, exhilarating state of blurred color and rushing wind.

Chapter Eight

ight cascaded from a thousand candles, making the
tapestries vivid. Garlands of spring flowers hung from
the railing of the musicians' gallery. Brocade sewn with
gems swirled amid silk bordered in silver or gold, a continuous
stream of colors swept by currents of dancing and graceful
gestures. A sibilant murmur of conversation flowed beneath
the music, laughter making little eddies here and there.

A stately basse dance ended, and Isabel curtsied to her
partner. Beyond the other dancers she saw King Henry
strolling, surrounded by a covey of his chosen companions and
followed by an assortment of hangers-on like ducklings after
their mother. Though glittering and bejeweled for the evening's
entertainment, her father was not a sun at present, but a
massive thundercloud, frowning with his small lips pressed
tight.

"What a lovely gown." Lady Raight approached, smiling
serenely. Isabel saw the burly, coarse-faced Lord Simon Raight
in a distant part of the hall, and knew Cecily had seized her
chance. "What news of Hugh?" she whispered.

"I saw him today. No ill news, but nothing good, either."

Cecily nodded, smiling at the dancers as a new tune struck up. "Do you think," her anxious murmur belied her calm smile, "they're discussing our matter?" Her eyes went to the King. Sir Thomas More was talking earnestly, and Sir Giles Colford nodded agreement, but King Henry's frown grew more baleful by the minute.

"Or the King's Great Matter," Isabel answered. "They say the Pope has answered His Grace's request by appointing two legates to judge the legality of his marriage to Queen Katherine. One will surely be Cardinal Wolsey. No doubt the other will come from Rome. Yet will the Pope's judge decide against the Queen with her nephew's troops occupying Rome? His Holiness cares nothing for English marital quibbles, he's caught in the pinch between the Emperor and France."

But Isabel saw it was useless. Gossip could not distract Cecily. She pressed her hand. "Keep up heart. I'm not giving up."

Cecily squeezed her fingers and moved on.

Watching the dancers, Isabel once again considered Adam Colford's meeting with Des Roches in the stables, a meeting he had bribed the witnesses to keep secret. As young Ned had pointed out, that suggested neither he nor the Frenchman knew the theft was occurring nearby. It gave her the impression they were wrapped in some entirely different conspiracy—not an unlikely thing at court. Or was that a ploy, too? One way or another, it proved Colford a schemer. That was no surprise, but it hardly simplified matters.

At the moment, Colford was talking with the tortuously self-serving Duke of Norfolk. His amber doublet was elegantly slashed and a hat with a brooch of garnet and jet showed off his dark auburn hair, but on even more obvious display was the man's vanity. Adam Colford would be a very peacock if his arrogance did not forbid even the distant intimacy of admiration. All evening he had completely ignored Des Roches. So completely that Isabel suspected they had agreed to it. The Frenchman, recovered from his rheums, was flirting with a few of the Queen's younger ladies-in-waiting, as if no serious thought had ever strayed into his mind.

Queen Katherine watched over her charges, ten-year-old Princess Mary on a stool by her side. Plain but demure in her blue velvet, Isabel's young half-sister sat with such obedient decorum she might have been a little straight-backed statue. Isabel sympathized. Her own rare childhood visits to court, all the etiquette that had been mercilessly drilled into her, didn't compare with the rigors a princess must observe. When Mary glanced her way, Isabel smiled, and an answering smile momentarily brightened Mary's polite boredom. As for Tom Seymour, Isabel searched in vain for him.

The dance over, a troupe of minstrels made a way through the gathering, playing on lute, rebec and recorder. People drew aside in anticipation as behind the musicians came men hauling stout silken ropes. Their white surcoats figured with red hearts proclaimed them the servitors of courtly love. Exclamations sounded as a gaily colored platform rolled into view. Upon it rose a mound covered with flower petals overlapping in cunning varicolored patterns. On its summit was a real tree, its spring foliage still fresh, and bound to the trunk with a silver cord, a maiden. Making woeful faces, she wrung her hands. Emblazoned on her skirt was her name, *Virtue*. The reason for her distress was obvious. Three fierce dragons raged around her, their scales gleaming copper-red, their manes flowing like scarlet flames. Ruby eyes gleaming wrathfully, they snapped ivory teeth. They had four legs each and lashed their tails furiously. The flank of one bore the legend *Jealousy*, another *Envy*, and the third, *Slander*. The workmanship of all was exquisite. Isabel applauded the spectacle with the rest of the crowd.

Virtue trembled as Jealousy menaced her with gaping jaws, but Envy threatened the guests with his fangs, and the nearest quailed with shrieks and laughter. "Rescue! Rescue for poor Virtue!" called a pack of young men, Des Roches among them. He laughed without a trace of care or guilt. Of course, being a diplomat, he was by definition a dissembler.

A knight rushed from among the startled crowd. He took a valiant stance, his breastplate reflecting the multitude of lights, his sword a firebrand of jewels. On his surcoat was the title, *Steadfast Heart*. At the sight of him the dragons thrashed their scaly tails and flourished their fangs, but undaunted he charged, and in an artfully contrived battle, vanquished the evils that imprisoned Virtue. As he slew each he slashed open their bellies to release a deluge of sweetmeats. Finally, having overcome the foes obstructing true love, he untied the maiden and knelt before her. The King applauded the spectacle with pleasure.

"Can't you guess the inspiration for *that*?" Isabel overheard a lady near her whisper to another. She glanced at Mistress Anne Boleyn.

Anne's smile was poised, but her sparkling black eyes revealed her delight. It was a dangerous game she played, refusing the King her full favors, yet she was winning so far, no doubt of that. Not only did her royal suitor accept the limitations she imposed, he was praising her for them. As for Isabel, she meant to hold aloof from the dangerous battle between Queen Katherine and Mistress Anne. In a way, she couldn't help feeling both were interlopers. Yet all who knew Anne Boleyn either fell under her spell or hated her, and even when Anne's wit stung, Isabel liked her. Anne was not all cascading dark hair, flashing eyes and refinement learnt at the

French court. For a time they had both waited on the Queen, and amid the vapid giggling and sighing over jewels and handsome young courtiers, Isabel found in her an exercise for the wits and a testing of serious thoughts, too. Anne owned a copy of Tindale's new, very controversial translation of the Bible into plain English anyone could read. If she did keep King Henry in tow, things could become interesting.

Isabel's musings broke off as out of each slain dragon emerged the two gentlemen who had supplied their legs. Amid music and the showers of sweetmeats tossed by Sir Steadfast Heart and Lady Virtue, Tom Seymour rose from Envy's forelegs and jaws. He brushed off his doublet, his rakish grin touching Isabel with a volatile mingling of wistful protectiveness and desire. Impulsively she raised her hands. In a flash Tom bent for a sugared plum and sailed it neatly through the air. She caught it. To respond so quickly, surely he'd been aware of her all along. As she put the sweet into her mouth he sent her a gaze tinged with pain. It was she who had willed their separation, said his eyes, not he.

Isabel turned away, her heart beating fast. Yet anger followed. Hugh needed friends, and where had Tom been?

As the platform was rolled out, its musicians were overpowered by a fuller strain from the minstrels' gallery. "My lady?" It was Tom's voice.

Isabel turned quickly. Tom bowed, offering his hand. It was only a dance. Surely, even under the eyes of all, no harm could come from taking it. His warm fingers closed around hers and together they swept into the line just as the galliard began. She wished it had been a slower dance. She did not want to raise her voice to talk with him. Yet the sight of his handsome face was hers to bask in, and the graceful uptilt to his eyes, and that wickedly sensuous mouth.

"Two endless months, and no word from you," Tom spoke

just below others' hearing, even as he completed his *cinque passi*. He landed in a graceful posture. "This spring is the longest I've ever endured."

"You know why," she murmured, and let the music carry her into light skipping.

"We've committed no sin. Nor will, if you don't wish."

"I don't wish? Do you think it's up to me?"

She saw his glance at her, and the hope that sparked in his eyes. She shook her head.

Tom kicked lively, showing off his fine hose, his hold on her hand remaining miraculously graceful. "I can live on your company alone," he answered when he was no longer airbourne. "Don't deny me that, at least."

"Even if we could be happy with that only, what of the dragons? Jealousy, Envy, Slander, not to mention Greed, Climbing Over Others' Backs, and Love of Trouble For Its Own Sake," she answered. "Any of those monsters knows how to make innocence seem guilty—look at my cousin Hugh's plight."

"No one thinks Hugh is guilty."

"If that were only so," she returned, stung at his passing it off so easily. Surely he did not realize how callous he sounded.

He saw it had hurt her. "I hope with all my heart he'll be proven innocent," he answered earnestly. "I know he's more brother than cousin to you, and I'd rather endure any pain than see you suffer."

"The pain of speaking up for him?"

"The pain of keeping quiet. Just before the robbery I saw Hugh near the tents."

Isabel paused. "You were afraid of incriminating him?"

"Of course not. I don't believe he's involved. Yet I would not contribute any scrap to those who do. Placed as I am, I can do little, but if I can ease your troubles by listening, I'll do that gladly."

"Not here."

The music ended, but his hand lingered. "Your half-brother the Duke of Richmond remains at court another week," he murmured. "As you know, my own brother Edward serves him. Visit your brother, and there find me."

Then he was gone. With an effort, she forced herself not to look after him. Leaving the floor before anyone could claim her for the next dance, Isabel positioned herself beside a wall tapestry and inconspicuously checked the less riveting objects of her attention. The French secretary, Des Roches began the dance with one of the Queen's ladies-in-waiting. She did not see Lord Colford, but the Duke of Norfolk stood talking with Anne Boleyn's father. That was natural enough as were brothers-in-law, but both were also French sympathizers. Perhaps she ought to pay more heed to them.

Where was Lord Adam Colford? Isabel scarcely hoped he'd do anything incriminating here, but even some tiny omission might prove important. For instance, Colford's and Des Roches' continuing lack of even polite conversation. Also, the Duke of Norfolk's seeming avoidance of the King. And who left the hall with whom. Colford, for one, had used that tactic before, meeting secretly under cover of a public gathering.

A meeting important enough to bring the Frenchman from his bed when he was ill, and for Colford to lower himself to bribing stable grooms to conceal.

If it was her foolish inattention, her hopeless love for Tom, that had made her miss Lord Colford leaving the hall, and noting who else might also have gone out, she would never forgive herself. She tried to take stock of who might be missing, but it was useless. The crowd was too thick and in too much motion.

"Here we have a lovely example of a caryatid in the English style," a puckish voice interrupted her thoughts. "Good evening, Mistress Wall-Column." Will Somers made a bow.

Isabel sighed. "I would rather have a better morrow."

"Nothing yet?"

"Little enough. Did you see the Lord Colford go out?"

"Many times, from many places. But not from here, tonight."

"If I'd only noticed when, or if another left with him or near the same time."

Will frowned. "Take Sir Hugh's danger to heart, but don't let it addle your brain. Even the stiff-necked Lord Adam Colford must occasionally need to relieve himself." Motioning over a wine server, he handed her a cup. "Drink this. Search for whom you must, but don't lose sweet Isabel." His eyes focused past her. "Sweet Katherine is also low, methinks. Tonight I'm more needed than sugar in sack!" Quietly he added, "If I learn the slightest peep out of the ordinary, I'll find you." He hurried off to cheer the Queen with his antics.

Isabel sipped the wine, considering the fool's sensible advice. He was right that she was over-eager. No doubt, just as he said, the high and mighty Adam, Lord Colford was conferring with nothing more momentous than the lacings of his codpiece. She had noticed he favored a prominent one in the fashionable and vainglorious Spanish style—not because she was interested, but because no one could fail to feel thrust upon by such a vaunting display of leather and gold needlework. She smiled in wicked amusement at the notion of him in the courtyard, overcome with wine and necessity and unable to tell its lacings from its elaborate stitchery in the dark.

The minstrels silenced in mid-strain. Everyone looked to see what the matter was, until the trumpets took up a familiar fanfare and a herald announced the arrival of Cardinal Wolsey. As usual, the Cardinal entered conspicuously, preceded by his gentleman with the Great Seal on its velvet pillow, and another with his cardinal's hat. Perched atop its cushion, this never failed to remind Isabel of a pompously exhibited radish.

Though the King was not at the moment dancing, Wolsey's interruption of the dancers was one of the most pretentious acts Isabel had ever witnessed. "Insufferable," remarked Sir Brian Harrow quietly, though whether to her or the Duke of Norfolk who stood at his other side, Isabel was not certain. Harrow came from Wiltshire, a fellow West Countryman, and so was probably some distant cousin on her mother's side. He was an envoy by profession, known for an astute tongue and agile sword, though for the moment his diplomacy seemed to have fled him. Outrage distorted his fine grey eyes and pleasant mouth, and threw his asymmetrical nose into lopsided, beaky relief.

"He planned this late entrance for no reason but to annoy," returned the Duke of Norfolk. "A petty ploy to lord it over his betters. But what can one expect of a butcher's son?"

Isabel remained silent. Pettiness did not confine itself to commoners' sons. In a church ceremony not long ago, Norfolk, bearing the golden basin of holy water, had accidentally slopped it into Wolsey's shoes.

"Does the King not see that such overweening pride will someday grip high enough to choke even him?" Harrow murmured.

King Henry gave the Cardinal a welcoming smile and signaled the musicians. They resumed, cutting Wolsey's fanfare slightly short.

"Perhaps he does," Sir Brian's wife, Lady Angela Harrow remarked in her rich contralto, accented with Italian. Isabel glanced at Lady Harrow, compelled as always by that fine voice. She had beauty too, of a tall, pale and dark kind. Harrow had married her while on state business in Venice, and fifteen years in the Wiltshire countryside had not detracted from her foreign glamour.

Norfolk made a sour face. "Bah! He strangles like a foul odor, does Cardinal Suet. How did such a churl manage to overmaster us all?" Since no one responded, the Duke answered himself. "Wolsey calculated His Majesty's horoscope, then used sorcery to bewitch the King until he doted upon him more than upon any nobleman—aye, even more than upon any lady!"

Angela Harrow glanced at the Duke in mild surprise, then at Isabel. With difficulty, both kept their lips from twitching. Isabel wondered if Norfolk really thought even the most superstitious would believe him.

"Why look so amused?" Norfolk gave them a beady eye. "Though His Majesty is no doubt dear to her, Lady Isabel is country-bred. She has no notion of the evil in this world."

"I have enough to observe that His Majesty is no one's dupe," Isabel retorted. With her eyes she indicated the Cardinal, who with his train was now walking in a more ordinary manner alongside the dancing courtiers.

Sir Brian Harrow smiled. "Any attempt at a procession would be ridiculous indeed to the accompaniment of that frivolous tune. Yes, I suppose it's well played of His Majesty."

But Norfolk regarded Isabel with a flicker in his small fox's eyes, as if he had tested her and learnt something.

With an exuberance that was probably deliberate, the dancers were widening their ambit so that Wolsey and his gentlemen were crowded toward her own group.

Isabel's recipe for the Cardinal was simple. Since he was too potent for sauce and too vengeful to use plain, there were only two courses for him, to serve him with an overabundance of sugar, or to swallow him as briefly as possible. Since it was too late to avoid him, she hoped her companions' tastes resembled hers. The Duke awaited his enemy with dignified reserve but, fortunately, no visible rancor, and Lady Harrow had composed her face to tranquility, but Sir Brian Harrow's eyes glinted like mica.

As Cardinal Wolsey drew near, his glance lit on Isabel. After cursory nods to the Duke and Harrow, he spoke solicitously. "A pleasure to see you here, my lady." Lowering his voice confidentially, he added, "And most wise of you, too."

His concern might have rung true, were he not the puppeteer behind Cromwell. But Isabel stilled her tongue before it could vent her wrath.

Seeing her mood, he stepped closer, shaking his head. "Let me assure you I am by no means convinced of Sir Hugh Lovell's guilt. I only seek the truth—and, of course, to recover the crown."

Wolsey gazed mildly into her face a moment longer, his own fleshy countenance unreadable, and despite its fat, without a trace of flaccidness. He paid no heed that he was practically standing on Sir Brian's toes, his scarlet-mantled shoulder crowding the smaller man. When the King thwarted his mood, Wolsey was subservient to his master, but often made up for it by subjecting gentlemen to ungentlemanly abuse. The only surprise was Harrow's lack of diplomatic calm. His agile fighter's body contained his fury as precariously as a drawn bow. As the Cardinal turned from Isabel, the scarlet hood hanging from his shoulders flapped Harrow's chin. Sir Brian's narrow nostrils twitched. "Do you not mean," he inquired, deadly quiet, "to *help* the *King* recover his crown?"

Lady Angela laid a hand on her husband's arm, seeking to silence him, but swiftly he blocked Wolsey's way. "Or is England's *other* ruler to have it?"

Complaints about the Cardinal's power were nothing new, but one did not speak them to his face. His cheeks flushed. Isabel watched with foreboding, torn between the desire to make peace and her longing for Wolsey to reveal more. When he spoke, his voice was supercilious. "Though you have long served as errand boy between policy makers, it's clear you understand little of these matters, sirrah."

Lady Harrow's face went pale. The insult was more than enough provocation for a fight. Her long, slender fingers dug so tightly into Sir Brian's arm that her nails went dark with crescents of livid white.

Yet Harrow did not burst into rage but suddenly cooled. The corners of his mouth quivered with some hidden humor. "Think you so?" With a flourish he swept his wife into the dance.

Isabel glanced at Wolsey, but he revealed nothing as he watched the honed edge of Harrow's dancing. At last, the Cardinal stirred. "I wish you an enjoyable evening, Your Grace. My lady." Like a great, scarlet-sailed ship amid small skiffs, he moved off through the crowd.

"I thought we should have blood spilled directly," the Duke remarked to Isabel with a small, arid smile, as if he would have enjoyed that. With a slight inclination of his head, he also took his leave.

Isabel turned to find several watchers hovering. She lifted her brows to indicate her relief, but kept her puzzlement to herself. Harrow's parting shot perplexed her.

From among the spectators, Sir Piers Knevet came forward and doffed his velvet cap with a bow. "My lady?" He was a thin, nervous man, an outsider in court circles who yearned to be an insider. Unfortunately for him, he had neither the wit nor the audacity. Yet if he wished a dance partner, he was lively enough on his feet. Isabel returned a nod and held out her hand.

He took it, but guided her away from the dancers. "By the rood, a touchy brace of squabblers!"

"A most disagreeable disagreement," Isabel replied lightly, wondering what he wanted. Gossip, probably. He all but twitched with yearning to be in the know.

"Indeed," he returned quickly. "My Lord Cardinal picks many quarrels, yet I knew of none with Sir Brian . . ." He paused in what he no doubt intended for a delicate manner. His meager lips parted in the center, making him look like a rabbit.

"You have some guess about it?" Isabel asked on the off chance.

He frowned and shrugged. "Some private matter between them, my lady. Nothing of any import, or we'd surely have heard of it."

"We? I fear, Sir Piers, all too much wafts in and out of the palace that neither you nor I catch a whiff of."

"So it may seem," he answered knowingly. "Yet those who think themselves important might be surprised, were all the cards laid face up. The King knows who's trustworthy, and many's the time I've done the odd service for him when he can count on no one else."

The very wiggle of him betrayed that he was vastly exaggerating. "Indeed?" Isabel tried to keep her smile politely neutral. Meanwhile, she searched the corners of her sight for Colford or Des Roches.

"Why, this month or more I've been keeping many papers of crucial importance for His Majesty—oh, quite unofficially, of course."

Isabel found his pathetic attempt to make himself important less amusing and more sad by the moment. "His Majesty values your loyalty. All here realize that."

He gave a little laugh. "I fear sometimes they talk of it."

"No doubt." Isabel struggled to take the sting out of her impulsive jibe, but did not entirely succeed.

His fingers tightened abruptly on hers.

"Come," she tried to make amends, "shall we take our places for the dance?"

"Perhaps you'll excuse me. I fear I've bored you as it is."
He bowed and escaped the scene of his shame. Isabel wished
she had been more kind.

Sir Thomas More and Colford's brother, Sir Giles, paused
to watch Knevet's retreat. "The swain flies from the damsel,"
Sir Giles jested, bemused. "What's this, my lady, a new custom
in courtship?

"If he flees far enough he'll seize me," Isabel returned,
framing a grimace. "It has to do with the new theory of the
roundness of the world."

She was rewarded by two unfeigned smiles. Sir Giles
Colford and Sir Thomas More were among the few men who
approved of education in women. They resumed their conversation, and she turned slowly, taking stock of all her quarry.

"These gentlemen are most remiss," a low voice spoke in
her ear.

Isabel whirled. Lord Adam Colford regarded her with
malicious amusement.

"Sir Piers was never weaned, and Sir Thomas More rarely
indulges in frivolities," his amiable tone was belied by a glacial
regard, "but my brother must be blind, allowing such a lovely
lady to remain partnerless for the dance." His hand closed
firmly over her arm, impelling her toward the dance floor.

Rigid with shock, Isabel took a place in the file of ladies.
Adam Colford positioned himself with the gentlemen, his dark
eyes raising in casual expectation to the minstrels' gallery, but
she sensed his intentness on her. Like her cat Eleanor watching
a mouse, she thought. The poised grace of him was like her
cat's deceptively lazy gathering before a spring. In Eleanor, it
signaled an intent to torment before the kill.

A pavane struck up. Facing Colford, Isabel automatically
moved in the formal steps, wishing it had been a livelier dance
to avoid conversation with him. His pacing beside her was

dignified, but his hold on her hand hard, as if he contained some emotion he wished to hide from her. She had seen his agile power in the tiltyard, but at close quarters the hard edged, disciplined strength of him dismayed her. Here was a man who regarded his body not as a habitation but a weapon. Though his expression was remote, his mouth as austere as a stone carving, she sensed that his disregard was a burning glass through which he focused some unknown intention upon her. Though he had also studied her with too much attention on the Tower wharf, she sensed that all had now changed. Mere conjecture had been replaced by a determined purpose—but what? What had happened since then?

If he expected her to quail before his cryptic silence, he would learn his mistake. "So," she sallied forth. "You have made peace with Hugh."

If her offensive surprised him, he gave no sign. Only one brow lifted in mockery. "You imagined I had some other purpose in the Tower?" It hardly sounded like regard for her cousin.

"I do not idle away my time imagining your purposes, my lord."

"No, my lady?"

She pretended to ignore his pointed barb. Perhaps it was only brought on by Ursula's visit to his cook. A horrific thought occurred to her. What if he was seriously considering marriage with her? But no, even a suitor motivated by political advantage would cram some semblance of chivalry into his gaze. "For aught I knew," she shot back, "you had some business with Master Cromwell."

He smiled, a mere curl at the corners of his well-shaped lips. Then he flowed like quicksilver through the next steps. She replied with a smile of her own. Whether or not he realized it, his mockery was an admission. He realized her curiosity in him was more than Ursula's excuses claimed. Now she knew that for certain.

And she knew her danger. Head high, she sketched her defiance of him with graceful steps. If he'd framed Hugh, she would see him in Hugh's place.

The music ended, and they bowed to one another with elegant antipathy. She turned away, but his grip closed on her arm, propelling her under the musicians' balcony and through a rear door.

She expected other couples to be strolling in the dim outer gallery, but was appalled to see the tall, arched windows empty of silhouettes. Lord Colford steered her to one, pinning her arm under his as if in formal courtesy. Help was within earshot, she had only to cry out. But then, muffled by the closed door, a faster dance began with bells and shrill pipes. Colford's grip tightened. "You've lost your chance, my lady."

Beyond the window panes the stars pierced earth's insubstantial vapors. Chin high, Isabel met the reflection of her murderer's eyes in the glass. His image, ghostly transparent, overlaid the void of the sky, but he was the first to look away.

"A true Tudor, in all but name." To her surprise, she heard admiration. Swiftly she turned, trying to wrench free. But he was trained to every trick combat could invent, and held her fast. "Courageous," he admitted, "but a thorough little hotspur. Do you understand how fragile life is, my lady?" The green of his eyes was oddly shadowed, like some secretive forest haunted by things she would rather not see.

No clever words came to her aid, but defiance scorched the back of her throat. "I imagine," she countered, "you'll find my death difficult to explain to my lord father."

"Unless it is an *imaginative* death." He vouchsafed her a small, unpleasant smile. "Therefore, lady, cease prying into my business. It can't save your cousin, and it could harm you."

"Or you?"

He narrowed his eyes, considering. Then as suddenly as he had seized her, he let her go. With a small, mocking smile, he dared her, "Then, if you must occupy yourself with foolish games, take them to their end. Accuse me to the King."

"I have no evidence against you, Lord Colford," she answered just as coldly. "Therefore, I am no threat."

"Oh, but you are." In his chill voice was honesty, and a warning. "But for His Majesty's fondness for you, I have no reason to tolerate such a threat. So bethink you of the danger. I warn you. Desist." He left her, brushing her like a breeze through December grasses.

Chapter Nine

Cautiously Isabel pushed the door to her rooms inward. A white bolt exploded at her, thudding with heavy impact into her chest. She cried out, arms flying up in reflex. The projectile nestled within them, claws sheathed, trusting her to catch and hold. Purring tumultuously, Eleanor of Aquitaine kneaded her with soft, warm paw pads.

"Your gown," Ursula scolded.

She was waiting up by a small fire. Isabel had managed to quietly rouse the servant who napped in the entryway to let her in, and creep past her aunt's chamber without waking her, but she was glad of Ursula's company. She did not want to be alone with her thoughts. Ursula brought her the cup of warm wine she'd mulled, but Isabel felt too profoundly exhausted to take it. For now, she was unable to do more than rest her forehead silently against the silky comfort of the cat.

"You're shaking," Ursula accused. "What have you been up to now?"

"Naught." Isabel drew a breath, and raised her head. "See, I'm unharmed. Mistress Catapult startled me, that's all."

Ursula watched her suspiciously. "I've never seen you affrighted of your own cat before."

She would have faced Colford again before she'd tell Ursula about his threats. Too many obstacles confronted her already without her own waiting woman's well-meaning hindrance. Eleanor mewed, her nose twitching toward the moonlit window. Isabel opened it and let her out, then pulled off her French hood. "I'm tired, Ursula. Help me out of this gown."

"So, Sir Wolf-whelp didn't seek you out?" Ursula meant Tom Seymour. "That's why you're so glum?" Ursula gloated like an attendant vulture as she unclasped Isabel's necklace. "I told you what his love was worth."

"Say the Duke of Norfolk danced with bells upon his toes and you'll be twice wrong," Isabel retorted.

"You're hardly overjoyed about it." Ursula drew off her rings, dropped each with a clink into the jewel box and snapped it shut. Isabel got the distinct impression that with each she mentally muttered a spell, and it was Tom Seymour she thus removed and shut away.

A quiet knock sounded. Isabel made a face at Ursula. Facing her Aunt Margery, pretending all had gone hopefully when her aunt needed solid results, was almost more than she could manage. Ursula gestured her into the inner bedchamber, and Isabel retreated gratefully into its darkness. She'd think of something hopeful to tell her aunt after a night's rest.

"A message for my lady." It was the voice of Matthias, Hugh's page.

Isabel poked her head out to see what he wanted. Ursula let the boy in and closed the door softly behind him. Seeing Isabel, he bowed and held out a folded scrap of paper. "The man who brought this wouldn't say who it was from," he told her dubiously.

"Never you mind," Ursula retorted, hand out. "Give it to me." Matthias dropped it in her palm.

Glad she'd removed nothing but her sleeves as yet, Isabel came out to see what was afoot. Ursula opened the paper, then held it up with as much exultation as Cardinal Wolsey's attendant with the famous scarlet hat. Nothing was on it but an X in a circle, scratched crudely as if by one unaccustomed to using a quill. "It's from my cousin," Ursula said. "You know, the one who had that little spot of trouble last year."

The one always in trouble, Isabel could have added, but held her tongue. Every family had its black sheep, as she had good cause to know, being somewhat one herself. "An X encircled. An alchemical symbol, or the map of a buried treasure?"

"You think it unlearned? Reading and writing can be dangerous," Ursula returned archly. "If my cousin Nibs could write some fancy note, Cromwell could snag it. It's the sign we agreed upon. This," she poked it with a thin, forceful finger, "means he's found our earless man."

By night, Isabel had never ventured into the poor quarters of London. Though the moon shone ringed like the X on Ursula's message, the crooked streets were deep crevices of shadow.

At whiles she sensed, as much as saw or heard, vague movements in the murk, rats foraging among the refuse, or a cat stalking the rats, or perhaps some larger and more perilous hunter. If so, they slunk away. It was easy lone prey they awaited, or drunkards with their purses, not a sober party of four who might well be armed beneath their cloaks. Indeed, two of them were. The two Lovell retainers Matthias had brought with him, Fuller and Jenkyns, were as different as night and day. Jenkyns, past forty, lived quietly with his wife and abounding brood. Twenty-year-old Fuller, the servant girls said, had a dozen welcoming beds throughout London. Her aunt trusted the fighting skills of both.

For now, their presence was formidable enough, but when they found the earless swordsman, more might be needed. Ursula had elected to look like a respectable woman, though not rich enough to rob. She had insisted Matthias bring an old leather jerkin and breeches to disguise Isabel. Despite the risk they planned to take, Isabel strode around the small room, pleased with the freedom of movement the male getup allowed. Over that she threw the woolen cloak the page had brought, such as an apprentice might wear. With her hair pinned up and her face shadowed by the hood, Isabel was confident she could fool a casual observer, but she dared not raise the hood to see fully. Doubtless, her face was well known to the spies of Cromwell, or of Colford.

The tavern where Ursula's cousin awaited was in a hive of cramped hovels where the odors of refuse, moldering straw and human waste were so thick Isabel's eyes smarted. At this late hour, few were openly abroad. Fuller walked a pace ahead to peer into the black mouth of each alley and doorway before they passed, and Jenkyns brought up the rear.

Once or twice they passed other vague shapes in the dark, as wary as they. Ursula pointed the way, surprising Isabel with her knowledge of this Hades. Though she knew her waiting woman was a poor man's daughter, she had not imagined a past like this. Ursula motioned at a narrow lane and they turned the corner to find a trio of ragged young men entering the lane's opposite end. Laughing with drunken carelessness, the three began remarking insultingly. When Isabel and her companions ignored them they took loud umbrage. Isabel still hoped they would content themselves with verbal attacks, but the foremost of them lunged. More quickly than her eye could follow, Fuller was in front of her, and the ruffian sitting in the muck of the gutter.

Apparently, that message was too subtle for the other two. One drew a knife with a dirty wrapped cloth for its haft, its blade long and jagged. Isabel froze, but Fuller trod almost upon her toes, shouldering her and Ursula to the wall. Despite its dampness they pressed against it, making as small a target as they could. Jenkyns sent one spinning, but another set upon him, and the one with the knife slashed at Fuller.

For a terrible moment it seemed the jagged blade must drive deep into his chest, but Fuller's foot darted forward, hooking the man's ankle. The knife hand went up, wrist caught fast. Fuller wrenched away the weapon as the ruffian went down. Jenkyns dealt another a blow on the chin, and he sprawled atop his companion. The third had better sense than to try further. They left him uttering vileness and picking his cohorts out of the muck.

As soon as they turned out of sight, Fuller flung the knife away with disgust, but Isabel noticed he kept a redoubled watch behind.

"This is the place." Ursula pointed out a doorway beneath a shabby hanging sign. Pulling her hood lower, Isabel entered in the protective midst of the others. At first she could hardly see through the haze. A badly vented fire and heavy smoke from cooking mingled with the sour tang of cheap ale. Two long tables filled the tavern, the benches ranged with an ill-assorted clientele, poor laborers and street hawkers in patched jerkins rubbing elbows with fellows in doublets of good cloth, but threadbare or besmeared, men stricken by the hard times of the last year.

"Beware foists and pickpockets," Ursula muttered, following the direction of Isabel's gaze. She turned toward the far end of the table where an old man of about fifty sat facing them, tankard in hand. "My cousin. Remember, lamb, let me do the talking."

Isabel nodded. They settled themselves on the benches, Jenkyns on Isabel's outside, and Fuller close by Ursula's cousin. The cousin frowned at that. "Puttin' on airs, ain't you, Urs?" he grunted. "Wise to bring along two of your lady's men, but what's the use in lumbering yourself with a lily-faced page?" He tipped his head toward Isabel.

"Good to see you too, Nibs," Ursula returned sweet as green lemons.

"This is no family visit." Nibs glanced at the brawny man beside him. "Since you want it, I've found a fellow who'll help you for a price, but I don't like it. The man you're after is rough company. The roughest."

"No rougher than some of 'em wearing gold chains on their shoulders," Ursula answered. Isabel marveled at how her manner of speech had changed, and envied her ability to fit in.

"Aye, or red hats on their pates! Now mind, the man who'll direct you to 'im doesn't know who you work for. If 'e did, 'e might refuse, no matter what the profit."

"Rest easy, he'll not find out. I'll only ask a question or so."

Nibs grunted, neither easy nor at rest. "Another thing, Urs. I don't think the crop-eared man knows what's up. I'll wager 'is friend's selling 'im without a by-your-leave. If 'e be a hunted man, take sharp care."

"That we will," Ursula agreed, with a frown at Isabel.

She gave no sign in return. Before setting out, she had told Jenkyns and Fuller that the use of fear, or even force, might be necessary. Now she had seen more, she feared that force would be all too inevitable.

"Watch your backs," Nibs gave a last, gruff piece of advice. Then his stubbled face hardened, and leaning back, he nodded. A big, slovenly man ceased trading sallies with a woman in threadbare finery, and thrusting her away as if she were rubbish, ambled over.

From within her hood, Isabel summoned a boy's stare of cocksure challenge. When the fellow had studied each of their small company to his satisfaction, he jerked his thumb at Nibs, who was only too glad to take himself off. "So," the newcomer said in a deep, phlegm-obstructed voice, "three pounds in silver for a certain man lacking his ears?"

"Only to talk wi' 'im," Ursula answered evenly. "Three for 'im, and three for you."

"Why d'ye want him?"

"Do a little job."

"I don't know that 'e'll agree. Carne don't seem to need money o' late. In fact, he said not to tell nobody where 'e's gone. Seems 'e did a job for somebody else, and when 'e went to collect the final fee, the knave tried to kill 'im." He subjected them all to a squinting scrutiny. "You wouldn't be part of that, now?" The scrutiny passed to Fuller.

"Part of what?" Fuller returned his stare.

"The King's men are looking for Carne too. Scouring London, as a matter of fact. You wouldn't be part of *that?*"

"'E's given 'em all the slip?" said Ursula. "That proves 'e's good."

The man nodded. Seemingly, her answer was enough. This Judas cared nothing for his friend's fortunes, only his own.

"Is this Carne as fast with a sword as they say?"

"The best. He learnt it as a soldier against the French. The time 'e got 's ears lopped is the only time the law's caught him. Wouldn't of got caught on that job either, but 'e was drunk."

"Just so he's not drunk when we need 'im," Ursula

answered, unobtrusively handing the coins wrapped in a rag to their informer.

Under the table he opened it enough to make sure of the silver. "Head east, then second lane to your left. You'll see an 'ouse with a whitewashed door. One o' the lower window shutters hangs skewed. Carne's there, alone."

Ursula nodded. They left the unappealing fellow to himself and went out to the street. "Go on, my lady," Jenkyns said. "I'll keep an eye on things here for a bit."

Isabel silently thanked her aunt for providing her with such fine guards, though she probably had little notion what dangerous use they'd be put to. After a little, Jenkyns caught up with them. They found the house easily, one of many cramped dwellings jammed so tightly along the crooked lane that there was no space between them, a collection of higgledy-piggledy angles and colliding roofs. Only a narrow rivulet of moonlight penetrated the lane, and no sound broke the quiet. Isabel searched the windows for a light within, but the shutters were bolted, but for the snaggled one on the ground floor. Through its gap only darkness showed. Despite what their informant had said about Carne being alone, their caution increased. "Knock," Isabel told Fuller.

As he moved to the door, sword in hand, Jenkyns positioned himself before Isabel and Ursula. The quiet knocking sounded like rolling thunder to Isabel, but not as deafening as the thudding of her heart.

No movement. No sound from within. The guard knocked again, but the dark house stood silent. And, Isabel felt, watchful.

"Break it in," she ordered quietly.

With sudden violence, Fuller lunged. The bolt splintered, and the door crashed loudly back. Against the darkness of the room, Isabel saw Fuller's outline, stealthy and alert, checking behind the door before he entered. Beyond him, all remained silent.

When he nodded, Isabel cautiously advanced, Ursula beside her and Jenkyns closing in behind. She stepped over the threshold into a small room, dimly lit by the moon through the gap in the shutter. Jenkyns shut the door, and Ursula opened the shutters. Earless, Carne might be, but probably not deaf. If he was here, he knew of their presence. Darkness would aid him, not them.

By the streaming moonlight Isabel made out a table, a few stools, the squat shape of a pot by the hearth. No embers glowed. A strong breeze flowed toward an inner, doorless opening. "There must be another door open in the back," Ursula said beneath her breath. "He's run for it!" With one accord they made for the back room. Its door stood gaping on a back alleyway, but as they hastened for it, a faint cast of yellow caught the tail of Isabel's vision, some light behind that was not moonlight. She paused, and turning back to the dark room, saw a stairway next to the door through which they had come. At its top, candlelight dimly glowed.

If she waited for the others, Carne might escape. Alone, she could do nothing to stop him. On the other hand, solitary, she was not a fearsome figure, and perchance, he would be more inclined to talk to her alone. She had the silver to persuade him, and if need be, the weapon of her real identity. As Lord Colford had conceded, the King's wrath made her murder a dangerous undertaking. Taking her resolve firmly in both swordless and shieldless hands, Isabel mounted the stairs.

As she neared the top she saw a landing, and a door ajar to a single room. A candle burned on a table, its steady flame revealing the foot of a bed as she climbed, and the sill of a shuttered window. And on the floor near the threshold, a tumble of discarded clothing.

Then she reached the top, and saw. Not a shapeless pile of cloth. A man. His arm was flung out, his legs awry, his head pitched back as if to stare at the opposite wall. Across his exposed throat curved a vivid scarlet gash. As she came closer she saw blood still flowing from it to gather in a wide pool where the floor boards sagged. The scarring of an older wound showed through the dead man's blood-soaked hair, the stump of flesh where an ear had once been. Isabel stepped back from the sight and the overpowering metallic smell of blood. But she forced herself forward again. On the near side of the room a chair was overturned, and crockery lay smashed, as if he had struggled with his killer. Isabel opened the door further to enter, but it met the resistance of Carne's outflung hand. She could move it, but was loath to touch his dead flesh. His eyes gleamed moist in the candlelight. The candle on a small table wasn't far burned down. "Not long ago," she murmured.

Her voice filled the stillness of the room as the scent of blood filled it, too full. Sweat trickled between her shoulder blades, and abruptly she knew what she feared. Someone was watching her. With the swiftness of panic she turned. The black pit of the staircase was empty, but her certainty sharpened to a pain beneath her breastbone.

A door shut below. Steps thudded with terrible loudness. "She'd better be, or I'll skin your hides," Ursula threatened.

"I'm here!" Isabel ran down the stairs, and was enclosed by the safety of her companions. "I've found Carne."

It was Jenkyns who caught the meaning of her tone first. His mouth stretched to a thin, grim line.

"No," she agreed, "he can't say a thing to save Hugh. Not with his throat cut. Yet we may not be too late. Someone's upstairs."

"Stay here, my lady," Jenkyns ordered, and dashed up the stairs. His head and shoulders were dark against the flickering light, leaning slightly as he shoved the body aside with his foot. He pushed the door against the wall with sharp crack, then disappeared into the room. After a moment he called, "It's empty, my lady."

"It can't be," Isabel argued, throwing back her hood and running up the stairs. "Someone was spying on me. I felt it in my bones."

"There's nowhere anyone could hide, my lady." Jenkyns turned, indicating the meagerly furnished room with his sword. Even the space under the bed was filled by a large chest. Though the dim light guttered wildly, the room was clearly empty but for themselves.

Isabel frowned at the flame, its smoke a thin, horizontal line trailing away from the window. Skin prickling, she saw the window was open. Rushing to it, she leaned out, peering past the open shutters as far as she could up and down the lane below, but no one moved in the darkness. "He's gone," she breathed, defeated.

"The murderer was gone before we got here," Jenkyns said, not ungently. "Look at the corpse—no, you'd best not, it's no sight for a lady. But the blood's only seeping. A wound like that'd be gushing, if it was fresh. This slaughter was done while we were still at the tavern."

"Then how is the window open? When I found him it was closed."

The guard shook his head. "Couldn't have been. Where would the killer hide?"

Isabel glanced around the room again. "Behind the door." As Ursula reached the landing and put her hand on the door in shock at the sight, the realization of what she was saying struck Isabel. She had stood exactly so.

"Don't fright yourself with imaginings, my lady. We're here, and no harm's come to you," Jenkyns answered with steady reassurance. Fuller nodded agreement, but Isabel thought she caught doubt in the glance they exchanged.

"Alone with that, who wouldn't imagine things?" Ursula turned away from the corpse, shuddering. "Let's begone before his friends show up."

"No," Isabel said firmly. "Since Carne can tell us nothing, maybe the room can. Jenkyns, search the body. Fuller, close the shutters and lock them, then stand guard at the door, just in case." She began tugging the chest from beneath the bed. Ursula joined her and they wrested it free. It was unlocked, so Isabel left her waiting woman to it and crossed the room to a smaller chest that stood open against the wall.

Inside was a jerkin and some shirts and hose, clean but snarled as if someone else had searched before her. Carne's killer had expected to find something.

"It's unlikely we'll find the Sun and Stars here," Ursula said, but continued to rummage with a good will.

"The man in the tavern said the first attempt on Carne's life came when he tried to collect his final fee. Most likely, he turned over the crown immediately after the theft and collected the first payment then." Isabel pushed the shirts aside.

"Looks like he'd hardly settled in here when his former master found him out and finished the payments for good," Ursula answered. "Carne's silence mattered very much to someone."

Isabel lifted a wad of threadbare hose, and paused, hand and cloth motionless over the glitter of gold. A pouch of coins lay half spilled among the dead man's clothing. She felt no doubt at all she was looking at the initial payment for the theft of the Sun and Stars. Yet if the murderer had searched here, why had he not taken it? The gold pieces were of some foreign coinage. She did not recognize them, save that they were not

French. She covered them with a shirt, giving herself time to think.

Was it possible the murderer had not searched for the gold, but put it here? These foreign pieces were distinctive, easy to identify. Apart from her having no rightful claim to them, if they were discovered in her possession Cromwell could accuse her—or anyone who found the body—of having received them for some part in the crime. But that hardly seemed sufficient reason to leave them here. How could anyone have known who would find Carne's corpse? If she had not showed up, the people of this neighborhood would most likely have found him, and the gold. What point in that? No, that was hardly the answer.

Perchance, she had interrupted the murderer's search. Aside from the value of the coins, their distinctiveness might be equally incriminating for Carne's former paymaster. In that case, the murderer would be back for them. Isabel glanced at the bolted window. "Have you found anything?"

Jenkyns grunted a negative.

She was glad she had not alerted her guards to the gold. They were good men, and she did not wish either of them to be tempted, or be caught with the coins later.

"Nothing," Ursula said. "Even if he could read, he was too smart to put anything in writing. He, or the one who hired him."

Isabel knelt a moment longer, considering. She might set a trap to lure the cutthroat into returning for the coins. But the sight of Carne, a hardened fighter who had bested the King's guards, lying in his own blood was enough to dissuade her of that mad notion. Two men at arms were too few, and they had already risked themselves overmuch for her tonight.

Making sure neither was watching, she slipped her hand among the clothes and took one coin. Then she closed the chest. "Come, we should make speed."

Carne's open eyes glinted at her as she passed, as if with malicious laughter. If he had gone to Hell without his ill-gotten gold, he had still taken his secrets with him.

When they opened the door, the night was as still as ever. The darkness had a bluish tincture, but the moon had set, and shadows had engulfed the lane. They pulled up their hoods and stepped out. No cock crowed as yet, and no one was astir but two dogs growling over some refuse. Beneath her cloak, Isabel slipped the coin from the pocket within the jerkin and into the small velvet purse she wore beneath it. The four of them made their quick, silent way to the mouth of the lane, and paused, wary of being seen coming out of this place into the wider way.

A rasp sounded, no louder than a pigeon taking off from the eaves. Isabel glanced up to see a darkness hurtling at her. She leapt aside, pulling Ursula. A sharp edge struck her arm and a heavy object crashed on the paving stones. She cried out in pain, then again louder as a man's shape clambered away against the starry sky. "On the roof!"

Fuller ran along the house fronts, desperately searching for a way up, but was left like a hound at the foot of a tree while the attacker escaped over the closely crowding roofs like a squirrel on interlacing branches.

"A chimney brick." Ursula picked it up, grunting at the weight. "He threw it straight at your head, the villain!"

"Are you hurt, lady?" Jenkyns asked, sword in his hand, not taking his eyes from the shadows.

"What, by that mere nutshell?" Isabel eyed the hefty brick, grimacing as she moved her arm.

Fuller returned, boiling with frustration. "It's no good. He's got away."

"Let's go, this place is too apt for an ambush," Jenkyns urged. "Steer clear of the eaves."

"He was aiming at *you*," Ursula muttered as they hastened along.

"If he was behind the door when I found Carne, he may have thought I glimpsed him and could identify him."

Ursula's whisper was sharp. "Because he saw you?"

Isabel shuddered, remembering how she would have opened the door and forced the murderer to act, but for Carne's dead hand. "Perhaps a glimpse through the crack at the hinges, but I had my hood up. Most likely, he recognized me in the street by my voice. But if he tells his master about me, *he* may gather more."

"If I were the cutthroat, lady," Fuller broke in, "telling my master about you is the last thing I'd do."

"Oh?"

"He botched the job of killing you. For all his master knows, you saw him and can identify him. That's hardly likely to earn him a reward. If I was him, I'd go back and report the job done without a hitch."

"I hope he sees it your way," Isabel answered, but she was too weary to feel much hope or fear at present. The man who might have cleared Hugh was dead, and she had gained no answers but a paltry foreign coin. They dared not return to Greenwich at dawn, disreputably dressed and with her bloody arm. They sought the Lovells' house, and by the thin light of dawn found only one kitchen servant abroad, to Isabel's relief. Before she faced her aunt's waking and worrying, she took Jenkyns and Fuller to the courtyard. "I want you to hire horses and make straightway for my manor at Treverbyn—that's in Cornwall, the most remote I have. Go there immediately, and stay till you're sent for."

"That cutthroat may have recognized you despite your disguise," Jenkyns protested. "You need protection."

"By daylight and among people, my identity gives me that. But if Hugh can be framed, so can you. I don't want you where he is."

"We can help you better here," Fuller objected.

Finger to her lips, Isabel glanced at the house. "You can help me best with silence. Now, and until this is ended. My heartfelt thanks for your skill and kindness. God be with you."

Chapter Ten

Isabel awoke after too few hours' sleep. She tried to look fresh and speak hopefully for her aunt, then escaped for a walk down the lawn to the river. Mist rose from it, and below the landing ducks paddled, quacking to one another. The day promised fair, but her head felt leaden and a sharp pain skewered her shoulder whenever she moved it. The bruise was worse than she had supposed. Yet that was nothing. It was now the fourth day. Hugh had only today and tomorrow.

That thought stirred her to full waking. And to the almost equally disconcerting thought of Lord Colford. His menace had been no courtly game, and no foolish prank. Nor an impulse of the moment. Everything she had learnt concerning Adam Colford suggested he considered carefully before acting. His seeking her out to frighten her was a deliberate act, with a purpose. That he meant his warning she did not doubt. He had done all but lay hands upon her then and there. *But for His Majesty's fondness for you, I have no reason to tolerate such a threat. So bethink you of the danger. I warn you. Desist.*

Isabel smiled. A fine quandary he must be in, to be sure.

Alive or dead, either way she was a peril to him, to judge by his manner. Yet was it guilt in the matter of the Sun and Stars he wished to conceal, or some other, unconnected connivance with Des Roches?

Also worth sifting, as she paced along the embankment looking out over the broad river, were the implications of Carne's murder. A friend of his, though none too good a friend, had sold his name and hiding place. But only to her, or to another as well? According to the man's tale, Carne, a formidable fighter, had feared those who should have paid him. The killer had known to look for the gold Carne had already received, had found it and, interrupted in the act, remained on the rooftop to take it when they were gone.

At least, that explanation seemed more likely than any other that occurred. If the killer had simply learned Carne had gold and slaughtered him for it, would he have hesitated to kill her when she blundered in? Would he not have thought her also after the treasure? While the two of them were alone in the house it would have been easy to spring from behind the door, make short work of her and get away with the coins. She shuddered yet again at how unwary she had been. If theft had been the cutthroat's only motive, what of his later attack on her? Even if he believed she had taken the gold, smashing her skull from the rooftop would hardly win him the treasure, but only alert the others. No, it was no ordinary robbery attempt.

By now he might have the gold. She doubted the bolted window would have kept him out for long. If those foreign coins turned up again, they might lead her to the Sun and Stars. Yet if the miscreant returned them all to his master, the chance of that was small. So far, the person behind it all had been far cleverer than that.

With a cleverness that was well-meditated, cautious and cold.

Lord Adam Colford's sort of cleverness.

Isabel shuddered yet more violently, unable to banish the thronging impressions of Colford's predatory smile, the wound gaping in Carne's throat, the brick passing inches from her head. Last night she had felt reasonably certain the killer's paymaster could not know of her part in the night's events. Now, she was no longer so sure.

Like a lamp to a benighted wanderer, Tom's offer shone from among last night's chaotic jumble of images. *Your half-brother the Duke of Richmond remains at court another week. Visit your brother, and there find me.*

Unable to bear her burden alone any longer, Isabel hastened to her apartments. To her relief, Ursula was not there. It was not easy dressing fit for court without help. The gown of a lady of rank was not constructed with that in mind. Far less, that the lady who wore it might have a sore shoulder from a scuffle in the London alleys. Isabel tied her points and pulled pinches of her linen shift through the prickings in her bodice, making small puffs of an even neatness. Satisfied, she went to have her mare saddled, impatient at the thought of even the few miles separating her from Tom Seymour.

"The Duke of Richmond is with his tutor, my lady," announced the page.

"No matter," Isabel answered, shrugging as if it were news to her. "Don't interrupt His Grace's lesson, I shall wait." His Grace, her nine-year-old half-brother, was as much a bastard as she, but being a boy, he'd been given a dukedom and consideration as a possible heir to the throne—or, had been, before Mistress Anne put the possibility of a legitimate son into King Henry's head. As if a notion had just occurred to her, Isabel added, "I understand my brother has gentlemen skilled in the niceties of Italian horsemanship. Might I consult with one regarding my mare?"

"It's Sir Edward, our Master of the Horse you want, my lady, but he's not here at present."

Isabel cocked her head in disappointment, then had another idea. "What of his brother, Master Thomas? Is he not also an excellent horseman?"

The page showed her to a small oak-paneled room with a fire in the hearth. Not rushes, but a sumptuous patterned carpet from the Orient warmed the floor. Alone, Isabel moved her bruised shoulder gingerly and moved away from the fire. The morning was getting too warm for it, making its glow too reminiscent of a red-hot iron. An agonizing, red-hot iron searing into Hugh's flesh. Trying to banish the thought, she paced up and down on the carpet, but its rich crimson became the thick pool of Carne's blood.

After an eternity, the door opened. Tom stood framed in it, his coppery hair gleaming in the light from the window, his grey eyes shining with pleasure.

He made a deep bow. "Greetings, lady." Then closing the door, he spoke more quietly. "Isabel! What an unexpected joy to see you so soon. I was busy storing up the memories of how we danced, and the touch of your hand in mine." As if her presence delighted him, he looked at her long and silently, smiling. It took all her determination not to run into the shelter of his arms.

He frowned. "Are you ill? Come, sweet, sit down."

Gratefully, Isabel let him gently force her into a cushioned chair. He perched on the stool at her feet. "Is there some new trouble?" His uptilted eyes beneath their fine brows were gentle with concern, their clear lights cloudlessness itself after the shadowy, guarded secrets of Adam, Lord Colford's.

"Hades." She remembered the Colford's countering of her appeal to heaven. "I'm lost in Hades, surrounded by murky

shades and half-glimpsed monstrosities," she answered, fighting
back tears. She had come here meaning to reveal all to him, but
now, though she trusted him, she felt reluctant. Daring he was
on his own behalf, rash some said, yet what would he say her
deeds last night? If he thought she was risking too much, he
might straightway inform her father, if only for her sake. And,
his own? A hanger-on at court, a younger son in boring service
to a staid official, he ached for a chance to be noticed and
appreciated. What better way than to earn His Majesty's
appreciation for her safety?

She pushed the thought back where it had come from. He
would not betray her thus. Not knowing Hugh's life was at
stake. Her doubt made her sad, and she shook her head. "I
can't talk about it yet, but please stay by me."

"Say nothing at all." He took her in his arms. She breathed
in the scent of him, cinnamon and horses, and sighed. The
strength and shelter of his arms was all she wanted. Just this.

"This is what I've been wishing for since last October in the
garden," he spoke a counterpoint to her thoughts. "Since you
flew from me. The leaves were falling like flames of anger
swirling around you. Didn't you know I can control my
passions? I would not have seduced you."

"Tom," she protested softly, stroking his hair, "you always
tempt me. You're doing it now."

"Of course I wish to love you. But I would never try unless
you want it."

She smiled at his ploy despite the tears in her eyes. "You'd
be a knot of wood indeed, to think it's that simple."

"I wish you had more faith in me."

"I do. You want to be a soldier, to command in battle and
win fame. I won't destroy your chances." She pushed him away
and sat up, wincing.

"You've hurt yourself. What happened?"

"A fall from my horse."

He grinned. "Maybe you really could use some riding instruction. Soon and often. I'm available. Why not? Who knows, by summer you may be such a rider that we can go together to the wars. Would you like that, my brave Isabel? On a charger, in armor, knocking Spanish heads off right and left—"

"French heads, if my suspicions are right."

"What, King Francis is behind the theft of the Sun and Stars? All right, that sounds likely, but our king will have to swallow his anger. When the French and Spanish come to blows again, it's the French we'll back. Wolsey will make sure of that. Even while the King was at war with the French a year ago, the Cardinal was secretly negotiating with them. These past months he's been involved in some secret matter with the French diplomats. Lord Colford has recently acted as his covert emissary in France, they say, and before that, Sir Brian Harrow."

"Sir Brian Harrow? Cardinal Wolsey's secret messenger? But I thought he and Wolsey were enemies! Only last night, Wolsey tried to provoke Harrow into making a scene to anger the King."

"Oh, they're bitter foes now. Some dispute over an inheritance. Sir Brian was a claimant, and Wolsey gave him to believe he would support him—but ended up with the property himself. Harrow knew better than to take the matter to His Majesty. A direct attack on Wolsey never works. Harrow left the Cardinal's service. Since then he's acted as England's emissary to the Emperor Charles, and to Venice. But that's no secret, all know that."

"From Wolsey's service to his opponents'?"

Tom shrugged. "The King's, either way. Sir Brian has a reputation for honor. At least, Sir Giles Colford seemed to welcome his assistance, especially in dealings with Venice. Sir Brian's married into a powerful family there."

"Odd," Isabel mused aloud. "Whenever I rattle this matter, a Colford falls out." She frowned, considering what she'd heard of dealings between the two brothers. Far too little, except that they were amiable, but not intimate. Seemingly, they were on opposite sides in questions of Continental politics, and yet . . . "Tom, what think you of Lord Adam Colford?"

"I think my backside is still sore," Tom answered wryly. "And, truth be told, my pride."

The joust, he meant. A thousand years ago, before the world changed. "He fought you dishonorably."

Tom shrugged. "He's not the most gracious of knights, but he was within the rules. I let him anger me and grew careless. I'll even the score."

Isabel hoped he would not have the chance. She had a score of her own to settle with Lord Colford. "He danced with me last night."

"I noticed."

"No need for jealousy, he was quite insulting. He thinks me a spoilt brat." She smiled off the thought of his threat.

"Yet he sought you out to dance with you. Why? If Colford wants you, Isabel, His Majesty will look at his barony and his noble ancestry and think him fit for you. The likes of *him*, *lords* who never had to strive hard for anything, who have everything handed to them simply because they already have everything—" He broke off, breathing quickly.

Kneeling by her chair, he took her hand. "Don't let them seize away your chance for happiness. Marry me, Isabel. The Duke of Suffolk secretly married the King's sister and he reconciled himself to it, though she was a full princess. Come, love, let's marry today, *now*. Then what can they do about it?"

Isabel jerked her hand away and stood staring at him. "Only annul the marriage, execute you for treason and lock me in a nunnery for the rest of my days. Do you really wish to destroy both of us?"

Steps sounded beyond the door. Swiftly Tom rose, turning away toward the hearth. The door opened, and the page made a neat bow. "His Grace will see you now, my lady."

Isabel followed the boy. Her one anguished glance behind revealed only Tom Seymour's back. It was not fear of discovery that made him breathe so hard or refuse to meet her eyes. It was sheer fury.

She spent another hour playing with her young half-brother, moving painted figures that stood for armies over a map of Europe. After a while she could range them without her hands shaking, but now all she had counted on was gone. Had she ever known Tom Seymour at all? She had imagined him like Hugh, rash at times, but honorable. Had Tom ever loved her for herself? Or did that matter now?

Gone, or in danger of going. Tom was no rare bird among courtiers. In fact, he was the most common of species, and their love was of just his selfish feathers, showing itself toward an accused man by refusing to show anything. Such was the friendship of Thomas Wyatt who scribbled poems about betrayal but did nothing for Hugh, and such was the honor of idealists like Sir Giles Colford and Sir Brian Harrow. Indeed, Harrow had been involved in Cardinal Wolsey's wooing of the French behind the King's back. With or without Sir Giles' knowledge, could Lord Adam Colford be using Harrow? And if so, for Wolsey, or against him?

Chapter Eleven

"It's raining again," Isabel announced, entering the room where Ursula sat sewing. "And the day is already half gone." Ursula looked up, her angular face tired. "We must tell someone of Carne's murder. Can His Majesty doubt now that Carne is Sir Hugh's earless man, or that he did the dirty work of the theft?"

"I want to show you something." Isabel went to her inner bedroom and took the golden coin from its hiding place between two boards in one of the cabinets. "I found this in Carne's clothes chest. It had many companions of the same sort." She dropped it into Ursula's lined palm.

The older woman squinted closely at it. "I never saw any money like that. French, it must be."

Isabel sighed. "Here's where we ladle up strange bones from the soup. I know French money. Hugh brought back a full sample of their coinage. Whatever this is, it's not French."

"Not French?" Ursula wrinkled her forehead dubiously, unwilling to do away with such a perfect answer. "Well then, a ploy by the French King so the payment wouldn't be traced back to him. Doubtless, getting hold of any manner of wicked, foreign thing is easy in France. King Francis paid his English traitor with it, who in turn paid Carne."

"Reasonable." Isabel took the coin and carefully slipped it back in its hiding place. "Yet," she said, returning, "Surely Carne wasn't the only one who could name his paymaster. Does that mean there have been other murders we know nothing of? Carne can't have carried out the theft alone."

"The master of the plan may have taken part. With so many jousters, how can you be sure you've accounted for all?"

"I can't," Isabel admitted, sitting opposite Ursula. "Yet if I were the traitor, I'd make sure I was accounted for." She rose again. "No, following that winding path would only waste our precious time. Carne's henchman may have been another hireling—the one who murdered him last night, for instance. Or, not. And neither explanation makes sense of the secret conference in the stable between Colford and Des Roches." A notion struck her, and she whirled to face Ursula. "Unless Colford and Des Roches planned to act as reinforcements if Carne and his henchman needed backing?"

"Risky," her waiting woman replied, joining her hands and pressing the thumbs to her brows as if they ached. "With all the hubbub over the crown, it was bound to come out sooner or later that they were seen nearby. Unless they hoped the very unlikeliness of it all would be enough to clear them."

"Remember, Des Roches didn't go to the tiltyard with Colford after the King's accident. After all, he was supposedly not at the joust, but ill in bed. What if Colford slipped back among the spectators while Des Roches received the crown from Carne or another henchman? That plan would keep the thugs from making off with it for themselves."

"Last night we saw these scoundrels' abundant trust of one another." Ursula picked up her needlework. "But much good it did us. We know no more than before. Nor are like to."

Isabel clenched her fists until she felt the blood pumping in them. "I'll not despair! I've lost too much. I'll not lose my kinsman, too. Not when every path twists back to Lord Adam Colford. He's a very Minotaur!" She looked at Eleanor dozing on her cushion. The cat's white side rose and fell with her slow breathing. Her furry legs were stretched carelessly, confident of her safety, the paw pads tender and pink. Despite herself, she smiled.

"I think you'd best tell His Majesty what you've learnt, and hope Cromwell is honest enough to follow the paths you've discovered, though a powerful lord may be at their end."

"Or something worse? Cardinal Wolsey may be immune to any scheming of Lord Colford's, as long as he keeps the King's favor. But Cromwell is hardly important enough to be invulnerable, and knows it. The King of Crete must have had lawyers, too. 'Play it safe,' they no doubt urged one another. 'For the sake of our precious necks, goad His Majesty to sacrifice a few youths and maidens. After all, youths are an awkward, impertinent lot. And as for troublesome maidens—'" Isabel shook her head. "No, I'll not give up until there are no more paths to follow."

"What others can there be?"

One, Isabel realized. With the realization, hope returned like blood flowing back when bonds were loosened. She was not about to tell Tom Seymour's gossip about Wolsey to her nurse. How she'd gotten it, the improper hour alone with Tom, would take too much explaining, and the only way to satisfy Ursula she'd done no wrong would be to tell Ursula she'd been right all along about Tom Seymour, while Isabel herself had been a gullible fool. Instead she answered, "When Cardinal Wolsey insulted Sir Brian Harrow last night, Harrow flared. But then he considered and was amused, like one who knows a

few secret paths of his own in the labyrinth. Even the
Minotaur had one weakness, and in the end was vanquished—
and by a homemade, woman's trick. So be of cheer, good
Ariadne, and lend me your thread!"

Ursula gave her needlework a dubious eye. "What?"

"Devious Colford may be, but he'll find he's met his match
at embroideries and embellishments. I mean to weave a web to
unsnarl his tangled paths. Help me dress for the King's
presence."

At certain times, the King granted informal audience to
members of his court wishing to lay some matter before him.
As Isabel entered the outer chamber with her page, she saw a
full covey of lords and gentry, divine and secular, eagerly or
stoically awaiting their chance. They made a picture of many
textures and moods, whiling away the tedium of the wait in
conversation, heavy gold chains of office gleaming upon vividly
hued, padded shoulders, gilded cases of papers burdening
secretaries in clerkly earth tones or scholarly black. Ladies in
the Queen's service and gentlemen with or without official
duties idled, determined to press some matter, or get in some
word before an enemy had the chance. Interested faces turned
toward Isabel. In her time at court, observation had taught her
wariness of power rather than hunger for it, and all knew she
rarely meddled here. Yet now, their knowing glances said, her
purpose was quite clear—and quite hopeless. Some looked
away to discourage her approach, not wanting to be associated
with a lost cause. Isabel cared nothing for them. All that
mattered was that Sir Brian Harrow stood by the grandest of
the hanging tapestries, chatting with the Venetian ambassador.

By another stroke of good fortune, Lord Colford was nowhere to be seen.

Isabel sent Matthias to request an audience with the King. She watched the Chamberlain acknowledge the boy's words with a single nod, his face noncommittal. Though fortune had favored her regarding Harrow, there was a danger that with so many important people waiting, she might be put off. If need be, she would still try her strategy, but without the private audience it would have far less effect.

At length the inner door opened. The Duke of Norfolk exited bowing, more like a woodcock rattled from cover than a departing dignitary. When he faced the courtiers he had mastered his composure, but his long face could curdle cream. From the look of him, he'd annoyed the King and been unceremoniously dismissed. In consternation the Chamberlain cast his eye over the gathering for any who might restore His Majesty to a better humor. It lit on Isabel, and with relief he signaled her near. "I will announce you now, lady." In a lower tone he added, "If His Highness pleases to see you, tax him with nothing irksome, I pray you. Amuse him, will you not? Of late, his temper grows alarmingly short."

Innocently, Isabel smiled. "What manner of thing is temper, that by growing becomes less?"

The Chamberlain answered with a faint chuckle. "I wish I knew, my lady. A thing above prediction, I fear." He disappeared within.

A quick glance assured her Brian Harrow waited patiently on. He had looked briefly her way when she entered, but if her presence concerned him, he did not show it. But that meant nothing. Much of a diplomat's life was spent in the antechamber of one sovereign or another, and no doubt the more he noticed the less he revealed. A chill touched the back of her neck as she remembered he was not a man who relied only on words. Before he had cloaked it, she had glimpsed the dangerous fury of which he was capable. Yet if there was a chance he was the flaw in Colford's scheme, she would risk it.

The Chamberlain emerged and bowed her in.

King Henry stood by the window staring out at the sunlit lawn, his fingers restlessly turning one of his rings. His shoulders filled the whole width of the window, and his broad chest tapered to a waist beginning to thicken from its once youthful slenderness. His hard calves twitched as he shifted his weight, and the cluster of diamonds on his hat scattered sharp edged spectrums along the walls as he turned. His thin, red-gold brows were drawn into irritable arches, and his keen blue eyes darted to make sure the door was closed. "At least it's only you," he said while she was still in mid-curtsy. "God's blood! The hindrances and self-seeking I've had to endure today!" He wheeled back to the view of the damp garden. "How I long for an open prospect with no walls, neither palace nor cage. If the weather turns fair tomorrow I'll throw over this tedium for a good hunt." He flexed his shoulders and turned back, smiling. "What do you say to a day of hawking, just a few of us, with Mistress Anne?"

Outrage rose in Isabel, and terror of a royal command that might force her to waste Hugh's last day idling. "If you please, sir, tomorrow it may still be too muddy for the ladies."

"Hmm. Always thinking of naught but your gowns," King Henry answered indulgently. "Well, if it's to be manly sport, there's the shipload of wild boars the King of France sent me as a gift—last month, before this blasted ado began." With his jeweled hand he waved trouble impatiently away, but as if the thought of being robbed drove him, he began pacing up and down. It made the chamber far too small. Yet it was passing strange, Isabel thought, that he could speak of King Francis' gift without raging at his perfidy.

"Francis sent me the boars because he'd heard they've become rare in England," he continued, then turned and grinned. "What if, in return for his boars from the French woods, I send him a shipload of bores from the English court? But no, he has enough of those already, to judge by the sample he's sent as ambassadors."

Isabel raised her eyebrows artlessly. "Have the French diplomats displeased you, sir?"

"They have, daughter. They have, and they do. But we'll not speak of that. You wish some boon of me?"

She twitched from head to toes to know what had passed between her father and the French, but she knew him well enough to hold her peace. He could be kindly, but he would not suffer his will to be gainsaid. As she forced back the question that craved to burst from her, she realized he had said *me*, not the royal *We*. A good sign. Yet his irritability was not far submerged. She must take care.

"The boon of your advice, my lord father. On a matter of business."

"Business? Not selling any of the lands I gave you?" He gave her a sharp glance.

"No, my lord," she reassured him. "I'm thinking of buying."

"That's more like it." Ceasing his pacing, for the first time he regarded her with his full attention. "Doing well, are you?"

She phrased her answer deliberately. "Very well for money and honor, my lord."

"And happiness?" He paused, then realized why she had left that off, and frowned. The signal was as purposeful as her omission. He was in no mood to bandy words about Hugh. "Advice, you said?"

"I wish a character."

He smiled, relieved. "Some would say you have character enough, Isabel."

It was a lovely opening, and she snatched it. "Yet I have not Lord Colford's character."

"You should thank heaven for that!"

She laughed with him. "I do, most heartily. But should I trust him?"

Henry sat facing her and rubbed his short beard. "Lord Colford is surpassing shrewd and always has an eye to his own advantage. Business with him, eh?" He was silent a moment in thought. "Here's what you do. Get his word on the transaction. Straight out and covering all the contingencies, I mean. Adam Colford won't break his word—it's when he doesn't give it that you must beware."

Such pride in his honor seemed incongruous in a traitor, but it would not be the first time Isabel had heard of an aristocratic recreant salving his pride thus. Such were the conflicting demands of gentility and ruthless policy. "I see, sir." Isabel hesitated as if uncertain. "So you never entirely trust him unless he gives his word?"

"Me? That's different. We're his sovereign. He owes Us absolute loyalty—and by God, he'd *better* give it, word or no word!" King Henry pursed his small, delicately shaped lips, his frown deepening portentously.

If his unease has no significance, Isabel thought, Colford's a farmer and I'm an eel pie. She blinked in surprise. "*You* don't doubt him, my lord father?"

"I told you, I'm his king," he answered, ominously quiet. "There's an end to it." He got up, poured himself a cup of wine, and slowly drained it. "So. You're doing well enough to buy more land. Good. You're turning into a very resourceful manager of your estates, Wolsey says."

"Wolsey?" she asked, startled beyond caution. "How would my lord Cardinal know? Has he a spy in my household?"

"Likely," Henry answered calmly. He poured more wine for

himself and a cup for her. "He has spies in everyone else's, including mine. How else could he know all that he does? But you needn't fear him, he also is loyal. Come." He sat in the great carven chair and patted the stool at his feet as if she were a kitten. "Wolsey can have nothing on you. You've turned out well, daughter, a pride and credit to me."

Isabel sat, arranging her skirts gracefully on the low stool.

"And pleasing to look on. So much like your mother." He was quiet for a few moments. "*She* had a pair of bright eyes too, and a pert tongue. Do you know, Isabel, sometimes in the still of the night I remember her. I think on her, and I grieve." He lowered his restless gaze, watching the crimson of his wine reflect in the golden hollow of his cup. "Old King Henry, my father, sent her away from court, you know, and my grandmother—even Father feared that stiff old lady—scorned my Devonshire dove like ten thousand dragons. I pleaded in vain. And so," he said quietly, "my sweetheart bore you in disgrace, and died. But if these courtiers dare look down their noses at you, remember this. Your mother and I loved. If only I could have forgotten all the duty to King and country, all the policy and alliances—God's teeth, how I sometimes wish I were a simple squire, with no cares but tending a little West Country estate and breeding horses! With my first love as my lady, and a pack of fine, strong brothers for you." Shaking his head, he patted her shoulder. "What would that have been like, eh?"

That his dream of escape from cares included her mother startled Isabel. Her throat constricted with a sudden emotion she could not name. Regret? Grief for the mother she had never known? Loneliness?

Her father's eyes darted conspiratorially sideways at her. "After all, what has my marriage to the Queen got me? Naught but another daughter less clever than you and an alliance with

that betrayer, the Emperor Charles!" He snorted. "More wine?
No? I say this to you because you're outside all the petty
intrigues, not a princess, only a loving daughter. When you use
your tricks on me—you needn't look guileless, I know you
sometimes do, eh? —at least, it's not for power like Thomas
Boleyn, nor Norfolk's lust to see his enemies' heads on pikes."

"I can think of more pleasing sights than enemies'
skewered heads," she risked the mischievous back talk that
sometimes amused him from her, "still less, Norfolk's
enemies'."

But even as she spoke, an image came to her of Colford's
head displayed on the bridge, his proud eyes picked at by
crows, the dusky fire of his hair matted with gore—or
Harrow's handsome features so mangled, and Lady Angela an
anguished widow. Her hands went cold. Whether or not her
motives were better than the Duke of Norfolk's, she was
pursuing the same end. The stakes were no longer merely
justice for Hugh. Saving him must bring destruction to another.
The abrupt realization sickened her and for a moment her
resolve wavered. Yet if she could not reveal the traitor, the
same end awaited Hugh.

"Yes." Henry finished his wine. "A country estate, a wife
still in her prime, a pack of sons as merry and clever as you,"
he mused. "Instead, I have a queen older than I, already
barren, and no male heir at all. That could mean disaster for
England. My father ended a century of factions and bloodshed
and gave the people peace. By Saint George, I'll not leave a
legacy of chaos!"

Isabel was silent. She wondered how long he had lived with
the leaden undercurrent of such fears flowing below his high
spirits and glitter. She realized what he was telling her. One
way or another, he would surely cast off Queen Katherine,
who had never been like a mother to her but who had been a

good queen and suffered much in trying to give him a living son. One way or another, he would make Anne Boleyn his queen. And if she did not give him sons? Then what?

A violent desire for Devon seized her. For the narrow River Torridge flowing through the green valleys where sheep grazed and ploughmen sang as they strolled home tired in the evenings, and for white sails dazzling against an azure sea. For the managing of her estates her father had praised, discussing crops and dovecotes with her tenants, without fear of grief or tyranny.

Without seeing this side of the only parent she had.

"The people would never feel secure with a woman on the throne. They want the assurance of an heir as much as I do. They'll accept the change, for that, eh?"

Isabel hoped she wasn't expected to answer that, but he fixed her with his bright blue eyes. "Eh? Won't they?"

Isabel told him the only thing she could, the truth. "Some may not, sir. Many love Queen Katherine." And, though she did not add it aloud, many hated Anne's French-ified elegance and proud airs.

"Some may not?" He rose, towering menacingly. "Do you mean to say that they, and you, know better what's good for Our realm than We do? Well?" Turning his back on her, he paced again to the window. "If We decide, it will be done. And, dissenters or no, by God, the people *will* accept it! Do you say otherwise?"

Isabel lowered her eyes. "No, sir."

"They had better accept it all," he muttered. "The people, and the French." Isabel tensed another notch, listening intently, but all he added was, "Begone. Tell the Chamberlain I want Wolsey."

Containing her hurt, Isabel curtsied to his back. She had known there was danger in giving him the honesty he asked for, but had hoped a caution might be worthwhile help. Yet she sensed his anger was not all against her. He would not have reacted so furiously unless he too had doubts about his scheme. As for his anger at her, that would wear off in a day or two. But those were days when his feelings toward her might be crucial to Hugh's fate. If all else failed, he would have little patience with a plea from her now. As court etiquette demanded, she backed to the door, though he did not turn to see what she did. The injustice only strengthened her resolve. She waited until she had opened the door before answering in a clear voice. "Good day, my lord father. I shall do as you bid in all things."

Inquisitive heads swiveled her way, flowers craving the false light of intrigue. As she murmured to the Chamberlain the summons for Wolsey, she saw Sir Brian Harrow's interested face among them. With deliberation, she fixed her eye on him and strode straight through the gathering to where he stood. Despite his surprise, Harrow's bow was flawlessly courteous. His small, lithe frame, she noticed, suggested the sort of fighter who would prefer the swift agility of combat unencumbered by armor, and to whom feats of climbing and balancing would come easily.

As if too intent on the King's directions for a greeting, she began, "A word with you, Sir Brian." She led the way to the comparative privacy of a window embrasure, then gave a sudden turn to face him. Regarding him with a steady, close scrutiny, she cast forth her thread. "A riddle, Sir Brian. If a man's ears are severed, might he still speak?"

Harrow's eyes widened infinitesimally. At once he covered the unguarded reaction with a puzzled smile. "No doubt he could, my lady. They say the ears are no prating fools, for all they may hear." His smile was urbane, and his voice without emphasis. Yet he held himself very still.

"Then, what would you disjoin next?"

"His tongue?" Sir Brian indulged her game.

"Yet he might point a finger." Smiling as if in play, she continued, "Interfere with his finger, and he might point a toe." Heart beating uncomfortably, she stepped close enough to make him uneasy. "What of his throat? Would that not be safer?"

Harrow's half smile did not change. Only his continuing stillness gave him away. He knew of whom she spoke, she sensed it in every atom of her body. And he knew she knew. But he had been adept at innuendo while she was still in the nursery. Having lost the first point to her, he deftly refused her a jot more. Try as she might, she could not tell whether Carne's death was news to him.

"Safer," she cast a last desperate thread, "than stopping his mouth with gold?"

Harrow lifted his shoulders, a slight, elegant punctuation. "Such macabre riddles are outside my province, my lady."

"Perhaps, then, I should confer with one who consorts with Frenchmen. They are marvelous subtle at riddles, my father tells me."

"Frenchmen?" His voice was sharp. "Ah, my lady, beware the veracity of any who have lent ear, tongue or throat to the French." Swiftly he bowed, and was gone.

Isabel watched him go, then on an impulse, gathered Matthias with a glance. "Follow Sir Brian," she told him quietly. "Report to me everywhere he goes this day and everyone to whom he speaks. Don't let him approach you, but don't worry if he sees you. If he does, all the better."

Pleased by this intriguing task, Matthias bowed and was off. From the window alcove, Isabel watched the boy make his way out. If he followed her orders he would be safe, and no doubt Harrow would mark this shadow clinging to his heels. If pressure could avail, that, together with the impression she hoped she'd made on Harrow—that she had tested him for the King—might push him to act. But which way?

If her ploy had fooled him and he believed the King himself suspected him, the results were not likely, this time, to occur in London's back alleys. If he made a move, she expected it here at court. Turning the gold chain at her waist as if idly musing on its design, Isabel perched in the window seat to watch and wait.

She had been there for some minutes when out of the next embrasure oozed the squat shape of Master Thomas Cromwell. Heart lurching into alarmed thunder, she cursed herself for not checking the neighboring alcove for eavesdroppers before speaking. As he passed, Cromwell glanced into her alcove. If he was surprised to see her still there, he did not betray himself. Making his way between the chatting courtiers, he disappeared quickly out the door.

Bound whither? Isabel played with the gold chain, her face bored, but her palms sweated.

Chapter Twelve

S atan seeks to devour all souls," her grandparents' parish priest had once said, "but he chooses a separate, particular devil to pursue each." When the conversation in the antechamber faltered, Isabel glanced up to see Lord Colford in the door, his dusky auburn hair blown back in the breeze of his own haste. His fury cast a thick, audible silence over the room. Like some Egyptian cobra whose glance spews acid, he scathed the gathering with a vengeful eye, too bent on his purpose to notice whom his scorn offended. Soon he would discover her in the alcove.

"Know your own devil," the priest had advised, "that you may overcome him."

Isabel stepped out of the alcove. Her motion attracted the poisonous glance, and at once his scarcely contained wrath glinted like a storm-charge along his body, nigh a visible flash. So on the verge of some demonic conflagration he seemed that she felt an instant of terror he would march in upon the King unsummoned. She did not know whether her relief or fear was greater when instead he strode straight for her.

It took determination to hold her place. He made a small, tight bow, a mere mockery of decency. "My lady, I invite you for a private word on that seat yonder," he pointed out the window to a bench in the garden, and his voice deepened with malignant irony, "in plain view of this, and half the other, windows of the palace."

True, the bench and short stroll to reach it were far too public for violence. Yet if he meant well, she was a camel's grandmother. But she had set this drama in motion, and she was determined to play it to its end, however bitter. If only Cromwell had not spoilt everything with his creeping in the corners. Now she had no way to know whether Colford's arising from whatever hell he inhabited was at Harrow's invocation or Cromwell's. Isabel inclined her head in agreement and followed without a word.

The garden lay in overcast tranquility, empty but for a brace of the King's pet scholars arguing out of earshot, and the budding roses. Isabel seated herself on the drier half of the bench, leaving the other end, bird-bespattered and overhung by damp branches, for him. "So, my lord," she broke the silence. "Here we are, on this seat yonder, in plain view of the audience chamber and half the other windows of the palace."

He remained standing, the green leaves behind him burnishing his hair a hue deeper than wine, his face in shadow, and glowering. "Weary me with no pretense that His Majesty bid you flush Sir Brian Harrow from cover."

Never had Isabel heard her adversary so near the edge of his caution. She folded her hands gracefully in her lap and smiled. "Believe what you will."

His fingers twitched as if he would like to wring her neck, but the adamantine control, though cracked, remained. His voice was cold, but elegantly civil. "You, my lady, are a fool. Not a garden variety fool, but a superlative, an astounding, a wondrous idiot."

"You flatter me too abundantly, my lord. Surely, as you keep telling me, I'm no match for you."

He ignored that. "I warned you not to cross me. I've a purpose to accomplish, and your mock-heroic errantry endangers all."

Though only the lacing of her fingers hid their trembling, Isabel regarded him steadily. "I should hope so, my lord."

The civil facade burst. "The plague take you, my lady." His voice grated and his eyes narrowed. "Hugh Lovell's interrogation, and Master Cromwell's ill-bred insinuations. Do you think this theft means no more than that?"

Isabel gave him coldness for his fury. "No. It also means Hugh's head on a pole—or someone else's."

"So some perverse taste in you has settled on mine. Since the poets assure us a woman persecutes whom she most ardently desires, should I preen, my lady Salome?" He gave her a feral smile.

Those hard, mocking eyes, intelligent and penetrating, his clear-cut lips, their sculptured shape and arrogant disdain, gave no quarter. Even his handsomeness he used as a weapon, forcing her to see again that proud face lifeless and gored. Revulsion filled her, and hatred of him for so accurately dredging up her anger and doubt and trying to distort both into weaknesses to use against her. Leaping up, she dealt that insolent, cynical face a blow with all her force.

And lunged on empty air. He had sprung back and now stood holding in laughter. "What? Have I given you the horrors? A gentle maid, after all?" He sounded wistful, but his eyes, glinting with amusement, contradicted it. "I know your servant was only plying mine for information and I mean nothing to you. With commendable family loyalty, you will save Hugh and—oh, so regretfully—put another in his place. Even though you are far from certain whether that other is really guilty."

Isabel did not flinch, but his insight chilled her. Was it true?

Every ounce of laughter drained from his voice. "Does it even begin to occur to you, my spoilt innocent, that more is at risk than one man's life?"

If he expected answers, it was he who must supply them. Every muscle taut, she waited in silence.

When he saw she would give him nothing, he raised an eyebrow, conceding her the point. "I warned you," he continued, his tone as hard as if he had acknowledged nothing. "I tried to frighten you off, as did Cromwell. Our tactics were ill-chosen. I now see they have only inspired you to persist until your meddling threatens to lay all my work, and Cromwell's, and Cardinal Wolsey's, to waste. Just when our trap is laid fair for Harrow, you have frightened him off."

"You, Cromwell and Cardinal Wolsey!" Isabel sat down so hard her teeth clicked. "What do you want with Sir Brian Harrow?"

"By now, that should be evident, Lady Hothead. The same that you do. We suspect he's behind the theft of the Sun and Stars."

"Weasel words!" Isabel flung up at him. "You suck out the truth and offer me an empty shell. I know the Cardinal and Harrow are enemies, and I know how my lord Cardinal creates scapegoats."

His lips pulled back as if to bite, but his voice was deadly calm. "It is you who are far too agile. You force me to reveal what I should not. To stop you, I will satisfy your curiosity. But if I find your tongue's as busy as your nose, I'll go straight to the King. Know this. If I suffer for what I am about to reveal, so shall you."

"Ah, a tale. Most chimeras have one at their end. A last resort, it's also called."

He countered her jab with an ironic semblance of patience. "As you have no doubt heard, a year ago and more, Emperor Charles broke faith with King Henry. After accepting money— a good deal of it—from England's treasury to fight the French for possession of Italy, and after capturing King Francis and rendering France ripe for joint conquest, the Emperor refused to honor his end of the bargain. Quite likely, he never intended to keep it. After all, if Charles can't afford France himself, why should he hand it on a silver platter to anyone else?" He smiled cynically. "Be that as it may, the Emperor broke faith and threw over his betrothal to Princess Mary for a better match, yet he believes he can hold us to the treaty. As he knows, we need our trade with the Netherlands, and the Netherlands belong to Charles. Our King, however, believes we have equal need of an alliance we can depend on."

"Old news," Isabel told him. "Or do you think to take employment as a tutor in ancient history?"

"I speak of the future. Our little island is not so powerful as Spain or France, yet we could direct Continental policy. The two great powers weigh equally and we can tip the balance. Even while King Henry planned war, he ordered Wolsey to begin secret negotiations with the French."

"What? You claim my father broke faith before the Emperor did?"

Colford gave a slight shrug. "No cunning ruler relies on a single strategy. Negotiations for an alliance between England, France, Venice and Rome are proceeding in earnest. Cardinal Wolsey has been managing the English side, and under him Cromwell, Sir Thomas More, and me. For a year I've been working for His Majesty on negotiations that include returning the Sun and Stars to the King of France."

"That crown is my lord father's emblem of glory in war. He'd simply hand it back?" she asked skeptically.

"With mingled reluctance and eagerness. King Francis wants it badly enough to pay through the nose."

"If the payment comes anywhere near the size of King Francis' nose, the terms must be extraordinary indeed," Isabel retorted.

"We offered it to him as a free gift. A sign of our good faith. After all, officially we're still in league with Spain against France. In these circumstances, our proof of our reliability must be considerable. Our offer surprised Francis, and in gratitude he has granted several important concessions, the opening gambits for an alliance. If King Henry fails to hand over the crown now, do you imagine the French will believe his excuses? If French confidence in our good faith is destroyed, so is the alliance. And with it, Cromwell's career, perhaps even the Cardinal's. Certainly, it will destroy mine. We need the crown. And soon. His Majesty becomes daily more galled by the strain."

"If that were true—" Isabel caught herself, and finished the thought silently. If his tale were the truth, it would account for not only the King's moods, but his reaction to the question of Lord Colford's duty and loyalty.

Yet, a plausible tale, even a true one, did not necessarily make Colford trustworthy. She went over the fabric of his words in search of the slightest hole or thin spot.

"—It might explain the pacing of a wrathful—and rather disgruntled—lion?" Colford completed her half-spoken thought with his own. "Indeed. If His Majesty continues to be thwarted, sooner or later he will spring and rend." He smiled humorlessly. "It's the way of lions."

"So," Isabel tried him, "I'm to believe that when you heard of the crime and came down from the stands, you said nothing to implicate Hugh?"

"Believe it or not, as you wish. But you know full well I was not in the stands."

"Nor alone in the stables."

It was his turn to be startled, and wary. "Bravo, my lady," he said at last. "So, you know about my tryst?"

Perchance, his nebulous phrasing was a trick to find out exactly how much she did know. "Yes," Isabel answered as if turning his tactic back on him, waited a moment to throw him off balance, then casually added, "And that you and Des Roches bribed the grooms to conceal it."

His face gave him away, but he recovered swiftly. "Not from you in particular. But the head groom, a certain Harry Hackett, came to me yesterday. Lady Isabel Holland had been asking questions, and would no doubt pay him for the truth, he said. Therefore, the price of his silence had risen."

"Blackmail," said Isabel. "So that's what set you on to me last night."

"That. And what Cromwell overheard in the Tower. And your serving woman's questioning of my cook, which my manservant reported to me."

"And?"

"Is there more?"

"If you don't know, my doings must still be somewhat a secret," she taunted.

"But no less dangerous to you, if the wrong person discovers them."

"Bald Harry, the groom, never sought me out again. Did you pay him?"

"The fit wages for blackmail, a fist in the teeth and a healthy fear in the belly," Lord Colford answered.

"Which, doubtless, you vastly enjoyed bestowing," she retorted.

"What, enjoy bruising my fist on a blockhead? To answer your unspoken question, the groom's information is no danger to you, only to me. Des Roches is an agent sent by the French

King to handle certain delicate aspects of the negotiations. Wolsey knows of his part in them, but no others do, not even Sir Thomas More. Des Roches and I do not discuss our business in the usual sessions. We meet as if casually. The Emperor has several agents at this court, and sympathizers as highly placed as his aunt, the Queen. Des Roches was to have been at the joust, where we'd arranged a brief word in the stables. He was taken ill but kept our appointment, as it was urgent." His mouth tightened briefly in one of those small, vitriolic grimaces she began to recognize as a habit of his. "Hardly so urgent after all, when as it fell out, the subject of our discussion was snatched from under our very noses. I've regretted my lack of vigilance, and bitterly. The King's plans must remain secret, even if the Sun and Stars is never recovered and the French abandon the negotiations."

"So my father can fall back on his treaty with the Emperor Charles?"

"Just so. That's why I warn you that you tittle into outstretched ears at your grave peril."

"At yours, you mean."

He showed his teeth, but this time not without humor. "Exactly. Like it or not, you have linked yourself with me in this."

"Indeed, I like it not. Yet if you're telling me the truth, King Francis has no reason to steal the Sun and Stars. If he's to receive it as a freely given gift . . ."

"And since he wants the alliance more than he wants the crown," Colford added.

"Then, none of it makes sense any longer. I've wasted the whole four days."

"So I tried to warn you," he said unkindly.

"You're a scorpion. You sting for pure delight."

He smiled.

"Is it any wonder I've treed the wrong quarry? Thanks to you, I've discovered nothing, and Hugh is closer than ever to a fate he doesn't deserve. May you have joy of your accomplishment."

"You suspect Brian Harrow," he contradicted.

"Only because I thought he had to do with your brother and you. Why do *you* suspect him? His enmity for Cardinal Wolsey?"

"And other reasons."

"For instance?"

"Cromwell and I can hazard a guess or two," he evaded.

"A very scorpion, in a very, very dark cavern. You think I'll prattle of it?"

"My lady, it is beyond me to predict what you will do. Your point, however, is valid. I understand that if you are to cease endangering my investigation, you must trust me—" Seeing her expression, he added, "—at least, enough to leave it to me. I fancy that if I offered you false honey, you would know it for mere bait. So instead, you must drink down the vinegar of my real nature, like a prevention against the plague. My interests lie in keeping the King's favor. That means catching the thief without allowing the King's reckless brat to get herself killed. Since fear hasn't rendered you *hors de combat*, I will immobilize you with information. Especially since whatever my doubts at first, I now suspect Hugh Lovell is innocent."

What sort of convoluted mind would it take to suspect a man of being innocent? But aloud she only asked, "And Cromwell? Do you trust him?"

"Trust Cromwell?" Colford let out a startled laugh, his eyes suddenly glinting as the late afternoon light grazed them. "My lady, I prosper because I trust no one. As for Cromwell, the eyes in his own head know better than to trust him. Yet in this matter his advantage is clear. His ruin will only be prevented if the crown is recovered. The only difference between his view and mine is that he thinks Hugh part of the plot."

"You've just destroyed all evidence against the French, so why suspect Hugh at all?"

"Ferrero." Under cover of watching a bird swoop from the ivy, Colford observed her reaction.

"And what may a Ferrero be?" Isabel asked, ready to burst with impatience at his deviousness. "An Italian card game? Or some new game of yours, my lord?"

"Giovanni Ferrero. Hugh never mentioned him?" His voice raked her with skepticism. "In Paris, they swore eternal brotherhood. Hugh saved his life from some street ruffians and the two became fast friends. Ferrero is a Venetian envoy."

"A man known to Sir Brian Harrow?"

"A relation of Harrow's Venetian wife."

"What have Venetians to do with the Sun and Stars?"

"Much, the Doge of Venice may feel. The Sun and Stars was made by a Venetian jeweler in the pay of the Venetian ruling house. Old King Louis of France never properly compensated them for the crown."

"Yet another claimant!" Isabel shut her eyes, letting her head fall back. "God's fingernails!" At last she opened her eyes to see Lord Colford regarding her speculatively, but he still said nothing. "So," she asked, "you went to Hugh in the Tower, pretended to repent of your old quarrel, and drew him on to fond reminiscences of the old days in Paris. He, not suspecting, told you all about this Ferrero."

"Yes," he answered without a qualm.

"A loyal friend you are indeed, Lord Colford."

Adam Colford's gaze was hard. "I got the information I needed."

Her gorge rose in a resurgence of dislike. "And what's that, pray tell?"

"I have told you all I safely may. Suffice it to say I've found no evidence that Harrow is in Venetian pay—yet. Possibly, by stirring him up you've aroused a tempest that will wash something to the surface. But like any storm, it may wreak violence. Go to your aunt's tonight, and stay there."

"You think to command me?" she challenged, her back thoroughly up.

His eyes went so dark that only a small point of light flecked each one. "Do you wish the thief caught? If so, don't force me to waste my time protecting you."

"Protecting me? You never have, nor was it necessary."

He acknowledged it with a slight tilt of the head. "Harrow didn't steal the crown himself. He was seen watching the King joust, so others committed the theft and killings. Though Sir Brian is a cautious man, his colleagues may not be. They're still on the loose and we have yet to identify them."

"You have?" Isabel did not even try to hold back her triumphant smile. "Then I'll tell you the identity of one of the thieves, and where he is now. That is," she added sweetly, "if you wish my help."

An instant of pure, unguarded surprise was her reward. Then he raised an eyebrow, letting the elegant show of skepticism be his agreement. She suspected that if he had spoken his request, he would have choked on it.

Chapter Thirteen

It was almost worth the unpleasantness of having Lord Adam Colford in the Lovells' house to see Ursula's expression. "Send for wine, good Ursula." Isabel pretended not to notice. "Don't call Matthias, I've sent him on another errand."

Colford unfurled his cloak and held it out without a glance at Ursula, who looked at it as if the Devil proffered his pitchfork, but took it. "We have claret here, my lady."

With a gesture, Isabel invited him to sit. He was about to, then noticed Eleanor slept curled where he was about to seat himself. Without a word he swept her off. When Ursula had poured wine for both of them, he spoke to Isabel. "This business is not for others."

"I see no others," Isabel returned evenly. "What is safe with me is safe with Ursula. Besides, it would be most improper for me to entertain you alone, my lord."

She had him there, and he knew it. His slight flicker of a grimace came again. Isabel smiled. Ursula, she noticed, kept her face as unreadable as that of a stone sphinx, and she settled as immovable as one in a chair against the wall.

Colford's variety of sitting was more leopard, his body gracefully composed but with a hint of taut alertness. The crimson velvet of his doublet was like a plush fur over the supple musculature of his arms and shoulders, and his hose displayed a horseman's calves, powerful yet compact and trim. But many men at this sporting court boasted a physique as well-honed. What drew attention to Colford in stillness, Isabel decided, was the absoluteness of that stillness. She had never seen him waste a single motion without purpose. Yet that quality in him was the farthest thing from slackness. Rather, it seemed the collected motionlessness of one waiting in ambush. His breathing was quick, as if even in his silent waiting he contended with some force imperceptible to anyone else.

Each of us is beset with our own devil, indeed, Isabel mused. *And perchance, some have the ill fortune to play host to three or four.*

Lord Adam Colford set down his wine cup. "You claim to know the identity of one of the thieves."

He had done as she asked, even to showing her the royal commission charging him with the powers to discover and arrest the thief of the Sun and Stars, whatever rank that person might hold. Even the Dukes of Norfolk and Suffolk were not immune, if Lord Adam Colford found evidence of their guilt. Surprised by this proof of her father's confidence in him, Isabel examined the signature closely. Its loops and angularities tilted in both directions so impatiently they nearly collided, with the R standing for Rex transmuted to a familiar, abruptly penned flourish. Without doubt, it was her father's. She met his skeptical gaze with her own forthright one. "I presume Hugh told you of the man with no ears he saw entering the competitors' courtyard as he was leaving?"

"That only? I've already proved his existence to my satisfaction. And finally, even to Cromwell's. During their search of the city, our men heard tales of a thief and swordsman with severed ears. Too many tales from too many quarters to be a lie. They give him different aliases, but describe the methods of a single man."

"One of the names is Carne?"

"It is," Lord Colford answered, unimpressed. "But we've turned London inside out and he's not to be found. By now, he's fled the city."

"In a manner. But he left his corpse behind."

Colford's eyes widened a fraction, their green tints suddenly apparent. "You saw it? Did you speak with him before he died?"

"I arrived too late, but not by long. His throat had been slit, but the blood was still wet—and abundant."

"Hardly a pleasant sight," Colford remarked with a trace of commiseration. "But how did you discover what none of my men or Cromwell's could?"

"You and Cromwell don't have Ursula," Isabel answered, and left it at that.

He regarded Ursula over his shoulder for several long moments. Ursula gave him stare for stare. If not for the dictates of propriety, Isabel could see she would be bombarding him with demands for proof of his good faith. And, no doubt, comments on his manners, as well.

"Surely, my lady, you didn't go into London at night accompanied only by an old woman?" From his tone, that was precisely what he thought she had done.

"You still take me for a fool, my lord? I'll wager on the two men at arms who accompanied me against any four of yours," Isabel flashed out in annoyance.

Colford smiled. "As I said before, not the garden variety. A resourceful kind, at least. So resourceful that doubtless you have an opinion on who killed Carne."

"A single man, agile enough to scale rooftops. We learnt Carne had received gold, but when he tried to collect the rest, he nearly got wages of a different sort. I think he collected the first payment upon delivery of the crown. That he agreed to turn over the Sun and Stars before collecting the last payment suggests he had worked for this master before, and trusted him to some degree."

"It sounds reasonable."

"After the attempt on his life, Carne went into yet deeper hiding, not only from your men, but from his former accomplices. To no avail. They caught up with him and paid him his final reward."

He smiled at her grim joke, but countered, "Or, a supposed friend murdered him for the money he'd already gotten."

"Maybe. But I think it unlikely that Carne let his murderer into the house. For one thing, the front door was bolted from the inside, but the back door hung open with its bolt broken. For another, we found Carne's body in the upstairs bedroom, not downstairs as if he had received company."

Colford arched a brow, considering her reasoning, then nodded slightly, accepting it. "These discoveries of yours may be of some use to me," he concluded thoughtfully.

"To Hugh, at any rate, I hope."

He gave her an acrimonious glance. "Surely a woman so lacking in natural delicacy as to scour London's bowels for an assassin did not entirely regain it just when indelicacy would be useful."

"If that insult means did we search the body and room, the answer is yes." Matching his brusqueness, Isabel quit his company to go upstairs to her room. She took the gold coin from its hiding place and returned, concealing it in her hand. "By the signs, the murderer searched for the payment Carne already had. He had either found it, or was about to, when we interrupted him and he hid. He made his escape at his first chance, without taking the time to gather the coins."

"You found them, then?"

"A treasure of them. No pay for any ordinary crime."

Adam Colford narrowed his eyes. "Then Carne's murder was no ordinary slaughter for greed, since the killer was less concerned with the gold than escaping unrecognized."

"I think he did go back for the gold. From a rooftop he aimed a brick at me, then scampered away over the slates. He was of middle size or less, and surpassing agile."

Colford's brow raised slightly. She could see he was thinking of Harrow. As was she. "You had the gold?"

"Probably the killer thought so. Yet there were four of us, and only one brick. It was only I who came upstairs while he was in hiding. He had no reason to fear anyone else had seen him."

"Ah."

"Yes."

"But you didn't see him?"

"By misfortune or good fortune, no."

"The time?"

"Not long before dawn."

Adam Colford fixed her with a penetrating regard, suspicious marks suddenly visible below his eyes. "Oddly done, to leave the treasure to the murderer."

"And take away his chance to incriminate himself?" Opening her hand, she displayed the foreign coin.

"A sample?" His eyes widened, suspicion giving way to a delight as startling as it was startled. "Yes, such valuable pieces in Florentine coinage must be rather rare in England. We'll notice if any more of these turn up."

"It's not Venetian, then?"

"Wouldn't that be tidy? But no. If you look for tidiness, I must disappoint you all round. The King's entertainment lasted until dawn. I remained until the end, and so did Sir Brian Harrow. He was not your agile cutthroat."

"That's as well, I suppose. Harrow knows who I am, and whoever the agile cutthroat was, I hope he'll be no cutthroat of mine." Despite her jest, she shuddered.

"Yes," he agreed absently, brows drawn down at some other thought. "May I keep the coin?"

"And welcome to it. I was in fear lest Cromwell find it in my possession. Far better it were in yours."

This time he glanced up, the corners of his lips twitching at her barb. At such close quarters they were remarkably shaped lips, the upper one with a sharply chiselled outline, the lower sensuous and full. It was a pity such an adornment was wasted on a man no one would want to kiss.

"Wise, my lady. At the moment, you do have far more to fear from Cromwell than I."

"Even though you know me to be innocent? With all your superiority to Master Cromwell, you can't manage him?" she challenged.

"I know naught of your innocence, save that not content with being threatened by menacing lords at royal entertainments, you visit London's cesspools and consort with corpses." But this time the glitter in his dark eyes showed he was not really suspicious, merely enjoying being difficult.

"What's our next move?"

"Not ours. Mine."

Footsteps startled them to silence.

Matthias trotted in, looking weary and marvelous pleased with himself. When he saw they had an important guest, he recovered with politic swiftness, summoned his best bow and doffed his cap with a flourish. "My apologies, my lady, my lord." He shut his mouth tighter than a clam, forbearing to spill his secret.

Colford belittled him with a glance. "What is this?"

Isabel ignored his rudeness. "You may speak before Lord Adam, Matthias. He's our friend—of a sort."

The page glanced at him doubtfully. "Well, my lady, Sir Brian noticed me before he'd got far from the audience chamber. I tried to act like I wasn't following, but when we drew near the tennis court, suddenly he took a side path. Since you said it made no matter if he saw me, I didn't dare lose him. When I turned the corner, there he was, on the walk a little ahead. He had slowed down. I kept on, but cautiously, so he couldn't lay hold of me." The boy's eyes shone with delight in his adventures and the fine tale they made. "Sir Brian turned toward the river, then again, till he'd made a full circle. He was testing to see if I was spying on him."

"Hardly," Colford quashed him. "He was showing you how idiotic your game was, and that he would go nowhere except to send your mistress an indirect message by it."

The proud son of a Devon yeoman family with no pretensions whatever to idiocy, Matthias went resentfully silent.

"Let the lad tell his story," Isabel retorted.

"I'm not preventing him," Colford answered, surprised.

Though Matthias was too well trained to contradict a nobleman directly, his tone did. "Sir Brian went to the chapel, my lady. Though he didn't pray, I felt wrong, spying on him there. What if he confessed, should I try to hear, or not? But he paid me no attention, and he didn't confess. For a long time he only sat and thought. At last he got up and left."

"I applaud your patience," Isabel said. "And then?"

"To the stables. He ordered his horse saddled and set off. I don't know where to, since I—well, I didn't know whether you wanted me to follow him away from the palace . . ." He trailed off uncertainly.

"You did well. It's safer so. That's all he did at the palace, then?"

"Yes, my lady." But the boy was still full of something unsaid.

"You noticed something else."

Pleased at the acknowledgement, Matthias drew himself up. "I did, my lady." He paused, making sure he had her full attention, and Lord Adam's, then glanced to the darkening rear of the room to make sure of Ursula's as well. With an art born of relish and anticipation, he delivered his prize. "Sir Brian left the chapel by the cloistered walk. As I followed some way behind, I saw a movement in the shadow of a column. A person in a cloak followed Sir Brian, keeping near the row of columns. Whoever it was, was very wary, and when Sir Brian glanced back once—at me, I think—the cloaked shape shrank between the columns and disappeared. When I passed, no one was there."

"Man, or woman?" Colford asked.

"The cloak was long, and the hood up, but I think it was a man, my lord. It was too tall for a woman. The cloak was dark blue. Good cloth, a gentleman's."

"Was he heavy, or light? Youthful or old by his movements?"

"Light and spry, my lord. Quick movements, very wary."

"You made no attempt to discover where he'd gone?"

Matthias smarted under the injustice. "I searched along the row of columns, but Sir Brian was getting away from me, and my lady said to follow *him*."

"There is only one of Matthias," Isabel reproved. "Though after this good service, I'd agree that's too few."

"Or too many," Colford snarled. "If you'd left the footpads'
work to my men, Harrow would not have been alerted, and we
might know all by now."

"Where were your men when we needed them?"

"What use sending them after Harrow when he knew full
well he was being followed by your boy?"

"My lady and my lord," Ursula broke into their swiftly
heating skirmish, but when his lordship turned to sting her too,
she was the perfect servant. "Do you please to sup now?" Her
eye was as hard as his.

"Not I," Colford answered. "I have wasted half the day in
idle chatter, and must make some progress."

"Idle chatter," Isabel repeated, tormented past all patience.
"So that's your name for what you've learned? Now you have
proof it was Carne who committed the theft, of his murder,
and evidence for its motives. You know of the Italian gold, and
of Harrow's being followed by someone other than ourselves.
Yet because I'm not a man, any dealings with me must be
frivolous? God's eyes!" Only refusal to prove his point kept her
from going for his own with her fingernails.

"Your conduct is all too frivolous, madam." His answer was
a precise, cutting edge of ice. "A proper woman should be far
more mindful of her safety, and as delicate in sensibility as in
manner. If a woman's intelligent, all the better, but preserve
me from female lawyers, battle commanders or spies."

"You were eager enough for the results of my campaign."

"Then be content that you've helped your cousin."

She would be content when Hugh was out of the Tower.
With a vast effort, she curbed her tongue. "May I know what
you intend now?"

"Must you?" He sighed. "Very well, then. Cromwell
suspects Hugh of collaboration with his friend Ferrero on
behalf of the Venetian claimant to the Sun and Stars, but

Harrow's relations to that party are even stronger. If I can prove not only a past, and a family connection, but recent deeds of Harrow's that open the way for this crime . . ." He frowned into the deepening dusk of the room, lost in his thoughts. It reminded Isabel vividly of what his cook had told Ursula. It was true; his brooding did make the shadows seem darker.

"How will you prove that?" Isabel dared speak into the spell.

Colford started, and glanced at her. Then he gave her a predatory grin. "By perfidy, of course. Harrow has been royal emissary to Venice twice in the last two years. Ostensibly, Venice is to be part of our league with France against the Emperor. If Harrow has done any negotiating to Venetian advantage at the expense of England, that can perhaps be discerned."

"If you knew the details of the negotiations. They're a royal matter, no doubt as secret as your own work."

"Yes," he agreed. "By royal command, the records are kept under lock and key in the charge of a trusted member of the Council."

"Do you have the authority to see them?"

"Perhaps I could get it. Though perhaps not, or only at the expense of alerting too many people to my interest in the matter. But there may be another way. The councilor entrusted with those particular records happens to be my brother Giles."

"Isn't that our misfortune? Surely, Sir Giles can't be bribed."

"No, he can't." The smile faded, and the brooding crept back. "And there's the sore spot. My brother's tedious scruples."

"I'm thankful some have them. Otherwise, we'd all be like Harrow and you."

Lord Colford smiled again, as if she had complimented him.

"Surely no perfidy is necessary. The King could send for the papers himself and let you examine them."

"It might take time to convince him. And he's surrounded by spies. Secrecy is too crucial. Not only in the matter of the Sun and Stars, but the nature of all my work for the King. Once that begins to come out, I lose my unique value to His Majesty—and its rewards."

To Isabel, her father's uses for both Colfords were clearer by the moment. Two brothers, the light and dark sides of statecraft, the official Council and the undercurrent of a ruler's secret schemes. Though Adam Colford's part might not be rewarded with ceremony, nor set down in the annals, it was a practical necessity. Her father could not have chosen an agent more suited to this work. Only, how far into darkness did this man's deeds go?

"But if Sir Giles won't show you the papers—" she began.

"I said he won't be bribed. But he might bend the rules—if I can convince him it's for an honest and worthy purpose."

"Surely, if you're Hugh's friend and think him innocent, that's worthy."

"That was another reason I visited him in the Tower. An explanation in case my inquiries became known. It would hoodwink many. But would it also gull Giles into thinking I would run such a risk for friendship alone? With nothing in it for me? He knows me better than that."

Isabel considered the small lines of suspicion that marred his otherwise fine eyes and well-drawn brows. In ten years his handsomeness would be swallowed by the harsh lines of his cynicism. Isabel imagined death itself would be less lonely than his unremitting distrust of everyone and everything. She would be glad when this was over and she need have no more to do with him. A whiteness in the gathering dusk drew her attention. Eleanor was stretching with elaborate, feline attention to each claw and muscle. Isabel smiled, then became aware Colford was regarding her as a ploughman might eye a thorn bush in his field. "There must be some other way," he muttered.

"Than what?"

He frowned, irritated that she had heard.

"Come, any idea so disliked by a being so devious as you must be a good, honest plan."

"Oh, it's devious, like me. A lie of a very pure order, but that's just the sort to convince my brother Giles." Still, he hesitated, searching for some other answer. At last he let out a small, peeved breath. "Your concern for Hugh is well known. Giles will believe in that. I can see no completely convincing plan but to take you along with me."

Isabel leaned forward eagerly, but she was puzzled. "Why should he believe you would help me? We're strangers."

"There's one obvious answer, isn't there? I'm infatuated with your irrepressible charms. But no. Even Giles would fail to believe that."

"My lord!" Ursula burst out, driven past endurance.

Lord Colford turned his displeasure from Isabel to her. "I merely meant that my brother knows I prefer ladies of the meek, dulcet variety. Yet," he added with a malicious smile at Isabel, "he knows a spark like yours can ignite my lust."

"If you think I'd lower myself to pretending infatuation for you, your conceit boils over into madness," Isabel retorted.

"If you cannot feign passion for my physical enticements, pretend your lust is for my lands. Or, you are using me for your cousin's sake. In which case I, of course, realize this, but hope to gain . . ." He concluded the thought with a wicked smile.

Though he was doing his best to eat his dish of crow well spiced, Isabel enjoyed the sight immensely. Season it as he might, he could learn more with her than without, and he knew it. As if he divined her thoughts, he added, "This arrangement lasts only for the one errand, you understand."

They would see about that. "Should we not be about it?" she answered. "Hugh has only tonight and tomorrow."

"Yes. Time grows short, and we must have the crown."

Chapter Fourteen

A t this hour my brother can usually be found in his office," Colford said as they followed the straight
gravel path that bisected a long lawn. Ahead a foun-
tain played, the last fire of sunset turning its white marble
opalescent and its water to molten flame. Isabel smiled. It was
at the fiery prisms amid the water, not at Colford, but he
joined her pleasure in the sight with a swift, almost furtive
smile of his own. Then, as if they had shared nothing, he continued, "By daylight and candlelight, Giles is hard at it, toiling
over the Netherlands trade agreement—of which His Majesty
intends to take as much advantage as possible before breaking
ties with the Emperor."

"Does Sir Giles know how short-lived the fruits of his
labors will be?"

"He must guess. One becomes resigned to wasted work
when one serves an impulsive sovereign, but he likes to work
toward a worthy purpose. Perhaps he makes ready in case the
wind of policy changes again."

"Policy is an empty, puffing wind indeed, blowing people like Cromwell aloft, while honest men must become mere weathercocks. And here we bluster along bringing our own puffery of stratagem and counterfeit."

"We'll tell him no lie, except that we like one another."

"A tempest, no less. By the by, I would prefer you to play at greed, not lust. It's you who want my lands."

"Lustful or calculating, either way I'm indefatigable." He sounded so cynically pleased with the possibilities this role might offer that distrust instantly filled her. Yet the rules of courtly romance were on the woman's side. If he pressed too forwardly, she would ridicule him with all the weapons available to the unattainable mistress. In fact, she hoped his spite would provoke some overly bold insinuation. To make a fool of him before Sir Giles would be sweet revenge for his insults.

"You smile, my lady. You suppose me riddled with greed but impervious to lust?"

"I would never deny your aptness for any sin, my lord." Yet as she spoke, it did occur to her that she had not imagined him prone to lust, nor any impulsive vice. It was the cold sins that haunted that guarded face and cultivated, chill voice.

Sir Giles had the privilege of a small office near the council chamber. Lord Colford raised his hand to knock on the door of carved oak, then paused. The corners of his lips twitching ironically, he instead held the hand out, rings flashing in the dusk, to Isabel.

If he thought to discomfit her, he little realized how human and petty such games made him. Without doubt he was a dangerous man, but she began to suspect that unlike his kin the scorpion, his flaunting of his stinger did not necessarily presage peril. His real sting, when it came, would be without warning. This brandishing of his barb was merely to amuse himself. Not about to give him further entertainment, Isabel took the offered hand as readily as if it belonged to the most chivalrous knight in Christendom. He raised the other and knocked.

Sir Giles Colford himself opened it. Fairer in coloring than his brother and shorter by a little, he was dressed in near-equal splendor, his jacket a sober blue-grey, but on his belt peridots sparked, and his gold chain of office glittered on his shoulders. When he saw his brother he smiled. If finding him hand-in-hand with Isabel startled, he was courteous enough not to show it. "Adam! Lady Isabel Holland, good evening." He sounded wondrous pleased to see them. As he bowed to Isabel and motioned them in, the reason for his gladness was revealed.

It sat anxiously at the table, chin in hand, a cup of wine half finished at its elbow and a hare's insatiable seeking in its pale-lashed eyes.

"Sir Piers," Lord Colford greeted the reason for his brother's eagerness to be delivered, and turned to Sir Giles. "We're disturbing you," he said generously. "We should leave you with your guest."

Piers Knevet had pressed his best polite face into service, but clearly agreed.

"Not at all." Giles Colford acknowledged the slight, mischievous twitch of his brother's lips with only the quickest of glances and firmly drew him in. It confirmed Isabel's guess that Sir Piers had been after some favor. Knowing him, no doubt it was an unrealistic one.

Realizing that the dread Lord Colford was coming in after all, Knevet showed all the enthusiasm of a lost soul for twenty demons bearing pincers and skewers. "It is I who should depart, my lord," he said. "Supper awaits me, I'll hazard a guess." In his haste to escape Lord Colford's scorn, his thin elbow grazed his cup. For a breathless moment it teetered, then tipped. With an abrupt dart he caught it, spattering wine over Sir Giles' doublet.

"Oh! Many, many apologies, Sir Giles!"

"No matter," Colford reassured him, dabbing at the drops with his handkerchief.

Strewing apologies like garlands, Knevet bowed past Isabel, then paused before his host. "Sir Giles, I implore you not to forget. I pray you, petition the King that I be relieved. It's been nearly two months."

"Yes, of course." Still wiping, Sir Giles gestured him an absent farewell.

"What could Piers Knevet have that the King could possibly want to relieve him of?" his elder brother asked with wicked perplexity.

Sir Giles smiled as he took fresh cups from a cabinet and poured them wine. "Only His Majesty's displeasure. His offense was so piffling I doubt the King remembers it." He rubbed his neck to loosen the muscles, and sighed. "At the end of a tasking day, surely one ought to be spared some people."

"Put all the Knevets together and you might have the brains to support a hat." Adam Colford smugly sipped his wine.

"A middling-sized one," Sir Giles replied, but without his brother's rancor. "The other Knevets are athletes and have that way to the King's heart. Piers—" He shook his head.

"—Should cease trying," Adam Colford disposed of him with finality.

Seeing the two Colfords together at close quarters, it struck Isabel how unlike they were in form as well as temperament. Not only were Giles' fawn hair and blue eyes a contrast to Adam's dusky auburn and forest green, their features were not much alike either. Giles' mouth was wide, without the fullness or chiseled outline of Adam's, but his chin was cleft while his brother's was not. He caught her looking and paused. "I was thinking what a contrast the two of you look," she excused her staring.

"Adam favors his mother, I take after mine." Sir Giles glanced at Colford. "At least, in outward appearance."

Isabel also glanced at Lord Adam, but he only returned her look, saying nothing.

She sensed some restraint in them both that had not been there before. Though she had heard nothing against Sir Giles' birth, being born on the wrong side of the blanket oneself made one all too careful of treading what might be delicate ground. Despite her curiosity, Isabel hesitated.

"Adam's mother died when he was quite young, and our father wed again," Sir Giles answered her unvoiced discomfort.

Another piece fell into place. Ursula's information that Giles alone looked after the widowed Lady Colford was no longer a condemnation of Adam Colford, if Giles alone was her son. Yet Isabel had not missed his denial of any but outward resemblance to his mother. Nor Adam's silence.

It was Lord Adam who broke it. "This morning I spent an hour with the grey colt." He gave Giles a smug, badgering smile.

Giles' mouth quirked in annoyance, an expression after all not unlike his half-brother's. "How goes his training?"

"He learns fast. He's developing wondrous strong hindquarters." Of a sudden, the elder Colford's dark eyes widened, as enthusiastic as a boy's. "I suspect this colt may prove a champion at the capriole, brother."

"A graceful form and a valiant spirit," Giles praised, and added enviously, "You had a stroke of luck, discovering him first."

"Not luck. Genius." Lord Adam glanced archly at Isabel. "I have an eye for such qualities, would you not say?"

Apparently, their rivalry did not extend to women. Sir Giles' glance held benign agreement, but no covetousness. "The two of you cut a gallant figure in the pavane last night, my lady," he directed the remark courteously to Isabel.

Without a single word, merely by a flash of tooth, the varlet of a lord managed to hint that he had received more than a dance. If Sir Giles had seen them leave the hall for the deserted gallery, no doubt he now thought her a loose, giddy flirt. Lord Adam had her neatly. Yet if she was to be branded a vixen in Sir Giles' sober mind, at least she would take the villain down with her. As if one thought led directly to another, she addressed Sir Giles. "When I told Lord Colford of my trouble, he was so kind as to suggest you might help me." Better a user of amorous fools than a wanton.

"How might I do that, my lady?"

She put the full strength of her feelings into her voice. "My cousin is innocent."

Sir Giles turned to Lord Adam, who supported her words with a brief, inscrutable nod.

Giles Colford studied him, then turned up his open hands on the table, accepting his brother's supposed interest in her happiness, but reserving his own opinion. "My lady, if you're certain Sir Hugh is not guilty, why such alarm for him? Do you believe he has enemies who will prevent a fair trial?"

"The note that drew Hugh to the tents was a forgery," Isabel answered.

"The business Sir Hugh refused to reveal to the King?"

"The forger knew nothing of it. That's clear."

Sir Giles frowned. "May I ask how you know?"

"I don't," Isabel lied firmly. Hugh's affair with Cecily was one piece of information Adam Colford was not going to lay his hands on. "Hugh gives his word that the matter had nothing to do with the crown. He's a man of honor."

"So I always believed," Sir Giles answered. "I know he was once your friend, Adam."

"He still is," Lord Colford corrected. "That is one reason I'm here." His tone implied there were others, but so subtly

~ 156 ~

that Isabel could only make matters worse by contradicting. "We must discover his enemies."

"And then you'll have the thief? It's worth considering, at least. So, Lady Isabel, who might bear Sir Hugh ill will?"

Before Isabel could answer, Adam slipped in, "Sir Brian Harrow?"

Adept indeed, Isabel thought. And another lie. It revived her uneasiness. What manner of life might force a man to be so covert even with his own brother? Or was secrecy an addiction to him, a lust far greater than any he had threatened to pretend for her?

Sir Giles only stared at them in surprise. "Sir Brian?"

"A friend of yours?"

"A colleague."

"What opinion do you hold of him?"

"He's remarkably apt at bargaining. At times, the man is nothing short of brilliant."

"I mean, personally."

Sir Giles leaned back. Large hands folded on the table, he considered carefully. "Volatile," he said at last. His disapproval of that quality suffused the single word.

"What of his loyalty?"

"His Majesty trusts it, and rightly, I believe. Without Harrow, Wolsey would never have had such success abroad, for all my lord Cardinal likes to imagine himself the Great Arbiter of Europe."

"Ah yes, the Great Arbiter." Lord Adam exchanged a wry smile with him. "But your adept bargainer may have dealt himself into a secret agreement with the Venetians, perhaps through his wife, perhaps through a kinsman of hers, one Giovanni Ferrero. If Harrow did sell himself to the Venetians, the records of his negotiations in Venice last year might show some indication of it."

Giles frowned. "You want me to show them to you? You know I can't open state secrets without authority."

"Old state secrets," his brother urged.

"You know you must get the King's permission, or Wolsey's."

"And you know both think Hugh guilty," Adam Colford argued. "What reason could I give? That this lady's eyes shine wondrously?"

"I regret it, brother, but that isn't enough for me, either."

Adam Colford raised his regard silently to his brother's face. "Granted. That reason is not enough for you—whatever it may be to me."

So bitter was his sarcasm that Isabel blinked. His brother, too, sat in tense silence, his blue gaze locked with the seething shadow realm of Lord Adam's. He lowered his head, brows bent, and stayed thus for a while. Then he collected himself. "This means so much to you?"

"It does," Adam Colford answered.

Giles sighed. Without another look at his brother he disappeared into an inner room and emerged with a ring of keys. "Wait here." He left by the outer door.

Isabel gazed out the window, avoiding her co-conspirator. She knew she should count this a victory. Yet the air in the small room hung oddly heavy, and when she covertly glanced at Adam Colford, he had braced one hand on the table, as if he needed it for balance. She tried to convince herself he had bullied his younger brother with his forceful will all their lives. But that did not describe what she had sensed. Whatever invisible coercion he had leveled at his brother, Sir Giles had not been cowed. He was his own man, equal to any browbeating of his brother's. Whatever his reasons for deciding to help, Isabel knew he felt them to be valid. Yet whatever unknown currents flowed beneath the confrontation, Isabel was certain of one thing. Sir Giles felt a strong loyalty toward his brother. She wondered if Lord Adam's silence was shame for getting what he wanted by trading on that loyalty.

It seemed long before the door opened and Sir Giles entered carrying two leather-bound volumes. He shot the bolt behind him and laid them on the table. "These are the records of Harrow's last two embassies to Venice."

Opening the first book, Lord Adam began quickly reading. Isabel could see only pages of small, closely written script, illegible from where she sat. She did not move her chair closer. Sir Giles had taken matters into his own hands in allowing even one unauthorized person to read the accounts; she did not wish to double the gravity of his infraction. Besides, she admitted to herself, her lack of diplomatic experience gave her less idea of what to seek. For what seemed a very long time Colford's face showed nothing but concentration, and there was no sound above the turning of pages.

Giles had lifted the decanter to offer Isabel more wine when Adam abruptly leaned forward. His eyes widened a fraction, then narrowed thoughtfully. Slowly, he smiled. Isabel could almost see his stinger twitching in malicious glee. "Sir Brian Harrow may be leaving us soon."

Giles looked at him sharply. "What do you mean?"

"For Venice. And this time, perhaps to stay. You're aware he holds a post there?"

"Some function to do with the harbor. Yes, he informed the King of it. I believe he's had the position for years, an unofficial piece of his dowry. It's mostly honorary, not lucrative enough to concern His Majesty."

"That may change. Look at these licensing provisions. Now, this page. Who do you think will grant the licenses? A fine Venetian plumage to feather Harrow's nest. But the little gifts would be more important than the fees. He would only gain the full benefit by living in Venice—a life he intends to take up once he's delivered the crown to the Doge?"

"It's hardly conclusive," Sir Giles replied. "You know how many English courtiers receive pensions from abroad at no harm to His Majesty. In fact, for economic reasons he encourages it."

"I cast no criticisms upon your supervision. Until this little private coup of Harrow's is laid next to the theft of the Sun and Stars, it seems harmless enough." Lord Adam's lips quirked with annoyance. "But I haven't found what I hoped. I can see nothing amiss in Harrow's negotiating. Discounting his greed, he looks as loyal to the interests of England as a minuscule and uncommonly glib Saint George."

"So it seemed at the time." Sir Giles was disturbed. "Still, look at this." Opening to another page, he pointed.

"More little provisions? Ah. This time, benefiting the mercantile empire of Lady Harrow's father, old Antonio di Fabiani."

"For a family of Florentine origins, the di Fabianis wield remarkable influence in Venice."

"Florentine?" Isabel said sharply.

Sir Giles glanced at her as if he had all but forgotten her presence, but his brother's quick, acute regard said he also was thinking of the Florentine gold.

"Indeed," answered Sir Giles. "They stem from an old Tuscan house. Why?"

"I think I remember Lady Angela mentioning somewhat of it," Isabel equivocated.

"The Doge's agent Ferrero is kin to Lady Angela Harrow," Adam steered the talk back to its former course.

Giles lit more candles against the dusk and put a log on the fire while Adam glanced down the rest of the page. "It looks as if Harrow made what amounts to a side deal."

"Against the King?" Isabel asked.

Lord Adam's smile could have corroded steel. "Hardly. In the event France becomes hostile to England, our trade with Venice is to go on undisturbed, regardless of Venice's treaty with the French."

"Contingency planning." Giles shrugged.

Ignoring him, Adam Colford put the record books aside. He stared into a shadowy corner of the room.

Apparently familiar with this mood, Giles remained quiet.

At last, Isabel could bear this incommunicative brooding no longer. "It means something more to you than you're saying."

Adam glanced at her, considered doubtfully, then finally decided to speak after all. "Only if Harrow is as loyal to the King as he appears, and Hugh is innocent." A sardonic smile darkened rather than lit his face. In a low, dangerous purr, he suggested, "Think on this: What if there was no theft?"

"No theft!" Isabel looked at Giles. "Then, where is the Sun and Stars?"

"Where would it be?" Adam asked, his amusement bordering on quiet rage.

"In the royal coffers!" Isabel objected. She silenced her arguments in time not to spill all their doings before Sir Giles, but gave Lord Adam an angry look. That he would suggest such perfidy no longer astonished her, but the notion that her father would murder Hugh to keep the crown was unthinkable.

Giles, however, had no reason to remain silent. "You're suggesting it's all a sham, that the King would perjure himself?"

"Dare any of us suggest that? Not I." Suddenly, as clearly as if they were written on the air, Isabel could see his broodings. If he was right, doubtless Wolsey knew the truth. And Cromwell? All of them, duping him, using him for their own purposes. Colford's eyes glinted dangerously. Then he noticed them watching, and his lids lowered. Yet the fury had not left him, he only concealed it.

"Look at Lady Isabel," Giles argued. "As you see, she believes no such thing of her lord father, and in truth, neither do I."

"If it's so," Colford reflected, "and Master Cromwell knows of it, then he's asking some very dangerous questions."

"Not in his nature," answered Sir Giles. "So, if all this were true, Cromwell must be one of the dupes. Which is another argument against your theory. If His Majesty were tricking us all, would he put a sharp witted-ferret like Cromwell in charge of discovering the truth?"

"Perhaps," Isabel stuck Colford with the point of her anger, "we should no longer trouble your good brother. It's a poor repayment of our debt to you, Sir Giles, to keep you from your supper while we incubate evil spirits."

The elder Colford gave her a malevolent glance at this description of his mood, but the younger pressed his lips together to disguise his amusement.

"For my part, I believe the crown was stolen, and I think Sir Brian Harrow guilty," she said.

Sir Giles reluctantly nodded. "Though that would be a shame. Harrow was a valuable asset to the King, and several times helped me gain the advantage over the Spanish emissaries."

Adam Colford pushed away the books and stood. "I *am* in your debt, Giles," he agreed with her statement, yet made his thanks his own. "I have asked much of you."

Giles' brows lifted in a denial that momentarily heightened the fraternal resemblance. But though his hand raised as if to clasp his brother's shoulder, he stopped just short of touching him.

Again Isabel felt she had ventured onto thin ice over some murky, unknown depth. Though the two brothers wished each other good night with the quiet accord of some strong bond, the air was thick with unspoken tension.

Chapter Fifteen

The sky glistened with stars like a great leviathan arisen black and wet from the abyss. A pretty metaphor indeed, Isabel thought mockingly, for a fair evening lit by a multitude of heavenly lights, and a stroll beside a man handsome enough, who despite his plaguing had played the suitor with courtesy and without seriously compromising her reputation. She glanced at Adam Colford, but he did not speak nor lift his gaze from the ground.

"You feel guilty." She broke the silence with an odd sense she took a great risk.

"I?"

"For hoodwinking your brother."

"No," he replied without rancor. "We have never been so intimate as to make such an insignificant connivance difficult."

"Then," she said with sudden insight, "it is Sir Giles who feels guilty."

He gave her a quick, startled look. In the dim illumination of the stars she could make out the twist of his mouth as if in humor, an unwilling acknowledgement. "Say on, Madam

Delphic Oracle. Or is your knowledge no sorcery, but bought of a spy?"

"I told you the extent of my spying on you," she retorted, insulted.

"So you say." But he relented. "Your perceptiveness is the equal of a brace or three of spies."

He was evading her, and nearly with success. Again she felt an inexplicable uncertainty in her recklessness. "What has your brother done to you that he owes you so much?"

"Giles is blameless in the matter." Stopping, he turned to her. "If you mean to pry into our affairs, at least I would not have you conjuring false phantoms. Though Giles can't help but feel responsibility, none belongs to him." He smiled. "Perchance you haven't noticed, Isabel, that I lack somewhat in easy fellowship."

That you suffer from a surfeit of offensive disdain? But she did not say it.

"My brother takes this too much to heart," he continued. "When Giles and I shared quarters during the royal progress, unfortunately—for both of us—I cried out in a nightmare. He knew what I dreamed. The irony is, though he himself is blameless, his existence caused my private hell."

He started forward again, leaving the long straight path, and struck off across the grass. Yet he moved slowly, waiting for her. "Lest you conjure false apparitions, sorceress, I'll clear my brother's name. As he told you, my mother died and our father remarried. This occurred when I was four years old. I found my new 'mother'—changeable. Her manner depended, I soon learnt, on whether my father was present. If she'd had no children of her own, she might have remained merely unloving, but once she had a son, she resented me in earnest." In the dim of the night Isabel saw him smile bitterly. "I was to inherit nearly everything, you see. Giles was only a baby when she first tried to kill me."

Shocked, Isabel paused in her tracks.

"She pushed me from a window. I was only six, but I remember it clearly, the sudden, hard thrust from behind, and dangling high over the paving stones, clinging to the sill while she pried and jabbed at my hands. The sickening feeling of falling. But fortune was against her. Naught but some ribs were broken. Servants came running, and she was forced to invent a tale. They believed her. I told my father the truth, but she had got to him first. When I insisted, he locked me in a dark room for punishment. I had ever been churlish toward her, he accused. Now I would love her, or suffer his wrath." Lord Adam smiled again, and Isabel felt a chill. "That was my entry into adult existence. The knowledge that what I had taken for the world was but a bright surface. A glittering, near-flawless surface where I was my father's pride, heir to a barony and green lands that stretched far as the eye could see, where I could stamp my foot and order the servants about like a small tyrant, master the horses and weapons to make me a hero, and win fame at court. But beneath it, a darkness yawned to swallow me, haunted by the misshapen monsters of lies, and truths forbidden, where power and riches were mocking deceptions, reasons for death to pursue me. For young as I was, I understood that her new kindness was only a mask. She was biding her time. With the baby's every new inch of growth, her determination grew that all would become his. To outwit my death, I learnt a double vision, to move through the world of light, but also to search the darkness. To be ready for its dangers."

Before them, the familiar walls and peaked roofs loomed against the stars, and beyond, rising higher, the twin towers of the palace gates. Their familiar security seemed alien, a gateway to the shadow world of which he spoke. Or, she thought, they were on the wrong side of the portal, and the court but a shadow realm where pretty deceits masked vicious truths. Lord Adam turned partly away from the buildings with their lit windows, toward the blackness of a small grove where fallen blossoms ornamented the grass like scented snow.

"She did try again, didn't she?" Isabel asked quietly.

"Of course," he answered, as if she had asked whether he ever had a tutor or the mumps. "My vigilance served me well, until she used my own inquisitiveness against me. Discovering a forbidden door in the cellar unlocked and thinking myself alone, I investigated to see what secrets I could discover. Instead I found myself trapped. I had mastered my fear of dark rooms, but this time was different. My father did not know where I was. I would die in a windowless, subterranean cell of stone, with no companions but dank earth and the small, shapeless crawling things. And I thought I'd known darkness before.

"I will own, it taught me interesting lessons. Absolute fear. Eternity. But not isolation. I was no more alone there than in the midst of others who would not hear the truth. Actually, I spent only two days there. In the search for me, one of the old servants had the wit to remember the disused cellar, unlikely though the chance seemed. Yet even then, the truth did not come to light. Not for my father. He would tolerate no word against his wife. Any servants who suspected the truth dared not press it. After all, I had little of the childish confiding or trust that wins affection. The final attempt occurred when I was eight. Her cruelty, and her madness, had grown apace. She poisoned me so cleverly that even I did not realize it. She fooled the physician as well. It was Father who discovered it. Finally, he had begun to doubt her. He placed her under guard and tended me himself. When I was well enough, he sent me to a monastery 'for my education,' as he termed it. Though we both knew better, he would never speak to me of what had really happened."

"Even after you were grown?"

"Madness and scandal, in the Colford family?"

They emerged from the trees, and in the moonlight she saw him smile. If it was an attempt at sophisticated irony, it failed. Too much of the hunted child had emerged from the depths of his eyes to their surface. The reflections of terrors controlled but not vanquished floated like the sheen of starlight on the darkness.

"Yet it was the truth and your father's love that saved you." Isabel solaced not the man, but the child whose fear dilated his eyes.

"It was his disillusionment with a lie," he answered. "Oh, friendship and loyalty can be real, I'll grant you that. I watched Norfolk weep heartfelt tears as he condemned his closest friend to death."

"The Duke of Buckingham, you mean? There was no choice. He plotted against my father."

"Did he? I was one of the judges too, and heard the evidence. It seemed likely Buckingham would have rebelled, given time, but his only actual offense was in his tongue—and in standing too close in line for the throne. And now, here is this matter of the Sun and Stars, and your cousin."

"For whom you feel friendship, whatever you may say. This time, you aren't condoning a wrongful death."

"That remains to be seen. As does Hugh's guilt or innocence."

"You still doubt him? Is there no one you trust, no one you believe is what he or she seems?"

The terrible, fearing, knowing eyes closed. "Only Alice." When Isabel remained quiet, he explained. "My wife—for one short year."

"She died in childbirth?" It came out before Isabel was aware.

"No. A fever. She was unlike all others I've ever known. Alice spoke little and said only what she meant. So gentle was she that I never heard her raise her voice. Perhaps she was no great wit, but she delighted quietly in everyday matters. And she cared to please me. Though it was an arranged marriage, I even allowed myself to imagine she liked me for myself. As for me, I gained peace in her arms."

"In short, you loved her. And still do."

Though he would not speak the words, she could see it was so. Odd that this harsh, arrogant scorpion of a man had loved with such gentleness.

Adam opened his eyes, their haughty fire quenched.

Instinctively, she moved closer to warm him. His fingers pressed firmly against her cheek, turning her face up to the starlight. "You are nothing like Alice. You most definitely wear a mask." She scarce heard his whisper. "What are you behind it? Not the spoilt, naive royal pet. You are not what you pretend."

"Nor you," Isabel whispered.

The vulnerability in his eyes had an unaccountable, terrible beauty. It overwhelmed her with a sorrow as fierce as joy, a fearful sweetness that filled her until she wanted only to taste more. Raising her lips to his, she felt him lean to her in the dark. The soft heat of his lips brushed hers.

He gave a start and stepped back.

Isabel opened her eyes to see the vague mass of a cloaked figure moving away on the walk. It paused uncertainly. "Apologies for my intrusion, Lady Isabel. I heard voices I thought might be yours, but didn't intend to disturb your privacy."

Isabel gripped Colford's sleeve. "You wished to speak with me, Sir Brian?"

In the dim silver light she saw Harrow glance about him and approach. Unobtrusively, Adam's hand slipped to the hilt of his sword. Harrow's, however, moved away from his, making his peaceful intentions clear. "If it's convenient?" Despite his embarrassment, his voice delicately conveyed urgency.

"It is convenient," Adam said firmly. His hand stayed on his sword.

Harrow drew near and eyed Adam thoughtfully.

"Lord Colford stays," Isabel said.

Harrow's eyes caught the starlight briefly as his glance flicked between them. "I realize you're no enemy, Lord Colford. Since we spoke yesterday, I've been in indecision. I imagined events would fall out differently and felt no alarm that the King's displeasure would light on me. Now that it has, I dare wait no longer." He paused, then as if plunging into fire, continued. "You see, if I tell the truth, I have much to fear from my enemies, but nothing to fear from His Majesty."

"Go on," Adam ordered sharply.

Harrow made another quick survey of the darkness, but no one was to be seen. Nevertheless, his voice lowered to a murmur. "Since my return from Venice—"

A thin whistling pierced the air. Harrow gave a sharp, eerie cry. Adam flung Isabel to the ground and flattened himself beside her. Though he had dumped her into the chill dew, Isabel pressed herself into it. She too had recognized the whine of an arrow.

She and Adam were easy targets. There was no cover within crawling distance. She went rigid with fear as a second keening sounded. A shaft lodged in the grass inches from her shoulder. With a curse of great resentment, Adam flung himself sideways, covering her with his body. "You're too high," she hissed, "too exposed."

"Silence."

Isabel's heart hammered against the anvil of her ribs as she pressed as flat as possible, ears straining to hear the next shot. A moment passed, and another. All was silent but for Adam's shallow, wary breaths against her neck. Beside them, Harrow lay unmoving. Catching a muted rustle from the grove behind them, Isabel raised her head a fraction to see over Adam's arm. For a split second she glimpsed a mass against the branches, then it disappeared, leaving only stillness.

Chapter Sixteen

Sir Brian Harrow stared at the stars, Isabel and Adam, all of them one to his unseeing surprise. The arrow bristled stiffly from his chest, a stick edged with feathers, an all the more terrifying end to a life for seeming so inconsequential. Isabel shuddered violently, and again, unable to stop herself.

"This position has interesting possibilities," Adam murmured, his lips warm against her ear.

Isabel pulled the shreds of her courage about her. "My thanks for saving my life. Now, please get off."

"That's better." He sat up. She saw concern in his glance, and also that he had purposely goaded her out of her terror. Releasing his hold on her, he bent to Harrow. "Point-device!" With caustic mockery he echoed King Henry's praise at many a hunt. "A fine eye and a steady hand."

"That isn't amusing," Isabel told him.

"It isn't meant to be," he replied grimly. "Harrow's fallen prey to an expert archer. This time, I think you needn't look for a hired cutthroat, but a sporting gentleman."

"Of which there are all too many at this court." Isabel closed Sir Brian's eyes.

"I thought I glimpsed movement in the trees. Could you make out anything?"

"Someone moving stealthily. The shoulders were of average span for a man, but his head was hidden by a cluster of leaves. He's gone now."

Adam examined the arrow closely. "I know this fletcher's work, but he makes arrows for half the people at court. A careful slaughter as well as daring, wouldn't you say?"

"You don't suppose the archer considers his job only half done?" Isabel said doubtfully. "Shouldn't we get inside?"

"Had he wanted us, we were all too exposed."

"Then, you may be right that he wasn't the man on the rooftops." Isabel fought successive waves of queasiness. "That is, if the second arrow was only meant to keep us pinned down. But did the killer wish Sir Brian dead, or only to silence him?"

"Harrow suspected he was being followed. Remember the way he kept looking around him?"

"It was not the King he feared," she answered. "Nor, seemingly, us."

"Then he shouldn't have dawdled so." Colford's tone was harsh with annoyance, but his hand on Harrow's shoulder was compassionate. "Well, we can do nothing for Sir Brian, and dark though it is, we are in rather public territory. On the chance we've been seen by someone other than the murderer, I think it wise to conceal nothing."

"We have nothing to conceal," Isabel answered in surprise.

"No?" In the starlight, she made out the faint hint of a smile. "Not that in a fit of idiocy I prated nonsense to you, and had not Harrow interrupted us, I might have lost my head and kissed the King's daughter?"

Isabel stared at his dark shape. They had nearly kissed? And she had wanted to? She took a steadying breath. "Of course."

"Well, time we raised a hue and cry." Standing, he gathered a lungful of air. "Guards! Murder! Ho, Guards!"

"I shall sail to Madagascar and climb a tree," said Isabel.

Adam roused himself from his ponderings, weary but inquiring.

"I find there's little difference between being an investigator and a lemur," she told him. "Acrobatics and jabbering all night, with no choice left but to snore all day." She covered a yawn, leaning her elbows on her aunt's empty dining table.

"Let us hope it won't come to that," he answered, but already it was late, and nothing felt more impossible than sleep. The guards summoned by him had in turn called forth Cardinal Wolsey and the Duke of Norfolk, who as Earl Marshal of England considered the matter his jurisdiction, not the Cardinal's. Sir Giles and Sir Thomas More were also summoned, and Thomas Cromwell appeared, unbidden but drawn by some mysterious sixth sense. Though as a mere servant of Wolsey's, he kept silence at the back of the room, Isabel was aware of him throughout the interview, pale and squat as a toad, devouring every word, every nuance, that buzzed by him.

By tacit agreement, she and Lord Adam had recounted only the events of Brian Harrow's death, and even then Isabel thought it prudent to leave most of the telling to him. If the Cardinal was pleased at the demise of an enemy who no doubt knew a few awkward things about him, his grave face and his hands' dignified stillness gave no hint of it. His first glance at

Colford held a trace of question, which Adam answered by an almost indiscernible nod. Thereafter, the Cardinal steered his questions well away from Lord Adam's secret work. Instead, with great deliberation he considered each detail of the killing itself. Taking his cue from Wolsey, More confined himself, lawyer-like, to confirming by the angle of the arrow and Harrow's fall that the arrow had in fact come from the trees. He joined the force of his opinion to Adam's that guards with lanterns should be sent to search the grove for any signs the murderer might have inadvertently left behind. Sir Giles verified their presence in his chambers beforehand, but watching his brother like a kingfisher questing over a stream, made no mention of their talk about Harrow.

It was the Duke of Norfolk who rendered the interview awkward. Of all this collection of conspiracies he knew nothing, save that his arch-enemy Wolsey was appropriating a matter that should be under his authority. Though an excellent archer himself, he would have nothing to do with the discussion of arrows, angles and distances. "My lord," he addressed Adam, "you say Harrow approached you. Did he speak before the dart struck?"

"He spoke, Your Grace, but not enough to reveal his purpose," Adam evaded calmly.

"It is my place to decide what the deceased's words may or may not reveal," the Duke contradicted. "What exactly were his words?"

Adam glanced at Isabel and lifted a brow slightly in apology. "Your Grace, he expressed embarrassment at intruding."

Sir Giles looked equally embarrassed. Sir Thomas More, the King's close friend, shot Isabel a stern glance. After an awkward pause, Cardinal Wolsey cleared his throat. "It would seem, Your Grace, that other matters shall prove more vital than the private converse of Lord Adam and Lady Isabel. They did not draw the bow that killed Sir Brian. We are concerned only with who did."

For once, Isabel blessed the Cardinal for his worldliness—and his astuteness.

Besides the Cardinal, Norfolk was the only member of the company provided with a chair. Though he was the smaller man, he tilted his head back, sighting down his bony nose at the Cardinal. "Since neither the lord nor the lady saw the murderer clearly, his position in the trees is of small import. His motive, on the other hand, may reveal his identity." Having exposed the Cardinal's faulty methods, he delivered his *coup de grace*. "Remember, a great mystery hangs unsolved at this court. Any who failed to consider that this violence may have bearing on the Sun and Stars would be negligent indeed."

"Agreed," Wolsey returned blandly. "The killer's motivation would no doubt aid in discovering him—*if* we had any means of discovering *it*. Yet I doubt if it was to preserve this lord and lady from interruption."

Her face burning, Isabel glared at Adam Colford. His insinuation had deflected Norfolk's inquisitiveness, but she could not help comparing Hugh's steadfast chivalry with Colford's wretched lack of it.

"I confess I also have difficulty imagining the murderer trailing Sir Brian about the palace, ready to kill him when, but only when, he attempts to reveal some portentous matter," Wolsey rubbed it in. "Yet no doubt he did have some purpose for this murder, and we shall most assuredly probe into it when we find him."

"*If* you find him," Norfolk retorted sourly. "My lord Cardinal, it would be more suitable for a commander experienced in action—"

"—To occupy himself discovering why the palace guards—ultimately under his command—failed to apprehend the archer *before* the murder," Wolsey overrode him. "If he was a resident at court, he had no business skulking at night with a bow and arrow. If an intruder, why then the breach of security is most appalling. A hired assassin, breaking into the King's palace to murder a gentleman in the King's service? Assuming he did not shoot astray, and actually intend to kill the King's own daughter. Sweet Jesu," he murmured as if only now struck with the enormity of it. "What shall I say to His Majesty?"

The Duke paled and spent the rest of the discussion glowering and taciturn. In the end, each went to attend to his own portion of the matter. As Isabel and Adam left, Cromwell gave them the beady eye. Isabel felt that had she been a fly his tongue would have picked her neatly out of the air.

"What of the Duke of Norfolk's rummaging?" she now thought aloud. "Was it really only an attempt to show up Wolsey, or did he have other reasons for pressing to know what Sir Brian said to us?"

"Whoever the archer was, he couldn't have heard us from the trees," Adam agreed. "But if Norfolk's got anything to do with it, I'm entirely out of my reckoning."

"In or out of your reason, my lord, you and my lady must not remain supperless as well as sleepless." Ursula entered the dining hall with two plates of cold meat and white bread. He gave her a glance from the corner of his eye, not missing her impudent misquote. Yet, to Isabel's surprise he did not ignore her. "Good Mistress Whatever-your-name, if you must listen, sit here and do it."

Plainly welcoming the invitation, Ursula took a seat at the table. Isabel was pleased he realized her opinion might be helpful.

"Harrow's words," Isabel repeated them for Ursula's benefit as well as theirs, '*You see, my lady, if I tell the truth, I have much to fear from my enemies, but nothing to fear from*

~ 177 ~

His Majesty.' That scarcely sounds like the beginning of a confession to the crime."

"Those were his exact words?" Lord Adam frowned as if searching his memory.

"Think what you like of my lady," Ursula told him, "but doubt her memory at your own risk."

"Oh, I'll not risk anything with this lioness. Whatever she lacks of ladylike mildness, she'd make an excellent comrade under fire. You gave a pretty blush before Norfolk and saved us from all sorts of awkward speculations about our sudden insep-arability."

"I feel quite separable from you, my lord, and most displeased to have gossip run through the court that we did things we never did."

"I could say the same," Adam returned. "Just now, I'm in the market for a suitable and gainful marriage. I would not have whatever lady I approach shun me on account of an erroneous rumor."

He gave not the slightest flicker of acknowledgement that anything at all had nearly happened between them. Isabel suspected he was as alarmed at the vulnerability he had revealed as she was at the kiss that had nearly followed. She was relieved he wished to forget it, but that was no reason for him to scourge her vanity. But her pride was stronger than her vanity, so she covered it. "Harrow said one thing else. *'Since my return from Venice—'*" She looked at Ursula. "That was when the arrow so discourteously interrupted him."

"Much to fear from his enemies, but nothing from His Majesty," Lord Adam mused. "As you say, it hardly sounds like a confession—if he wasn't lying."

"But it did have the ring of an explanation. I believe it was the manner of a man telling the truth."

"And I will never be so incautious as to believe anything

based on no better proof than a person's manner," Adam rejoined. But he gave a small, caustic smile. "Though the part about danger from his enemies proved true enough."

"Must you always smile at death?" she asked.

"Always," he answered.

Knowing what she knew now, she had no answer. She returned to the more urgent matter. "Unless Cardinal Wolsey is behind the theft, Harrow had more enemies than we realized."

"Eat your supper," scolded Ursula. "I went to trouble to have it prepared, and it's getting cold."

Absentmindedly, Adam took out his fork. To hide her amusement at his obedience, Isabel cut her cold venison and fell to.

Lord Adam Colford ate as fastidiously as she'd imagined he would. "The alliance with France will be the culmination of many years' work for Wolsey. He'd hardly abandon it for a personal feud. What's more, it's Harrow who was wronged by the Cardinal, not the other way around."

"Sir Brian knew something against Wolsey," Isabel reminded him. "Whatever it was, it pleased him."

"If Harrow had something on Wolsey, he might well try to bring down his old enemy. Say if the Cardinal were not merely protecting my secret work tonight. Say if he were deceiving me as well as Norfolk and my brother." Beneath the surface of his eyes she saw the same dark flicker as when he had considered the notion in Sir Giles' chamber.

"So, *Wolsey* pretends the crown is stolen?" She considered the notion, and found it possible.

"Part of a chief minister's job is to be blamed when one dare not blame the King."

"Back to that, are we? Steal his own crown? Shame himself before his court and all Europe? Even if my lord father could

bear the taste of humble pie—which as you well know he
can't—two of his own guards were murdered. And what of
Hugh?"

"The pie may have a certain savor if you know its secret
ingredients. Besides getting his way and keeping the Sun and
Stars, what a last laugh he would finally have on his great rival,
King Francis!"

"No!" Isabel slammed her wine cup down. "He would
never murder Hugh in cold blood!"

"No? But does that leave matters at a pass any prettier? If
the crown is really stolen, but not by Harrow, who besides the
Venetians covet the Sun and Stars enough to risk His Majesty's
wrath? Not the Emperor, the King of Portugal, nor the Grand
Turk. Except for the honor it symbolizes to ourselves, France
and Venice, it's not such an extraordinary treasure as all that."

"What are you hinting? Come out and say it," she
challenged.

"You must see it yourself, deny it all you like. If it's no
scheme of the King's, we ought to look more warily at Sir
Hugh."

"Curse you for a suspicious, disloyal villain! As soon as
you're at a loss, all your friendship, all your trust, evaporates
like mist!"

"I suffer no trust," Colford answered as if it were a disease.
"At this court, let sentiment do your thinking for you and you'll
go down."

"Live barren of trust, and no one will mourn if you do go
down," Isabel hurled back. "I'd rather die on the scaffold than
give no love nor loyalty where it's deserved, and inspire no
friendship in anyone at all."

If her words cut him, he refused to show it. "Other than
Harrow, Hugh is the only Englishman at court who has sworn
loyalty and *friendship* to a Venetian. He was among the arming

tents. Note who's dead. The earless felon who helped with the theft, and Harrow who must have known more than anyone else of Ferrero's dealings with Hugh."

"Who killed them? Hugh, firing birdshot from his window in the Tower?"

"Any of Hugh's numerous, *loyal friends*," he rubbed it in, the same salt she had used on his wound. So, to be called unloved did cut him, after all. "Robin Tremayne, for instance?"

"No, not Robin."

"What of their covert business?"

"I tell you, it's irrelevant."

"Then what of you? Cromwell has his suspicions, and perhaps for once he's shrewder than I."

Isabel sighed, weary of him beyond words.

"Why not? You have the wit for it, and as you proved tonight, the nerve. Should I trust you simply because your fine furies make your breasts heave so enchantingly beneath your pearls?" He gave her a feral flash of his teeth, but then it was gone. He pushed away his plate. When he spoke again, his voice was ice. "As a matter of fact, I don't suspect you. But I rely on neither trust nor impulse. If I wish to survive and prosper, my reason is all I have. Until I know the answer, I shall examine every possibility."

"Be my guest. Meanwhile, I shall sleep." She rose. "What course do you mean to follow tomorrow?"

"I'm not sure," he admitted. "Wolsey will send for me, no doubt. I'll tell him most everything but my suspicion of the King and himself. But I haven't forgotten tomorrow is Hugh's last day. Innocent or guilty, I mean to spare him from torture, if I can."

Isabel stepped from the tinted lights and hush of the chapel to an early morning breeze infused with the warmth of the sun. The young leaves filtered the brightness, staining the cloistered walk as if she had left the blues and crimsons of the chapel windows for a wider hall of branches glassed with living, breathing panes of peridot.

"That was time well spent," Ursula said. "You've neglected your prayers since this started."

"I need God on my side just now," Isabel agreed. "And a few saints, while we're at it."

Ursula's voice dropped. "Saints, indeed! If yonder waits the help they've sent, your prayers have gone amiss."

At the end of the cloistered walk stood Master Cromwell with a cat-at-the-mouse-hole look. Isabel's stomach balled up, queasy and tight, but she stepped from the cloister to the paving stones. She was nearly past him when he looked up. "Good morning, Lady Isabel."

Despite his polite tone, his addressing her first was a breach of manners. It was up to a king's daughter to decide whether to speak. "Good day, Master Cromwell." Isabel continued past him.

But whether she would or no, he matched her pace. Ursula gave him an indignant stare, and though she dropped behind, kept close at their heels. "Forgive my lack of ceremony, my lady," Cromwell said in confidential quiet. "I'm most anxious for a word with you."

That he had known where to find her was far from reassuring. "About the murder of Sir Brian Harrow? Surely you should speak with your colleague Lord Colford about that."

Cromwell's pale lips twisted in what looked more like

resentment than humor. "Lord Colford, my colleague? My lady, the lord is a nobleman of distinction, culture and great pride. Do you imagine he would condescend to such a relationship with a lowly lawyer?"

"Some are worth his respect." Isabel knew insulting Cromwell was not wise, but could not resist her dislike of the man. "It depends on the lawyer."

"Perhaps. Or, upon the nobleman? The lord is not overburdened with friends." He glanced at her slyly. "Nor, may I hazard a guess, overburdened with admiring ladies? But never fear. The Duke of Norfolk, More and the rest seem convinced by your ploy. Last night Norfolk went away muttering about couples roving unchaperoned in the King's parks as if that were as bad as the murder." He smiled, but Isabel gave him no quarter. As if used to it, he calmly resumed. "However, my Lord Colford has told me what really occurred, and your errand beforehand. Most clever of his lordship. Particularly, the key." A delicate pause.

Isabel caught herself just in time. Inwardly she cursed Adam Colford. If he told Cromwell tales, the least he could do was inform her of them. Outwardly she strolled on, hands clasped before her in the approved style for young ladies, her eyes lowered modestly to the ground. "Yes," she murmured, "the key."

"I confess I'd like to have seen him purloin it from Sir Giles. Pilfering is not the sort of activity one imagines of his lordship. I take it Harrow's Venetian negotiations were inconclusive, and his confession to you—as much of it as he managed to get out before he died—cast doubts about his guilt in Lord Colford's mind."

"In mine, too," Isabel answered carefully. She understood Adam's withholding the truth about his brother's help from Cromwell—and from Cardinal Wolsey. While Cromwell would perhaps not divulge Sir Giles' disobedience of a royal command now, he would at some later time, if it suited his purposes.

Or Wolsey's. Giles and Cardinal Wolsey were opponents, at least so far as foreign policy went. Each had labored for years on a strategy directly opposed to the other's.

"Harrow now seems unlikely to have been the ringleader."

"Most unlikely," Isabel agreed.

"Which, unhappily, makes this errand necessary. You've been a great help to us, Lady Isabel. And, through us, to your most noble father. If you will, you can perform one more service."

"For my lord father? Or merely for you?"

"For Sir Hugh. As you know, the task of learning the truth from him falls on me. As will His Majesty's wrath should I fail. Forcing a confession from a man of Sir Hugh's mettle can be slow and uncertain."

"Especially if the man has nothing to confess."

"You look on me with loathing, as if I were one of those twisted creatures who take a prurient delight in torture. I assure you, lady, I'm not. The tongs and the rack are tools, like any other."

His matter-of-fact tone sent a shiver crawling up the back of her neck. Isabel's anger flared. "I'll not urge my cousin to perjure himself, Master Cromwell. All the false confessions your torture can extract won't make Hugh guilty."

"No?" From a purse he drew something small, and opened his hand. "Can these?"

On his palm lay two golden coins, mates to the one she had taken from Carne's chest.

"I see you recognize this currency," he answered her silence. "Lord Colford said you might." If a cold, staring fish in a market stall could feel triumph, it might bear such a smile as Master Cromwell's.

"Where did you get those?"

"From Sir Francis Weston, who was paid them yesterday by Sir Hugh."

"So you say."

"So Weston confirmed, after a Tower guard witnessed it. Even Sir Hugh did not deny it when I confronted him with the coins and witness. Yet even now he will confess to nothing else. My lady, you must persuade your cousin to confess all. If you bear him any affection, you owe him this." Cromwell moved closer, the coins glaring on the fleshy cushions of his palm. "Make no mistake. On this evidence he'll be convicted, however he pleads. But we must have the Sun and Stars. We *must*. Warn him, Lady Isabel. Sir Hugh is utterly in my power, and I will stop at nothing to recover it."

Closing his palm with a small, chill *clink*, Master Cromwell bowed to her and walked away.

Standing still as the trees, Isabel watched the squat grey blot of him dwindle. She imagined the metal of the two coins still burning cold in his palm.

Hugh had never been to Italy, where such coinage was used, and had showed her no Italian coins among the curiosities he had brought back from the Continent. If he himself admitted to paying out Florentine gold, how had he come by it?

And why, if he and Ferrero had sworn eternal brotherhood, had he never once mentioned the Venetian?

Chapter Seventeen

Hugh was sketching when Isabel entered his cell. He smiled and held his drawing out for her to see. It was of the manor in Devon where he had grown up, the details reproduced from memory with admirable accuracy. Clearly, he had spent a very long time on it. "Scarcely one of Master Holbein's masterpieces," he said, "but what do you think?"

"It's a fine likeness."

He resumed his work. "Did you speak with Cecily at the King's entertainment?"

"Briefly. She seemed well, considering." Isabel moved closer. "Time is short, but I must ask you some questions."

"Questions," Hugh echoed. Then he smiled. "Robin has been to see me. He said you danced with the dread Lord Adam Colford. And the two of you left the hall together?" He glanced at her slyly. "Not sweetening toward your friend Tom's nemesis, are you?"

"They can both go swim the bottom of the Thames, for aught I care."

"Good. I never liked Seymour." Hugh's charcoal made soft stroking sounds on the paper.

"Coz."

He did not look up.

Isabel folded her arms. "Did you hear me? I must learn a few answers."

The charcoal went silent, and he gazed full up at her. "My time is all but run out. I have today, and tonight. I'm spending that time as pleasantly as I may." He began sketching in blades of grass. "If you wish to talk of our old pranks before we came to court, I'll welcome that. But there'll be enough questions tomorrow."

"I'm trying to spare you that!"

"Nothing's been any use so far, has it?"

Isabel grabbed his shoulders and shook hard, sending the charcoal flying. But he braced against her, and he was far larger and more solid than she. She felt like a puppy worrying the heels of a charger. "If you despair, I'll march out of this cell in a rage!"

Sighing, he put aside his drawing. "Ask, then. But I'll answer only to please you. I've had enough of the soarings and down-plunges of hope."

She let him go and sank onto the other stool. "Cromwell says you gave Sir Francis Weston two Italian gold pieces."

Hugh frowned at her. "What is this bother about the gold? I owed Sir Francis a gambling debt and wished to settle up. I sent him word, he came to the Tower, and I squared it with him. What's so sinister about that?"

"It's not the debt that matters, it's the gold pieces themselves. Where did you get them?"

Hugh shrugged. "From Mother, of course."

"Those coins weren't in the collection at your house."

Hugh's frown deepened. "No. When I opened Mother's

package I noticed some of the money in it was foreign, but foreign gold is as good as English."

Isabel tensed. "You're certain the package came from Aunt Margery?"

"Who else would send me my green hose and a cask of our best wine?" Untangling his long legs from the squat ones of the stool, he went to his chest and rummaged out a pair of pale green netherhose knitted of silk, well worn, and two garters.

"If you claim those as acquaintances I doubt they'll contradict you." She feared her smile lacked cheer.

"What is it, Isabel?"

"I found your earless felon murdered. Coins of that same stamp had been paid to him."

Hugh's eyes widened in alarm, then anger. "And were confiscated by Master Cromwell?"

"No. By the time the soldiers searched his hiding place, the coins were gone. We think the murderer got them. All but one that I pocketed. This morning Cromwell showed me *two*."

"I can show you three more." Reaching beneath the clothes in his chest, Hugh picked among his money, then came and plunked the coins down loudly on the table. "There. Is it these that will cost me my life?"

"With all my heart I pray not," Isabel said faintly. With a numb finger she lined up the three gleaming coins in a row.

"If Mother didn't get them somehow, they were slipped into the package before it reached me. I think we can guess by whom."

"Yes. And there's something else. It's not for your French friends they suspect you. It's because of Giovanni Ferrero."

"Giovanni?" Hugh asked, more perplexed than ever. "Who thinks Giovanni is involved?"

"With the Sun and Stars? Surely you know he is. He's a good friend of yours, as they say?"

"We're no letter writers, but in Paris he was my friend, and I am his if we cross paths again. It's true we spoke of all sorts of things, but never the Sun and Stars. Why have they ceased suspecting the French?"

"I've promised secrecy."

"Not to Cromwell, surely." Then he leaned forward, tensing. "To Colford? He's in this somehow, isn't he? Who else would think to connect me with Giovanni? Isabel, what's going on? It's my life, I've a right to know!"

Isabel looked at him, taken aback by his outburst. But he was right. "Colford did tell me about Ferrero, and he told Cromwell," she admitted. "That, together with these coins, makes it look ominous. But Hugh, if Ferrero is your friend, why did you never mention him to me?"

"I never did?" Hugh thought a moment, then shook his head. "Maybe because most of our adventures weren't fit to tell a lady."

Isabel studied his face carefully, but it was only Hugh's face, his blue eyes angry but forthright, his blond brows lowered and his mouth pressed closed, but with no line she had not seen before.

"Why do you watch me so closely?" he said at last.

"No reason."

"Do I hear doubt? Even from you?"

"No."

"But I do, coz."

She stood. "I'm going. I mean to find the source of those coins. Whoever it may be, I will pursue them until they sit in this Tower." Without another glance at him, she crossed to the door and banged on it for the guard.

As the boat made its too-slow way downstream, Isabel thought out her battle plan. If she questioned Aunt Margery about the coins at once, it would be afternoon before she got to Greenwich. If she sent Ursula instead, she would not be able to see her aunt's reaction. Yet why should that matter if she believed Hugh? It was odd that he had not told her of Ferrero, but not necessarily sinister. After all, she had not told Hugh about Tom. Loyalty ran deep in Hugh. Whatever his friendship with the Venetian, he would not forswear his allegiance to his king and country.

Yes, Hugh's love and loyalty ran deep. As when he had refused the King's command to reveal the matter of Cecily. But that was also different. The well-being, perhaps the very lives, of Cecily and her son depended on his silence. Between two impossible choices, Hugh had done what he believed right.

As, perhaps, he would if he felt some equally pressing need to protect his friend Ferrero?

Isabel gripped the seat of the boat, wishing it would cease its giddy sway; having no firm ground beneath her was swelling her dizzy uncertainty by the moment.

Perhaps she should go to Aunt Margery herself.

Isabel wondered at herself. The shocks of murders and cold-blooded betrayals had shaken her until nothing in the world would ever be the same. Even the very sunlight seemed changed, a sparkling and flaring on mere surfaces, hollow and brittle as an eggshell. Had the last few days poisoned her reasoning or awakened it to the truth?

She did not know. Nothing was certain any longer.

Except for one thing. In the absence of proof, when reason

no longer showed the way, she must have faith in her instincts. Her instincts trusted Hugh.

She would not question her aunt herself. She would send Ursula.

As soon as the boat nosed the quay at Greenwich, Isabel was out and hurrying across the grounds. She had bid Ursula fish for palace gossip about Brian Harrow's death, and she was probably still at it. Isabel crossed the garden lawn, nearing the place where Harrow had left the path to speak to them. The grass showed no stain of his blood, and the grove of flowering trees, well-searched now, seemed deceptively innocent by daylight. She thought of Lady Angela Harrow, whose tall elegance and husky voice she had always so admired. At the entertainment, all the little signs between her and Sir Brian had borne the unmistakable stamp of love. Saddened anew at how much more a death destroyed than a single life, Isabel hastened away.

But this time no instinct had spoken to her. Sir Brian's murder did not clear him of suspicion. If he had known the identity of the traitor, everything suggested he had possessed that knowledge from the beginning. But then, why did he tell her he'd feared nothing until her ploy convinced him of the King's displeasure?

Lord Adam Colford's theory intruded into her thoughts, and his anger at the notion that he had been led a merry dance. That the theft was a decoy. That for the King's greed, two guards had been murdered, and Carne, and Harrow. And soon, Hugh. Everything in her fiercely resisted thinking her father capable of that, yet the deeper she searched herself, the more dismaying was the difference between her trust in Hugh and her mixed feelings about her father. Not that she agreed with Lord Adam that he would murder for sheer greed. King Henry was open handed to his friends, gambled freely with his

courtiers and paid up with good grace when he lost. He was
the antithesis of the miser king-in-his-counting-house her
grandfather Henry VII had been. Avarice struck her as far
more Adam Colford's flaw than her father's, and it was oft-
times the way of a sooty pot to smear its own grime on others.

Yet if greed was not her father's vice, what of vainglory?

Power and splendor, to prevail triumphant in his own eyes,
those things mattered to King Henry above all. When she
asked whether he would murder for them, the only answer she
could honestly give herself was to pray fervently it was not so.

But if it was, if her father did, after all, mean to sacrifice
Hugh to keep the crown and alliance both, a more dismaying
prospect lay before her than any she had yet considered. The
King's misdeed must be covered, yet Hugh's life must be
saved. However insurmountable the obstacles, however
formidable her opponents, she must concoct a scheme to clear
him, but throw false blame on no one else.

Entering a small side door of the palace, by habit she
climbed a staircase that led to the corridor from which the
Queen's chambers opened. Yet she had no business there, and
no wish to be milked for gossip or commiserated with by those
there whom she usually called her friends. Instead, she paused
at a window seat in the corridor. Having nowhere to go, this
place would do as well as any.

All was quiet. The Queen and her ladies must be out
enjoying the spring sunshine. She doubted she would be
disturbed here. Sitting in the window seat, she gazed blankly at
the opposite wall. Over its wood paneling hung a tapestry. In
the morning light its colors were faded with age, but its
needlework was fine. Its woven figures wore the outlandish
dress of a past time, the women's headdresses like wind-filled
sails, the men's hose parti-colored. One handsome swain in a

surcoat, with the hem dagged and tattered like a fool's motley, knelt to bestow flowers upon a simpering lady. An antic pair they made. Yet they held Isabel's eye, reminding her of something.

"Who cares for your blandishments?" she muttered at the foolishly costumed coxcomb.

The hanging stirred slightly in the breeze from the open window, the kneeling fellow in his jester-like parti-colors seeming to proffer the flowers anew.

Will Somers and his gift.

That was what the figure put her in mind of. The information he'd presented to her in the musicians' gallery. Despite its dubious significance she'd said she would keep it like a nosegay. A scrap of argument Will had overheard last summer, it was. *An Adam berating a Thomas.* Adam Colford reviling Thomas Cromwell for pawing among his papers.

Isabel could imagine the scene all the better, now that she knew him. Let Cromwell deny it till he was as green in the face as the toad he resembled, the suspicion of the man spying among his secrets would enrage My Lord Scorpion to a fine fury of lashing and stinging. Isabel wished she had heard the entertainment. Perhaps it enlivened that long, too-damp summer while the court traipsed the soggy countryside cramming itself into one courtier's manor house after another.

Isabel's hand closed on the cushion of the window seat.

Still clutching it, she began searching the notion that was coming to her. The farther she probed, the faster her pulse raced, until at last she could sit still with it no longer. Rising, she descended the stairs, seeing nothing but the darkness of her thoughts, and the pain they would cause if they were true. Hoping to find a flaw, she tested each memory of the last five days against her notion, but the harder she examined it, and the faster she paced, the more certain she was, until she stopped altogether.

She knew the answer.

She hated the truth she had discovered, and dreaded what she must do about it, but loathe though she was, her discovery left her no choice. With reluctant foreboding, she crossed to the wing where Lord Colford had told her he kept rooms and she could find him.

Chapter Eighteen

ord Adam had left two hours ago to attend the King, a
servant wearing his colors told her. No one knew when
he would return. Wishing only to get the deed over
with, Isabel made for the royal chambers.

Passing through the great guarded door of dark oak, she saw
the long outer gallery sprinkled with a fair scattering of people.
They stood by the gothic windows in little conversing groups,
sat upon the brocade-cushioned benches along the walls, or
moved along the black and white chessboard of the marble
floor.

Isabel saw mostly gentlemen of lesser official rank, private
secretaries and attendants wearing on their sleeves the badges
of Cardinal Wolsey, the Dukes of Norfolk and Suffolk, and
several lords and knights. It spelled no private audience but
some larger gathering that might continue for hours.

Suppressing an impatient sound, Isabel paused. As she did,
she noted Cromwell alone on a bench scribbling rapid notes. As
if possessed of some extra, eyeless perception of his own, he

glanced up at her and inclined his head. She was not about to approach him. This was not yet a matter for Cromwell, of all people. Not until she had heard two answers.

Beneath an open window stood Thomas Wyatt with others who were Hugh's friends in better days. Wyatt at least had the decency to be embarrassed and avert his gaze from hers. Unlike Sir Piers Knevet, who, predictably, hovered in the hopes of riding fortune's cloak hem. He whispered with one or two other hangers-on, casting curious glances at her, the only woman daring to intrude on this male sanctum of policy.

But frustrating as it was to be patronized as a court pet, it had its advantages. Though others might have urgent business with one of the lords closeted with the King, none of them would dare do what she was about to. Asking paper, ink and a quill of one of the secretaries, she swiftly composed a note, then folded the paper small. By this time nearly all the men watched her, so it was not difficult to catch the eye of Lord Adam's page. The boy approached, but when she murmured her directions he stared at her aghast. "Go," she commanded quietly. "If His Majesty is angry, just say you're intruding on my order. If you delay, you risk retribution from both your master and me. Off with you!"

With an ill-natured glower perhaps learnt from his master, which no doubt masked an understandable qualm about his task, the boy bowed and made his way up the gallery to the tall inner doors. Isabel watched while the guards heard him out. They cast scandalized glances at Isabel but she lifted her chin, nodding peremptory confirmation. They let him enter.

For the benefit of her audience, Isabel strolled casually to an unoccupied window and gazed out. She let none of them see she was battening down her hatches for a storm.

It came, as surely as if following an ominous red dawn. Lord Adam Colford's advance was the rolling of its thunderclouds, his eye its lightning. "What do you mean, calling me out of a conference with the King?" he hissed in a fury no less intense for being audible only to her.

"May we speak privately?"

He as much jerked as escorted her away from the avid spectators, down the gallery to a small, ornate door. Finding the chamber within empty, she hastened over the threshold before he could fling her in. He closed the door behind them with a thud. She turned to face him across the paneled room. It was little more than a closet, dim as a wooden box. A room suited to dreadful matters. "Two questions," she began. "First, while we were on progress last month, did you accuse Cromwell of trespassing into your private papers?"

As she had hoped, he put aside his anger long enough to consider. "So I did," he answered. "And halted his fingers' wandering among my property for a while, I hope."

"What papers were they?"

"I keep all my week's business in the same case. It occurred while we were at Woodstock, so if you wonder whether they included notes on the plan to return the crown, the answer is yes. But I use a cryptic method of making notes. Cromwell would understand little of them."

"When the case wasn't in your hand, no doubt you kept your papers as closely as an oyster its pearl?"

"You've already had your two questions."

"No, I'm still on the first. When I come to the second I'll let you know."

With an acerbic quirk of his mouth he gave in. "I kept them locked in a stout chest in my bedchamber and the key on a chain beneath my doublet. But this is pointless. Cromwell knew all the plans for the Sun and Stars. No harm could come of his spying but breach of privacy."

"Yet you're sure someone pried among them? You hadn't merely disarranged them yourself and forgotten it?"

"They weren't disarranged," he retorted. "I always set a contrivance against spies. A small sign that can't stop intrusion, but will warn me if it occurs. If your all-consuming curiosity hopes to discover what sign, it must remain unsatisfied. I wouldn't put it past you to steal a glimpse into my paper case."

His offensiveness made it a little easier. Yet she still had to steel herself for the blow she was about to deliver. "This is my second question: Woodstock was cramped quarters for us all. Did you share your bedchamber?"

He gave her a scathing look. "That is most definitely none of your business."

"Please," she appealed.

"As it happens, at Woodstock I shared quarters with my brother."

His words dropped the full weight onto her shoulders. "Can he read your cryptic style of notes?"

"Giles?" Adam Colford stared at her. "I thought you had reached the height of your fever-delusions with your suspicion of me."

"You were keeping the truth from me then. Now that I know, my suspicions are all too rational."

"I must return to His Majesty's business."

"Let us say—for the sake of the argument—that Sir Giles did manage to get your key long enough to open the chest in your shared room and read your papers. An ironic twist on your tale of pilfering Giles' key, if it's so."

"Not ironic. Impossible. But—for the sake of the argument—let us concoct the fantasy that he did waft the key from around my neck by magic. Giles understands my manner of making notes. Our father liked cryptic writing and taught us both his own system. But if you imagine Giles would stoop to Cromwell's habits, you're much mistaken."

"I don't. Cromwell would pry simply because a chest is locked. Sir Giles, perchance, would do so only if his purpose outweighed his reluctance. And he did have a purpose. By then, whispers were abroad of the King's rapprochement with the French. The King was about to choose between the two great powers of Europe. If your brother is anything like you, he's not the sort to let years of his best work land in the midden."

"You express yourself with such delicacy, my lady," he mocked harshly. "In fact, my brother is nothing like me. He would do what he believed best for England, whatever the cost to himself."

"Would he, indeed?" Isabel received the information with a sense of confirmation. "If he looked at your papers, he would learn of the plan to return the Sun and Stars to King Francis. If he wished to destroy France's tenuous trust in us, he now had the means."

"You're clutching at cobwebs. Were Giles a scoundrel, there might be something to it. If anything, my brother is moral to a fault."

"I've not seen nor heard aught to contradict that. Yet for the sake—"

"—Of occupying me with fantasies and bringing the King's displeasure down on my head—"

Resolutely, she pushed on. "Let's assume that all Sir Giles needed was to wait for the Sun and Stars to become vulnerable. Many people knew my father was to joust, and the gentlemen of his chamber would all know what crown he was to wear that day. That Hugh would attend the tournament was certain. The injury that kept him from competing was immaterial. It was only necessary to add Robin's supposed note to put him in the vicinity of the crime."

"A hole in your reasoning. If it were Giles, wouldn't he find Harrow a better decoy than Hugh?"

"I don't know," Isabel admitted. "Sir Giles himself was in the stands during the joust. I saw him come down to the King's aid. That means he would need to hire at least one other to assist the earless felon Carne with the theft. Who, I don't know. The man who killed Carne?"

"From your description of his monkey-scamper over the rooftops, the cutthroat knew the neighborhood. He was another ruffian like Carne. But it would take at least one person familiar to the guards to get the thieves into the arming tents."

"Odd that Hugh saw no one, either known to him or unknown, but Carne," she admitted. "Well, leave that for now. Whoever they were, they killed the two guards, took the Sun and Stars and delivered it to Sir Giles, who paid them in Italian gold with the same purpose that led him to put the blame on Hugh. Yet a few days later, for some reason he changed his mind.; He decided to do away with Carne and repossess the gold. I wonder why."

"And that suggests forethought?" Adam replied. "Whoever the traitor—if there is indeed a traitor and a real theft—he could not have foreseen your stumbling upon the gold, far less intended it to happen. Therefore, the Florentine coinage was not a decoy. Which points the guilt not at my brother but an Italian source."

"I did not stumble. I searched. Sir Giles must have known the danger of someone getting hold of it at some point. But on to last night. When you and I came seeking Sir Giles' help, how that must have pleased him! Surely he guessed your covert involvement with the Sun and Stars would obligate you to secretly investigate its theft. When we turned up on his doorstep he knew for certain. He probed to discover whom you suspected and also into the matter of Hugh's forged note. He wrote it without knowing the real dealings between Hugh and Robin, and wanted to make sure he'd made no mistakes there. When you mentioned Harrow and asked to see the records, Giles could afford to make his reluctance convincing. After all, he knew you held the ultimate weapon over him and would use it if you must. Having leveraged his guilt unfairly against him and regretting it bitterly, how could you doubt his honest reluctance? But that reluctance was only a show. He was eager to show you those records."

"Eager!" Lord Adam's nostrils flared disdainfully.

"He had to shake your suspicions of Sir Brian Harrow, don't you see? He was about to eliminate Sir Brian. If we had continued to think Sir Brian guilty, his death would lead us to search for some highly placed cohort. We might have begun to consider Giles. After all, they did work together. No, he had to send us in another direction, so he carefully chose what he showed us. He knew your assailable point. Betrayal. To be used for another's purposes. Remember how he himself pointed out the page that kindled your doubts of the King?"

For the first time, uncertainty crossed Adam's face.

"At all costs, he needed to keep Harrow from talking with us. The tall, thin man my page saw following Sir Brian from the chapel doesn't sound like your brother, but I think it was Giles himself who followed us from his chamber and shot Sir Brian. He's an excellent archer, is he not?"

"As are many at court. You yourself pointed that out."

"He had a clear aim at us. That second arrow came within inches of me. Yet once you shielded me, he stopped shooting."

"And who but Giles would wish to spare me?" He favored her with his most cynical smile, but she could see he was disturbed.

"Having silenced Sir Brian, he paid some Tower guard to slip a few of the telltale gold pieces into my aunt's package for

Hugh. Now that he had incriminated Hugh and planted doubt in your mind whether it would be in your interest to investigate a trail that might lead to the King, he could rest easier. Soon Hugh would also be silenced, and you would find it doubly politic to cease probing. Your next move would be to reassure Des Roches and the other French of your belief in His Majesty's good faith, but could you do it convincingly without the crown, and no longer believing the King *was* acting in good faith? Sir Giles' purpose would be achieved. We would be forced return to the Spanish alliance. His policy would prevail."

"You keep ignoring a large knot in your argument," he reminded her coolly. "The gold coins. Giles doesn't know we're aware of them. For obvious reasons, we've held that information in the strictest secrecy. You, your serving woman, me, Cromwell. No one else knows. Not even Cardinal Wolsey."

"Unless we guessed wrong about the cutthroat, and he did tell Giles about me."

"In which case, slipping them to Hugh would be a fool's errand." Adam paced the narrow width of the room and stood in thought, his back to her. A wren alighted on a branch outside the window and began merrily chirping. Its carefree noise grated Isabel's nerves raw.

At last, he turned. "I do not accept your hypothesis. Hugh would stand to gain a fortune for the Sun and Stars. The King—well, we're agreed that he might wish to keep it. But Giles would gain nothing but a will o' the wisp change in policy. What could be more ephemeral than that? If you wish a sensible motive, look for greed or power. And so, to Hugh or His Majesty."

"You may not credit this, but for some, right and honor mean more than base greed."

"More than power?"

"You accuse my cousin and my father of perfidy."

"You accuse my brother."

So they had ranged themselves, she realized. At a standoff, too angry to accomplish anything. Meanwhile, noon drew on to the afternoon of Hugh's last day. Without warning, tears welled up with sharp force. She struggled grimly to keep them in.

Fortunately, he did not notice her weakness. "And then," he argued quietly to himself, "there's the horse. That's the final proof." He looked over at her. "You, who remember all, no doubt remember my brother's envy over my superb grey colt."

Isabel took a chance she could trust her voice. "The one you hope to make a champion at the air-borne leaps?"

"The very one. In my paper case at Woodstock was a letter from a dealer informing me of the yearling and his owner's willingness to sell. All our lives, Giles and I have waged a passionate rivalry over horses. It was the only antagonism we could safely risk, and in an odd way it held us together when our past and present differences would have driven us apart. If he saw my papers, he saw the letter about the yearling. Giles is resourceful. He would have invented some explanation for his own discovery of the yearling. He could never have resisted the chance to jump in before me to get such a promising horse."

His absolute conviction shook Isabel's certainty for the first time. Weariness overcame her and she closed her eyes.

From beyond the door came the sounds of voices, growing louder as they neared. Rising foremost, she recognized her father's.

"The audience is over," Adam said. "I have indeed missed it all. No doubt I shall suffer penance." But though his words were peeved, he sounded as weighted with cares as she felt.

"Let me take the reproach. After all, it's rightfully mine."

"Shelter behind a lady?" His eyebrow rose disdainfully. "I think not. I came of my free will, and I'll reap my share of royal displeasure with no help from you. And now, I'd better go to it." Without another word to her, he opened the door and stepped out.

Chapter Nineteen

hen the door opened, King Henry's voice silenced. As Lord Adam bowed the stillness reached ominous proportions. Isabel could vividly picture her father's glare. Adam's demeanor became stoic. Unfortunately, on him this attitude was nearly indistinguishable from arrogance. Isabel held her breath in foreboding.

"Well, my lord. We are glad to see your urgent business is discharged. Now, perchance, you may find a sliver of time for Our more trivial matters." It was King Henry's sarcastic tone, a rather high, nasal one that always made Isabel wince, and not entirely for its sound. It presaged retribution.

Lord Adam had the subtlety not to answer at once.

"Will my lord find it convenient now to attend upon his sovereign?" The King made his words a chastising rod. Adam's face was stony, his pride no doubt smarting at being called to order like a schoolboy caught playing truant. Yet in anger the King loved to browbeat, and all who served him knew his enjoyment of this sport was oft-times enough to dispel his ire.

Isabel suspected much of his annoyance came from his own hatred of sitting cooped up for hours on end, and what he really resented was another's escaping a boring session he had perforce endured.

"Well?" King Henry asked. Isabel pictured him standing, hands on hips, powerful legs stanced aggressively wide.

"I crave Your Majesty's pardon," Lord Adam replied, his voice uncharacteristically deferential, yet reserving to itself every iota of dignity.

"No doubt. Stay within call. We wish to speak with you anon—and with you, my lord Cardinal. You both know the matter I mean, so prepare your answers well." This new ominous note was more than irritation. Like hers, the King's time was running out.

Her time was running out, indeed. Some two dozen people had seen her vanish into this room with Colford and knew they had been alone behind a closed door for nearly an hour. It would do her far more harm than good to skulk as her father and his party passed by, as if she had some reason for shame. Lord Adam had wanted to take his dose of her father's displeasure in his own way, and he had. Now she must think of herself.

Isabel placed herself just within the doorway. Their footsteps advanced, and she caught the first glitter of her father's gold reflecting in the polished wood of the door. She curtsied sprightly and low, as one who respected her sovereign's temper but felt no guilty trepidation.

Two great, broad feet, encased in square-toed shoes of scarlet satin, strode into sight on the black and white squares of the floor. Toes of other colors came in sight, soft brown leather, purple velvet and green. One of the large red feet abruptly landed beside the other, and both turned their toes to her.

"It seems," said the scourge of a voice, "we've started not one fox from this den, but two."

Isabel knew better than to speak but looked up with offended reproach.

Her father's small, bright blue eyes glittered down at her with no trace of humor. "Or should I say, a vixen? I'll summon you before this day is out, girl, and by God you'd better have an honest explanation for your gallivanting!"

Isabel curtsied lower. When he was past, she straightened. Cardinal Wolsey, the Dukes of Norfolk and Suffolk, Sir Thomas More and others of the King's closest followers passed her. Sir Giles Colford was with them. He paused, gave Isabel a bow, and beckoned to her and Adam. Smoothing her skirts, and she hoped also her expression, Isabel stepped forward. "Yes, Sir Giles?"

"Good day, Lady Isabel." He took Adam's sleeve, steering him into a walk, too slow to overtake the King and his followers. Isabel joined them. "I pray you," Sir Giles urged quietly, "don't trifle with the King's anger. You know what a mood he's in of late. If, as I presume, brother, you left his presence for the business that brought you to me yesterday, tell him so. After last night's gathering, the Duke of Norfolk went tittling in His Majesty's ear."

"About what?" Adam asked sharply.

"The two of you, and your dalliance yestereve in the park. He ran to the King with the tale that Harrow's unfortunate demise broke up a wanton tryst. He made the worst of the grass stains and damp on your clothes and has puffed it all out of proportion from a harmless kiss."

"Particularly, a kiss that never occurred," Isabel agreed innocently.

"Did it not? Last night you gave us to believe it had." Giles looked surprised, but Isabel caught his new, smiling

~ 207 ~

guardedness. "Or, something of the sort. But if Norfolk likes to imagine you indulging heedless lust on a public lawn, it speaks more of him than you."

He had parried with skill, but Isabel saw the uncertainty in his eyes.

And in Adam's, a sudden widening. As he searched his brother's face, the two startled openings on his soul grew to twin torments of doubt. Denial flared but was devoured by a slower horror of certainty.

Sir Giles' frank blue eyes widened too. Isabel saw in them comprehension. The acknowledgement hung silently between them.

Very quietly, Giles said, "All my life I have given, and given, expiating an evil not my own. Has my love earned aught of yours?"

Adam closed his eyes to hide his pain. Giles laid a hand on his elder brother's shoulder. Then he lengthened his pace to catch up with the King's party.

Adam raised his head. "And what of Sir Hugh Lovell in the Tower, brother?" The clear, englacial resonance of his voice made not only Giles turn, but King Henry and the lords.

Sir Giles frowned, pretending incomprehension. "A most grievous matter. But what of him?"

"And what of the coins you foisted on him?"

Sir Giles started violently. His wondrously plausible puzzlement slowly changed to marvelously plausible disbelief. "Adam? You would speak such a lie, and against me? Surely even your incurable mistrust would not cast so desperately wide, nor use a lie as your net?"

Taking heart from the startled, incredulous faces of the King and his companions, Sir Giles continued, "Or, if it's no lie, I suggest you examine the deeds of the honest Master Cromwell, yonder. Whomever you find responsible, you'll find me absolved of any connection with the coins, still less any attempt to incriminate Sir Hugh with them."

Again, pain flickered in Adam Colford's eyes, but they hardened to the sheen of obsidian. "You hit the mark—once again. I do lie. But my net is of a different sort than you think. Like you, I suspect Master Cromwell of slipping Sir Hugh the coins. Yet how do you know of them—still less, their power to incriminate?"

Giles turned to the King, who regarded him, motionless.

Cromwell, who upon hearing his name had dared to move closer, now put on a self-righteous air. "You see, Your Majesty and my lord Cardinal, the purpose of my stratagem with the coins." Wolsey favored his servant with a noncommittal glance and returned his attention to the King. For Henry, neither Cromwell, nor the Cardinal, nor the whole gallery of them existed. All his brittle, weary, strained attention was focused on the two Colfords.

Sir Giles moistened his lips. "Your Majesty, do these gentlemen seriously imagine that even an honest man may survive at court without spies? I admit to having them, as they have them. It's from one of my brother's own men that I know of the gold."

"That won't do," Adam answered. "I've discussed the coins with but two people, Lady Isabel in privacy, and Cromwell alone on the Tower Green. None of my men could possibly know."

"Then my own man has misled me. Your Grace, the Cardinal and his faction are my opponents, for reasons you well know. True, I never counted my brother among my foes, but this transparent intrigue to bring me down—!"

King Henry's eyes glittered dangerously. "Is it indeed? Transparent? God's wounds, it's transparent! Clear as glass, your whole plot! So, you would have me trotting at Spain's heel?"

"Your Majesty," Cardinal Wolsey cautioned, laying a heavily ringed hand on the King's sleeve. "Discretion—"

King Henry shook him off. "Discretion? What need of discretion, Cardinal, when the Emperor Charles himself knows every atom of my strategy?" In a fury of betrayal he glared at Giles Colford. "Do you doubt that this agent of the Emperor's has told him all?" He flung out his arms in a gesture so violent the gathering fluttered back from him. "What use in cautious tiptoeing now? The Doge of Venice and a few paltry thousand pounds!" He snorted. "All the while the real stakes were the collar and leash of the Emperor. Not only the French alliance destroyed, but my honor before all Europe! Lord Colford, We find you have raised sufficient doubt. Guards, take custody of this man. And make no mistake, Giles Colford, the truth will be wrung from you with such diligence that all shall be known before dawn."

The two guards attending the King carefully moved in on Sir Giles. One unbuckled and appropriated his sword, but he suffered it with dignity. "There is no need. Since all is up, I have no reason to conceal the truth. Indeed, I wish to speak it out before Your Majesty, and all."

The King stayed the guards with his hand.

"Your Majesty wrongs me," Sir Giles spoke with all the candid clarity and purpose that had won him the trust of King, Council and court. "Though I'm responsible for the disappearance of the Sun and Stars, I am not the Emperor's agent. Still less am I a traitor. All that I do, I do for England."

Beside Isabel, Adam lowered his head, his shoulders rigid with grief.

"I am England!" Henry thundered.

"Then Your Majesty must be stopped from following the path of folly and ruin. Ruin to all Your Majesty and I have worked for, and of that most noble lady, the Queen."

"The Queen! Sirrah, do you accuse Queen Katherine of treachery?"

"Never, Your Grace. The Queen is absolutely innocent— and unaware—of my plan. France may use us, but in the long run what has France ever been but England's enemy? What is King Francis but a dissolute despot? The only good course, the only humane one, is for Europe to be united in peace. Only the Emperor stands a chance of that."

"Such far-reaching policy is His Majesty's concern, not yours," Cardinal Wolsey reproved sharply.

"It is all England's concern," Sir Giles contradicted. "Just as Europe must have accord to prosper, so must we. Your Majesty's affairs of the heart are not my business, but casting off Queen Katherine will throw England into discord."

"Our conscience—" the king bellowed.

"—Will not be shared by the Pope, under pressure as he is from the Emperor Charles, the Queen's nephew," Sir Giles dared to gainsay him. "Mistress Boleyn's Lutheran leanings are well known. These Protestants scorn the Pope, and what will she urge you to next? That way lie a hundred years of religious contention, people burnt as heretics, and lost lives."

"You dare defy His Majesty?" Sir Thomas More spoke quietly, but severely.

"I warn you, all is at stake. Say there is a second marriage and another Queen. And say, two heirs to the throne. What do you want, another generation of war between contending rulers? No, we cannot go that way! Unity under one church, one king and one queen is the only way for England to prosper."

"Your belief is blind, Giles."

Startled, Isabel looked at Adam. As did the whole gathering, but he ignored them, his whole formidable mind intent on his brother.

"Belief." Giles smiled, and shook his head. "You, of all people, will never understand, Adam. Finally, there is nothing but belief." Turning again to face the King, he spoke lower, yet carrying. "If need be, belief strong enough to die for. Since I am to die, I caution Your Majesty, you stand in danger of becoming a tyrant. When I was young, you appeared as a new King Arthur, but what of these crushing new taxes the Cardinal heaps on your people? Whether you will or no, I'll tilt the scales for England's benefit. You may tear my body asunder, but you'll never have the Sun and Stars."

Isabel braced for she knew not what. She felt Adam's tension beside her, and saw even the Cardinal's jaw clench in fear.

Yet no cataclysm followed. In silence, the King faced his accuser. "We hope what you say is untrue," he said at last, quietly. "But even if it were so, what are you? A man who owns allegiance to no one and nothing but his own opinion. If all did as you do, would there be peace? Or only a slide into chaos, will against will?"

Sir Giles met his eyes steadily, silently, his conviction undiminished.

"Take him away." The King motioned wearily, and the guards marched off Sir Giles.

"You are all dismissed," King Henry continued. "We shall send for you anon." His lips closed tightly. Isabel saw there the pain of betrayal. He had infinitely trusted Sir Giles. All began to move off, seeking their own thoughts and conclaves. Isabel knew new alignments would follow this upheaval. Fresh factions would surface, old enmities differently dressed up. Yet just now she could not bring herself to care. Beside her Adam stood, letting the others leave him alone, like a lone rock resisting an outgoing tide. She stayed behind, too.

"You will now call me the fool," he said, his voice hoarse, but controlled.

"I say no such thing."

"No? You'd be justified." He made an attempt at a cynical smile, but gave it up.

"Ephemeral," Isabel said softly, troubled. "All is ephemeral. France or Spain, Katherine or Anne, Papist or Protestant, is it really so important?"

"Our French alliance will be short-lived," he admitted.

Isabel searched Adam Colford's face.

"As you say, one or another." He shrugged. Whatever he felt, the shadowed green of his eyes concealed it. "So what's to do but as my king commands? It's to my honor, and to my best advantage."

Obviously, he took no comfort from such reasoning. Isabel was chilled, feeling that darkness was not a morass beneath the surface of the world as he had described it, but an infinite void pressing all round, and herself in a small bubble of light, as illusory as it was fragile.

"I must try to find comfort in that," he said. "Otherwise, I've brought my brother to the scaffold for mere opposing viewpoints."

The bubble burst. Isabel shut her eyes, fearing to see what the loss of her lifelong, protective innocence would show her. But she could not remain thus, eyes squeezed shut, for the rest of her life. With misgiving, she opened them.

Afternoon sunlight streamed through the gallery's gothic windows, and birdsong reached her. The world was still the world, after all. Adam gazed downward, lost in the coils of his memories.

"We've saved the life of an innocent man," Isabel said.

"That was your reason. What was mine?" He met her eyes. "Can I ever be sure it was not revenge?" He tensed against a wave of pain. Isabel reached out and gently touched his sleeve. He tightened into a yet harder rigidity, and walked away.

Chapter Twenty

As Isabel entered the council chamber, she saw the company of the early afternoon had reassembled. On a low dais at one end stood a gilded throne backed by a hanging of Tudor green with rampant golden lions. A richly patterned damask carpet silenced the steps of the gathering, and the afternoon light filtered through windows high in the wall, their top mullions containing the King's and Queen's arms in stained glass.

"The alliance is ruined, all the same," the Duke of Norfolk was saying to another lord. "Will King Francis trust His Majesty if he doesn't honor his promises? Would we trust the French, if the positions were reversed? Hardly!"

Isabel spotted Adam at the edge of the room speaking with Cardinal Wolsey. Whatever he felt, his face now showed no indication of it. Perhaps the other lords admired him for this. Isabel felt a chill at the polished hardness of his eyes.

"What's the girl doing here?" Isabel turned to see her father's good friend the Duke of Suffolk staring at her with bluff perplexity. The earl standing next to him shrugged, a large movement of broadly padded shoulders.

King Henry's voice sounded outside the door. The assembly quickly silenced. As he entered with Sir Thomas More, caps swept off and the whole company bowed. Isabel heard them continue their conversation as they passed and saw the lower half of More's gown stir as he bowed. The King seated himself on the throne, and with the others she straightened.

Gravely, King Henry looked over the gathering. "This day has laid a sore burden on Our heart. We counted Sir Giles Colford Our friend. To be thus repaid for Our trust, that's the worst to bear." He glanced at Adam. "Yet Our burden is lightened by the loyalty of this lord."

Adam's head inclined in the mere shadow of an acknowledgement, his sculpted lips pressed together.

"Troubles still beset Us," King Henry resumed. "Though We've caught the thief and Sir Brian Harrow's murderer, We have not recovered the Sun and Stars. With that task We charge each of you. As you all know, Giles Colford is a man of fixed purpose. Just how fixed We little guessed until today. We doubt simple questioning will reveal where he has hidden the crown." He let his eye travel over them all. As he noticed Isabel among them, he was briefly surprised but moved on without comment. "Now you know why the Sun and Stars is so crucial. We must regain it." Avoiding Adam, his eye lit on Cardinal Wolsey. "Whatever it takes."

"Your Majesty," the Cardinal confirmed, and glanced at Cromwell, who looked none too happy at the challenge of wringing it from Sir Giles. Isabel suspected he was yearning nostalgically for simpler times, and Hugh. Nevertheless, his pale, merciless countenance was enough to make Sir Piers whisper uneasily into the ear of the gentleman beside him. And no wonder, since Piers himself had been observed closeted with the traitor only yestereve. Isabel wondered what he would say if he realized how far his fatuousness cleared him of anyone's suspicion.

"For the rest of you, my lords, no matter how far away Colford has sent the crown—"

"Or how near," Isabel said almost before she was aware.

"Did someone speak?" King Henry's sharp eye lit on her. He knew well enough the exclamation had been hers, and meant she should silence herself. Several of the lords standing nearby glanced at her, edgy and censorious under the King's strained mood.

Yet the pieces she recalled might fit, so far as they went. It was worth a try. "Your Majesty, the crown is not far off," she repeated.

"What do you mean, girl? Who admitted you, anyway?"

"You summoned me, sir. At least," she said innocently, "I thought you meant me, along with the rest."

"And how do you know where the Sun and Stars is?"

"Not I," Isabel answered. "But there may be one in this room who can unearth it for you." Turning, she looked across the gathering at Sir Piers.

"Knevet? A traitor?" her father asked incredulously. His eyes darted to Sir Piers. The guards came alert, ready to seize Knevet at his command.

"Your Majesty!" Knevet protested. "Surely the lady only toys with me, but her jest is most unseemly!"

"My surmise is wrong?" Isabel asked him, disappointed. "You've nothing in safekeeping for Sir Giles?"

"Only a chest of papers, to foil His Majesty's enemies," Sir Piers defended himself angrily. "Harrow, especially."

"Harrow?" Adam Colford's voice cut through the chamber

as cleanly as a tempered sword. "Is that who you've been so skittish of?"

"And so you took to following him?" Isabel added.

"In self defense," Sir Piers answered, aggrieved. "But you couldn't be more wrong about those papers. I saw the contents of the chest when Colford gave it into my keeping. Oh, not to read, but to know there was naught else in the chest. Besides, Your Majesty, I've had them for more than a month, long before the theft."

"Some six days ago, Sir Giles called on you to examine them, perhaps?" Isabel hazarded. "In privacy, perhaps?"

Sir Piers' mouth dropped open. With a gasp of terror, he fell to his knees.

"God's blood, man! Get up," the King ordered. "Go see what's in your chest!"

Sir Piers sprang up, bowed, rushed to the door, bowed again, and ran, followed by a few of the guards.

Isabel turned back to find her father smiling. "Of course, sir," she added, "I may be mistaken."

"My Lord Colford," King Henry asked, motioning him closer. "What is the girl doing in this business? I take it she's been some sort of help to you, but what *is* she doing in it?"

"The truth be told, Your Majesty, I couldn't stop her. The Lady Isabel has admirable courage, remarkable wit," he gauged the King, who was nodding complacently, then added, "and extraordinary stubbornness."

"Indeed," her father agreed without turning a hair. "And this matter was your only business with her? No assignations behind closed doors or trysts on the lawn? You'll give us your word for that?"

"I scarcely need to, Your Grace," Adam answered. "The lady's honor speaks for itself."

"A commendable answer, coming from a man of such

proven honor as yourself," replied the King. He gave the Duke of Norfolk a pointed look, repayment for his tale-bearing.

A rattle sounded at the door, a whole collection of guards looking anything but disciplined in their elation. From their midst emerged Sir Piers to collapse panting on his knees.

"What?" King Henry turned a beady eye on him. "Not gone yet?"

"Please Your Grace, my house is just across the river." Between terror and triumph, Knevet motioned forward a guard bearing a small wooden chest. Opening it, the man removed an object wrapped in frayed linen. With a flourish, he pulled away the cloth to reveal the fierce sparkling of a magnificent diamond, set amid the glitter of gold and lesser gems.

A drawn-out "Ah!" sighed from the gathering as the guard carried forward the Sun and Stars and with a bow, presented it to the Cardinal, who in turn knelt to proffer it to the King.

Henry removed his velvet hat. With both hands he lifted the crown and solemnly placed it upon his head. Then he broke into an irrepressible, boyish grin.

"A thing of rare beauty," he proclaimed, to the applause of the gathering. "And a most noble prize of war. Now that We have it back, We confess it will be surpassing hard to give it up again. Perhaps We'll claim We never recovered it." He glanced at Wolsey's and Adam's startled unease and chucked, well pleased with his jest.

"For your services, my Lord Colford, We would not gift you with blood money, even if We imagined you would accept it. But We hereby command you to join Our Privy Council, where We are in need of your skills to repair the breaches of this day."

Adam did not look altogether pleased. "Your Majesty honors me too much."

"It's an honor, but you'll earn it." He meant it. The Privy Councilors had much power, but paid for it with prodigious work. It was a command not to be refused. "For that reason, ask of me a boon of your choosing. I shall be generous."

"Then, Your Grace," Adam answered evenly, "I shall seize the opportunity. There is indeed a treasure I would have, that surpasses the Sun and Stars. I would possess that treasure. I would make her Lady Colford."

As faces turned to stare, Isabel realized with shock that he meant her. The breath left her. Lord Adam Colford, he who of all people had seemed to appreciate her mind and spirit? He was asking for her without her leave, without even asking her opinion of the matter, as if she were a haunch of venison, as if her feelings were as irrelevant as those of a sweetmeat he wished to swallow. Isabel opened her mouth to protest, but her father darted her a warning glance. "Hold your tongue, daughter," he commanded. Frowning, he stroked his neatly trimmed beard, weighing the advantages and disadvantages of the proposed bargain. In utter, unavailing fury Isabel glared at Adam Colford's back.

"We'll give the matter thought." Her father gestured Colford back and motioned Isabel forward. "For you, despite your cleverness, no seat on Our Council." He smiled as the other men laughed pleasantly. Isabel refused to join them. "Yet I would reward you. Would you like a fine emerald? As pure and large as the ruby Princess Mary wears?"

It was his way of telling her he valued her as highly. Despite herself, Isabel felt the pricking of tears.

"Come now," her father encouraged. "Shyness doesn't suit you."

Now was her chance. Now, or never. "My lord father, I crave only one reward."

"Name it."

She took a deep breath. "To choose my own husband."

Behind her, she heard the buzz of condemning masculine whispers.

King Henry burst into laughter. "Has there ever been such a willful baggage? By Saint George! For a headstrong service, a headstrong reward! Daughter, I'm in a mood to grant your request—with one condition. When you do choose, I must approve of the match. But this I promise: you shall not be forced to wed against your will."

Isabel curtsied so low her skirts swept the floor in an arc. "My most heartfelt thanks, Your Majesty."

"Well, Adam," the King turned to Colford, enjoying himself immensely. "It seems you must take up your suit with the lady herself."

Lord Adam bowed his acquiescence. "Lady Isabel Holland, I humbly request your hand in marriage." He arched an eyebrow in a manner she found insufferably conceited.

He was that certain she would acquiesce? Every man in the room stood gawping at them, amused by the scene, and at the impertinent hint of desire in that arched brow. Isabel's indignation swelled, so galling she could have spit it at him. "Your Majesty," she declared, "Your leave to speak to Lord Colford in private?"

"You have it." Her father chuckled in a knowing way, infuriating her still further.

They backed from the King's presence to the door. Once out, Isabel spun and stalked along the corridor to an alcove well beyond earshot of the council chamber. It was empty but for the golden light of late afternoon striking the oak paneling of the wall. Stopping there, she wheeled. "May you have my hand? No, you may not have my hand. Nor my finger, nor the slightest pairing of my nail!"

"Not even a scratch?" Both his eyebrows lifted this time, but only slightly, with cool hauteur. "What have I done to earn such abhorrence?"

"Would you like the whole list or only the first one thousand items? First, the way you asked the King for me as if I were a bag of grain—"

"Treasure, I said."

"A lump, a thing. If you seek to spend your life with a woman, do you care nothing what she feels about it?"

He eyed her reluctantly, but had no choice now. "What do you feel?"

Too much, of horror, and triumph, sorrow, and a sweet stirring she did not dare name. "Seasick," she said, honesty prevailing. "Up, down and aslant. An overmastering desire to crawl into a cave and sleep for a hundred years."

"Understandable," he agreed.

"But no desire to marry."

"Are you so sure?"

"What on earth made you ask for me in the first place? Oh, I know the advantages of being the King's son-in-law. Or should I say, son-out-of-law, considering I'm no lawful daughter. But he's in your debt now, and you're on the Privy Council, a more sure way to power. You don't need me. I know right well you don't love me. I'm hardly the meek, dulcet lamb you're seeking."

"No, you're not." As he stepped toward her, his eyes caught the light, their darkness suddenly clear green to the bottom. "Yet I find you are, after all, a promise of joy and endless challenge that I do not want to do without."

"You'll take me for a challenge? Well, it goes both ways. As a challenge is the only way I can imagine taking you."

"We are agreed, then?" He held out his hand to her.
She did not take it. "My father must approve."
"We'll persuade him."
Isabel stepped back. "First things first," she said. "I may
allow you to persuade me." Turning, she let herself out the
door and closed it behind her. She scarcely heard her own light
steps passing along the gallery. Each window glowed incandes-
cent with the slanting sun.

Chapter Twenty-One

A fire crackled merrily, painting the great hall of the Lovell house with mellow amber, yet the windows were thrown open to the cool spring freshness. Isabel looked at the faces she had loved longest, gilded by the firelight and illuminated by joy. Aunt Margery, Ursula, and Hugh.

"So the Warden said, 'beat me at cards and I'll let you walk out of here.'" Hugh continued. "I thought he was having an ill-considered jest with me, but better to play, I thought, than sit dwelling on the morrow. I won the game. And then he got up from the stool and threw open the door! I only sat there. 'Well, go!' he said. 'You're the first prisoner I've seen yet who wanted to stay!'"

"You tell a tale, sir," Ursula accused him.

"By Saint Cecilia, I do not."

Isabel caught Hugh's eye. If he swore by Cecily, it was true. "I believe you, coz."

Hugh smiled back at her. "I know." To them all, he resumed, "Then he showed me the King's order for my release and told me all he knew of events. 'But,' I asked, 'what if I'd lost the game?'

"'We'd play another,' said he. 'And if need be, another and yet another. If you'd lost them all, you'd have spent the night in your cell!'"

Laughing with the rest, his mother rose, went behind his chair, and held him fiercely by the shoulders. Isabel joined her affection to her aunt's, reaching to tousle Hugh's golden hair.

But the thought came to her of Sir Giles Colford sitting now in the Tower, watching the night gather and knowing he would never walk out again, save to the scaffold and a traitor's death. Even knowing Sir Giles for a fanatic, it was hard not to admire his courage and forthrightness. And hard to ignore his warnings, some of which she knew might be well justified.

Hard not to like him, even knowing him for the enemy who would have killed Hugh.

In fact, the whole matter of enemies and friends was becoming exceedingly confusing. It was Cromwell who had sent her the first word of Hugh's release, in a message of goodwill that, in a manner she could only call considerate, detailed the few points on which she still felt curiosity. Having learned the Sun and Stars was in the King's hands and his plot void, Sir Giles had consented to talk to Cromwell. Indeed, Cromwell reported, he had confessed all, but for owning that his deeds were crimes. One of the questions which had most baffled Isabel, that of who had been Carne's cohort in the theft and the murder of the two guards, he had answered with a simplicity that checked any overblown notion she might have formed of her own cleverness. One of the two guards was in Giles' pay. Having conducted the earless man into the arming tents, he turned on the one loyal guard, making it a fight of two against one. He little dreamt that his henchman would turn and serve him the same.

As for Sir Brian Harrow, Giles had recruited him long before. Hearing of Sir Brian's grievance against Wolsey, he offered him a chance to foil the Cardinal. Thereafter, at home and abroad, Harrow had done much to sabotage his enemy, traces of which were in records Giles had *not* shown Lord Adam and her. Yet when Sir Giles hinted at a chance to undo King Henry's French alliance, there Harrow had drawn the line. He was in it to avenge himself on Wolsey, he said, not to betray his king. Though Giles had pretended to drop the idea, when the crown disappeared, Sir Brian had not been deceived. Unknown to Sir Giles until almost the end, Harrow had thought to recover the Sun and Stars and trap the thief himself, thereby showing up the Cardinal and winning the favor of the King.

His crucial mistake, Sir Giles had told Cromwell, was in waiting too long to kill Carne. For years, Carne had been his informant and operative in London, and served him as well. Giles trusted him, and had placed too much faith in his silence. Had the earless man not indulged in one of his rare lapses into drink and begun to talk, he would be safely abroad by now.

So, Cromwell concluded with a smug flourish of his quill, Sir Giles Colford's fatal flaw was his conscience.

Isabel could not help wondering whether that was not a far wiser observation than Master Cromwell imagined. What had been one kind of hell for the elder brother must have been only another sort for the younger. To bear his mother's guilt without having shared in her deeds, to know that his existence had nearly caused the blotting out of his brother's, must have shaped Giles, as the early knowledge of deceit had formed Adam.

Perhaps, in attempting to right wrongs, Giles had sought to expiate a guilt that nothing, even his brother's forgiveness, could transcend. Sir Giles had sent but one message from the

Tower, Cromwell reported. It was to Lord Adam, and Cromwell thought it most strange: *Hardest of all was to forego the grey colt.*

Isabel sighed. At least, Cromwell had written, since Sir Giles was withholding nothing, there was no need for torture. If his brother pled for him at the trial, the King would doubtless grant a quick death. Isabel closed her eyes, thinking of Adam Colford alone in his apartments, and the memories and regrets that must fill his brooding. A weary sorrow overcame her.

"So," asked Hugh, scooping Eleanor of Aquitaine up into his lap as she walked by. "You really mean to let that proud Lord Adam Colford court you, coz?"

"We'll see. He was publicly insolent to me before my lord father and all the important men of the realm. That will take some repaying. And, he insulted me in private more times than I can count."

"Perhaps you should refuse to be on speaking terms with him at all." Hugh smiled.

"Perchance, if he ate all his insults and spent a year or two proving they weren't so, and that he's enslaved by love of me, then I *might* let him court me. Or perhaps not. In the meanwhile, I care not what he does. I'm mistress of my own fate now and I have the flowers of my freedom to gather."

Boots sounded on the floor, and they all turned. "My ladies, Sir Hugh," one of her aunt's servants announced, "Lord Adam Colford."

Standing at the threshold he unfurled his short cloak. His hair, blown back by his ride, mingled like dark flame with the sable of his collar. As he came toward her, sorrow was in his eyes, and hope.

A Note from the Author

When it helped my story I have played a little fast and loose with history. I slipped an imaginary crown into the international affairs of 1528, scooted a few events by several months, and overlooked some real people in favor of invented ones. The fictional characters in *The Sun and Stars* include Isabel's cousin Hugh Lovell, the Colfords and Sir Brian Harrow. And, of course, my detective herself. Henry VIII had an acknowledged illegitimate child, Henry Fitzroy, and was rumored to have others—at least one of Mary Boleyn's children may have been his. But he had no known daughter named Isabel.

Yet in the colorful mosaic of the Tudor court even an imaginary person couldn't be an isolated individual. Friends, opportunities, enemies, a person's entire social, business and political support system, depended on family connections. To place Isabel more firmly in that world, I've attached her to a real family, the Hollands of Weare, Devon.

The Hollands were like most gentry of that era, locally important and kin to powerful people, but country people rather than courtiers. They were a junior branch of the Hollands of Upholland, Lancashire, and did indeed have Lovell cousins. Readers who love Daphne DuMaurier's wonderful novel, *The King's General* may be interested that Isabel's close cousins would include the grandfather of the Royalist commander Richard Grenville. Among her more distant connections are both the Boleyns and the Seymours. Like it or not, Isabel may soon find herself interestingly embroiled.

~ Elizabeth Adair

Coming soon from BearCat Press

The Forest of the Heart
by Elizabeth Adair

Devon. July 1528. On the evening of her wedding Isabel already wonders if she has made a mistake in marrying Lord Adam Colford. But the guests gathered at her country manor think the match a fine one and celebrate with unrestrained gaiety at the magnificent marriage feast. Minstrels play, wine has been imported from Aÿ-Champagne, and gossip abounds about King Henry's determination to put aside Queen Katherine and marry Anne Boleyn.

Yet beneath all runs an undercurrent of fear. In London the deadly plague known as sweating sickness has broken out. King and courtiers have fled to the countryside to escape infection and many of the guests have flocked to the celebration because the sweat has not yet reached the remote West County. No one mentions events of ill-omen at a wedding, and the merry-making is all the more clamorous in defiance of death—until in the midst of her laughter a particularly flirtatious lady collapses face down in her dessert, felled not by plague, but poison.

Isabel and Adam must come to terms with truths about each other as they untangle a coil of deceit and forbidden love, and as the rumor that Anne Boleyn has succumbed to the plague brings about a confession that ignites the murderous jealousy of Cecily's husband, Lord Simon Raight.

About the Author

Elizabeth Adair grew up on her father's tales of Man o' War, Citation and Whirlaway and her mother's stories about the wives of Henry VIII, Queen Elizabeth, Sir Frances Drake and Sir Walter Raleigh. Torn between becoming a pirate, a queen, a jockey or a horse, she realized a writer can be all of them. After a decade in California and some time in Egypt she returned to the Blue Grass of Kentucky where she writes, designs graphics and works on behalf of retired race horses.

Talk with Elizabeth at
elizabethadairauthor.wordpress.com

Also from BearCat Press

Helen of Troy by Tess Collins

The Appalachian Thriller Trilogy by Tess Collins:
The Law of Revenge
The Law of the Dead
The Law of Betrayal

Floats the Dark Shadow by Yves Fey

Coming from BearCat Press in 2012,
a mystery suspense novel of Paris, 1897

Floats the Dark Shadow

by Yves Fey

A thousand candles burned in the darkness of the catacombs. A thousand flames wavered, golden lights bending and rising with the doleful ebb and flow of the music.

Repelled and fascinated, Theo Faraday watched their flickering glow caress the curved domes of the skulls. Tinted by candlelight, the naked bones took on a sepia patina, like sacred reliquaries carved from amber. A shiver swept through her. Nothing—not her delight in the outrageous, nor the wickedly delicious thrill of the forbidden, not even the inspiration the images would bring to her art—nothing overcame her sense of oppression. They were deep in the earth and room after endless room of bones surrounded them.

The black hollows of the eye sockets seemed to watch the concert attentively—as attentively as the audience of chic Parisians, still clothed in mortal flesh and fancy silks, still breathing the dank, stifling air of the chamber. As the last notes of Chopin's 'Marche Funèbre' echoed, the gathering applauded with mock solemnity, saluting the musicians' skill and their own daring in coming here. Elegant in their tuxedos, the orchestra lowered their instruments with a flourish and rose, first bowing to their guests, then once again to their skeletal hosts. Theo smiled and clapped with them, fighting off her apprehension.

"They call this Empire of Death." Averill Charron leaned close and Theo bent to meet her French cousin. In the eerie light, the smile hovering at the corners of his mouth shifted from sweet to sinister and back again. His breath caressed her face and she caught a bittersweet hint of absinthe. The scent churned up a chaos of emotion—concern, frustration, anger, yearning.

A pang of jealousy.

How perfectly Parisian, she thought, to be jealous of a liqueur.

When had his flirtation with the green fairy become a love affair? Two months ago, four? He called absinthe his muse, but she stole as much as she gave. Under her influence, Averill's moods grew ever more erratic and his exquisite, fantastical poems ever more bizarre.

A fierce impulse surged through Theo's turmoil—to paint Averill as he looked now, bitter and sweet, taunting and tender. She envisioned him almost emerging from the canvas. Strands of black hair tumbled over his eyes, pale blue flames glowing too bright within the shadows. Patches of rose madder made a fever flush on both cheeks. Her fingers twitched eager to render mustache and beard in quick, narrow strokes of lamp black touched with indigo, a frame for the quick twist of a smile that mocked the world and himself.

Theo forced a smile in response. "The Empire of Death. So you've said."

"Three times at least, Charron," Paul Noret sneered from the seat on her other side. "Before, during, and after your nightly tryst with the green fairy."

Slouched in his chair, Paul looked too much at home in this underground kingdom, like a strange insect god, half man and half praying mantis. His body was long and bony, his face cadaverous. Shadows carved crescents into his lean cheeks, and scooped out circles under his eyes, which bulged slightly, and glistened. His hair was prematurely grey, the color of ashes, and aged him a decade or more. Paul was thirty four—thirteen years older than she was, and ten years older than Averill.

"You should sip the green ambrosia, Noret, and cavort with her yourself." Averill said.

Paul scowled. "Absinthe rots the brain."

"Ahh...but your poetry will soar."

"Not if your twig-bound twitters are any example."

There was a heartbeat of silence. A stinging retort sprang to Theo's lips but she bit it back when she felt Averill's light pressure on her arm. He leaned across her to taunt Paul in turn. "Twitters? When people hear twitters, they pause. They smile. They listen. If they hear barking, they shut their ears—or throw shoes."

Paul examined his scuffed boots. "These were acquired just so. They cost but a single barking couplet."

Theo relaxed, glad the jab had been too wide of the mark to cut Averill. They were all used to Paul's forays but always en garde. They ignored him at their peril. What seemed to be a feint might suddenly pierce the heart. They'd look down to discover their idea, their verse—or their art—mercilessly skewered. But that same skill made Paul chief critic to the group of poets and musicians who had invited Theo into their midst. Since the success of Le Revenant, Paul seemed to have doubled his criticism. Was it jealousy? Paul's poems were harsher but they too had won praise—everyone's work had, but no one as much as Averill. Perhaps Paul was forestalling vanity from taking hold when someone proclaimed Averill the new Rimbaud, the new Verlaine.

Absinthe had destroyed Verlaine.

Gazing around, Averill gestured dramatically to the skulls crowning the wide pillar of tibias and fibulas. "We have set ourselves in the Empire's heart, in the sanctity of the Crypte de la Passion."

"It is so perfectly decadent," Theo murmured. The word was a like a magic key—a key that opened many intriguing doors in Paris. Yet when Averill nodded yes, another part of Theo's mind whispered rebelliously, So perfectly horrible....

So horribly sad....

"Yes." Averill gave her another conspiratorial smile, as if he heard and agreed with each silent pronouncement.

The undercurrent of longing pulled Theo forward. She started to reach out to him then curled her hand tight against her heart. Averill's friendship was precious. She could not bear to shatter what they now had on a futile quest for a foolish amour. She made herself sit back.

"If you think this crypt was named for Christ's Passion, you are wrong, Charron," Paul reproved, his nasal voice smug. "The true meaning is more prosaic—and more profane. Whenever the gendarmes hunted the street walkers too aggressively, the women brought their customers down here. Whores have no hearts, and neither does this sepulchral maze."

Averill shook his head. "You are the one with no heart, Noret."

"Who needs such a soggy rag?" Paul rolled his eyes disdainfully.

"A poet, certainly," Theo countered.

"Exactement." Averill ruffled the boutonnière he had pinned over his heart. It was a curious concoction he had created from white paper cutouts. Today, yesterday now, was All Fools Day. For some obscure reason Theo had not discovered, the French nicknamed it Poisson d'Avril—April Fish Day. Their favorite prank was decorating the backs of unsuspecting passersby with paper fish. Averill collected these zealously, declaring the day Poisson d'Averill, and the paper fish a personal tribute. He wore the tattered little bouquet pinned to his jacket. Theo frowned. If she included that boutonniere in her portrait, should she attempt to show it was actually paper fish, and not a white carnation? Unbidden, a tall glass of absinthe inhabited the bottom corner of her imagined canvas, glowing a malevolent chartreuse.

Would Averill be angry if she painted that? Theo felt a war begin—her not wanting to put the glass there and the glass insisting. I am truth, said the glass. And I am so deliciously, evilly green.

"I find a brain far more useful than a bleeding heart." Paul arranged his lanky frame in the chair as best he could, crossed his arms and closed his eyes. His lips began to move silently. No doubt, he was composing a poem to prove his point—something perfectly cynical and quite as gloomy as their setting.

Averill sat up and looked intently about the candle lit crypt. Curious, Theo asked, "Searching for more Revenants?"

He gave her an oblique glance. "Not exactly. Just someone I thought might come tonight."

That was rather mysterious. "Someone from medical school?" Averill shook his head at that. He'd always said he had found no true friends there.

His gaze scanned the crowd once more, but whoever the unnamed person was, Averill did not find him…or her…. Turning back, he gave her a shrug and a smile. "It's not important, ma cousine."

Theo was so startled, she did not pursue the question of the mysterious someone. Her illegitimacy was an open secret, but propriety demanded that she be presented as her father's ward. Averill never called her cousin in public. He shrugged as if to say "Everyone knows".

Then someone behind them commented on the performance and Averill turned, inviting himself into conversation. Paul was scribbling a note by candlelight. With both her companions distracted, Theo watched the musicians. Their host and fellow Revenant, Casimir Estarlion, gave her a brief salute with his violin bow. She smiled in answer. As always, the baron looked both raffish and elegant. Artfully pomaded, his golden brown hair curled slightly, glistening in the candlelight. His eyes were amber, wide set, alight with the same sly charm as his smile. Theo was glad she'd accepted his invitation to this bizarre event, but grateful only one more piece remained after the interlude.

She saw Casimir quickly search for any other friends in the audience, but it seemed only the three of them had come. Not every poet felt bound to visit the catacombs at midnight. No, she was wrong. There were four of them, not three. In one obscure corner stood the most shadowy Revenant, a young man named Jules Loisel. He seldom spoke and was so shy he had not pushed through the crowd to join them. Theo might not have noticed him at all, except that he looked more incongruous than anyone else—a shabby brown church mouse with pointed chin and darting brown eyes. She felt a twinge of sympathy. Jules subsisted on stray jobs Paul procured for him from the publishing company he worked for during the day, drearily editing textbooks. Crumbs of crumbs.

Theo shifted restlessly. Despite the eager murmur of the crowd and the blazing candle light, she felt the murky shadows and musty odors of the crypt encroaching. She yearned to escape the oppressive atmosphere. Tomorrow she would go riding again. She closed her eyes and saw the fragrant green woods and pink cherry blossoms of the Bois de Boulogne. For an instant, she felt the vital strength of the little mare surging beneath her, the cool wind a sweet current flowing around her. When she opened her eyes again, the shadows had retreated.

Theo lifted her chin and smoothed back the tendrils that had escaped from her braid, adjusting the opal studded comb that held it in place. Tonight she sported her recent flea market coups. She knew her antique frock coat of sapphire velvet deepened the light blue of her eyes. Beneath it, a fine linen shirt and jabot foaming with Chantilly lace topped trousers and leather boots. Theo wanted her clothes to be festive, but she had not wanted to fret about silk skirts and dainty shoes while picking her way through dirty, dank, and claustrophobic tunnels.

Officially, the catacombs had been closed to the public decades ago. Visiting them was condemned. Unofficially, there was a thriving business in satisfying that perverse curiosity. Averill had insisted on the full tour before the concert. Theo had been startled when their guide met them with his ten-year-old son, but the boy took even more delight in the ghoulish maze than his father did, lifting his lantern to illuminate the carved mottos along the pathway. When Averill intoned their warnings of mortality, Dondre laughed and intoned along with him. "They were what we are. Dust. Toys of the wind...."

With his curling hair and expressive brown eyes, Dondre reminded her of Denis, the laundress' son who had vanished weeks ago. Theo's heart gave a sudden twist. Perhaps other boys were missing as well, else why was the detective in the alley still investigating such a hopeless case? That memory was far more depressing than the catacombs. With a shiver, Tho pushed it away and turned back to Averill and the others.

Together they followed the lantern deeper into the City of the Dead...

For more about *Floats the Dark Shadow* and its world, visit Yvesfey.com

CPSIA information can be obtained at www.ICGtesting.com
Printed in the USA
LVOW091727070712

289152LV00004B/2/P